HARLEQUIN S
Celebrates its ~~anniversary~~

Two decades of bringing you the very best in romance reading.

To recognize this important milestone, we've invited six very special authors—whose names you're sure to recognize—to tell us how they feel about Superromance. Each title this month has a letter from one of these authors.

Who better to write the foreword to Joan Kilby's *The Cattleman's Bride* than acclaimed author Margaret Way. Both writers live in Australia and both have the magical ability to make the land and its people come alive.

The Cattleman's Bride is the story of a man and a woman who must overcome differences as vast as the outback itself in resolving the dilemma that faces them. In that harsh and beautiful land, superficialities are stripped away as Sarah and Luke reach deep inside themselves and find a love that promises them a lifetime of fulfillment.

This is Joan's third book for Superromance. Her first novel earned her a RITA nomination for Best First Book, and her writing talents have merited a profile in the much-respected *Writer's Digest*. It's a pleasure to showcase Joan on this very special occasion for Superromance.

Dear Reader,

I was born and grew up in Vancouver, Canada, but have
lived in Australia for ten years now. My first impressions of
this beautiful land remain vivid—the colors, the scents, the
intensity of the sun, the enormous blue sky and the wide-
open spaces.

The outback holds an almost mythical place in the hearts
and minds of Australians, most of whom live in large cities
along the coast. As I got to know more about the outback
and talked with the people who live there, I was struck
by the fact that, despite the harsh environment and the
hardships they face, they passionately love their way of life.

As my heroine, Sarah, discovers, it's *not* an easy life, but
in the challenge lies the reward. Her greatest reward is
Luke—a modern-day pioneer, a battler who loves the land
and the freedom to be his own man. In each other, Sarah
and Luke discover that once-in-a-lifetime love that
transcends all boundaries.

I hope you find *The Cattleman's Bride* as enjoyable
and satisfying to read as it was for me to write.
I love to hear from my readers. Please write me
c/o Harlequin Enterprises Ltd., 225 Duncan Mill Road,
Don Mills, Ontario, Canada M3B 3K9, or e-mail me at
www.superauthors.com.

Sincerely,

Joan Kilby

FOREWORD BY MARGARET WAY

The Cattleman's Bride

Joan Kilby

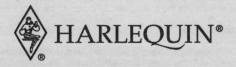

HARLEQUIN®

TORONTO • NEW YORK • LONDON
AMSTERDAM • PARIS • SYDNEY • HAMBURG
STOCKHOLM • ATHENS • TOKYO • MILAN • MADRID
PRAGUE • WARSAW • BUDAPEST • AUCKLAND

I would like to thank Karen Emmott for her generous and
enthusiastic response to my quest for information about
modern life on an outback cattle station. Thanks also to
Angus Emmott for his contribution. Truly an inspiration!

I would also like to thank Jacqueline Curley,
Heather Goldsworthy and Carol Ross for sharing their
stories. Miriam McArdle of the Australian Stockman's
Hall of Fame and Larry Lewis of the Barcaldine
Rural Fire Service also assisted.

ISBN 0-373-70941-2

THE CATTLEMAN'S BRIDE

Visit us at www.eHarlequin.com

Printed in U.S.A.

FOREWORD BY MARGARET WAY

When my editor, Paula Eykelhof, asked me if I would write a foreword for an upcoming Superromance, the year 2000 being the twentieth anniversary of the line, I agreed with pleasure—and with the sense of being honored for my own contribution to the big, bright, beautiful world of Harlequin romance novels.

Although I have written some 80-odd books for the Harlequin Mills and Boon Romance series, it was only recently, through Paula's encouragement, that I extended my boundaries to Superromance. *The Australian Heiress*, released in 1998, was the first. My second, already researched, is in the process of being written. It is again set in the Australian outback, and I hope it will be an exciting read with a fascinating and provocative theme. Ancient Egyptian presence in tropical far north Queensland? The hunt is on for treasure in the rainforests and crocodile-infested swamps of Australia's top end wilderness coast. Be assured that a great romance figures in this story, along with the skulduggery and high tension. I look forward to seeing it in the Superromance lineup for 2001—and I hope you will, too.

Although I greatly enjoyed writing for the Romance series and have done so for the past thirty years, Superromance has provided me with a fresh challenge. I derive considerable satisfaction from the longer story, which gives me the opportunity to weave a more complex plot, introduce more characters and let them speak as they develop a fuller personality.

Being a successful writer (for which I must thank my publisher, my excellent caring editors and my loyal readers) must be one of the best jobs a woman can have. I love getting involved with my characters. I love falling in love with my heroes (yes, I do), but one of the most delightful aspects of the job is bringing pleasure to a lot of readers.

And speaking of readers… I've recently had the pleasure of catching up on my Superromances. I read books by Jan Freed, Bethany Campbell, Margot Early and others—and I thoroughly enjoyed a diversity of compelling stories. On the newcomer front, I particularly enjoyed A *Father's Place* by a fellow Australian, Joan Kilby. This book has an important message to deliver through a very engaging heroine. Such messages can change lives. I'm sure that writing such an eloquent first book gave Joan enormous pleasure and satisfaction. I know she'll go on to even greater things.

A peaceful and prosperous 2000 (and beyond) to all our readers (with the fervent hope for better government around the world!).

Margaret Way

Margaret Way is one of the best-known and most-loved romance writers in the world. Her books are usually set in her native Australia, which she writes about with passion and immense skill. She's made Australia *real* for millions of readers. She continues to be published by Harlequin Romance—the original romance series. And her second Superromance will appear in February 2001.

CHAPTER ONE

"DOUBLE HAZELNUT MOCHA with a sprinkle of cinnamon and a dash of nutmeg, please."

Sarah drummed the steering wheel while the attendant at the drive-through stall in Eastside Seattle whipped up her coffee. She usually ordered espresso to wake her up on gray October mornings, but in times of crisis a jolt of flavored caffeine usually helped perk her up.

Okay, so her father's death wasn't exactly a crisis; she hadn't seen him more than a handful of times since he and her mom had split up when Sarah was a baby. The shock was learning he'd left her Burrinbilli, the outback cattle station where her mother had grown up. Half the station, that is. The station manager owned the other half.

"Thanks," Sarah said to the attendant, and maneuvered the steaming foam cup through the window of her Mazda.

Back in the stream of traffic, she sipped her coffee and fantasized about buying the penthouse suite for sale on top of her employer's office building. If she lived there she could be at work by now. Imagine, rising at a civilized hour, having a leisurely breakfast in the café next door, then taking a mere elevator ride up to the computer programming department where she designed educational software. Urban paradise.

The traffic inched along. The windshield wipers slapped away the rain. The fax machine rang. Sarah pressed the start button and glanced at the emerging paper—a request for details on the new software package she was working on.

She could sell her half of Burrinbilli and buy that penthouse suite.

Or she could do something really nice for Mom.

She pulled into the car park opposite her office building and hurried across the street. Minutes later she stepped onto the fourth floor to navigate the rabbit warren of cubicles to her workspace. Some people complained about the cramped quarters, but Sarah didn't mind. She'd plastered the divider walls with *Far Side* cartoons and pictures of her cat. With her coffee at hand and a family-size bag of Gummi Bears in her drawer, what more could she ask for?

She pulled the letter from the executor of her father's estate out of her briefcase, punched in the phone number of Burrinbilli, then swung around to gaze at the old photo tacked to the wall of her cubicle, the receiver tucked under her ear. The little girl standing on the steps of the veranda and squinting into the brilliant sunlight of western Queensland was her mother.

Mom had raved about Burrinbilli for as long as Sarah could remember. Endless blue sky, the creek where she fished for the freshwater crayfish she called yabbies, the wide shady veranda that wrapped itself right around the elegant 1880s homestead.

And best of all, to Sarah's mind—Lake Burrinbilli.

The telephone rang and rang. Sarah wondered be-lately what time it was in Australia. Was it five hours ahead or nineteen behind? Either way, that meant... Uh-oh. She started to hang up the receiver.

"H'llo." The man on the other end stifled a yawn.

"Hi!" she said. "I've just realized what time it is there. I'll call back later."

"Who's this?"

"Sarah Templestowe. My father was Warren Temp—"

"What can I do for you?" His sleep-roughened twang suddenly had an edge like a boomerang.

"I'm looking for the station manager, Luke Sampson."

"You found him."

"Hello. Nice to meet you." *Slow down, Sarah. Breathe.* "I guess you'll have heard from his executor. That he left his half of the property to me, I mean."

"I heard. Sorry about your father."

"It's okay." She felt uncomfortable accepting condolences for a man she'd hardly known. The man who hadn't cared enough to do more than send a Christmas card and visit once every five years. Warren Templestowe might have been her biological father, but her stepdad, Dennis, had been the stable, loving man who'd always been there for her.

"I was going to call," Luke said. "Offer to buy you out."

"Oh, no," she said. "I want to buy *your* half."

A long silence ensued. "Hello?" Sarah said, thinking she'd lost the connection.

"A week before your father died I made him an offer on the property," Luke informed her. "I've got a bank loan arranged and the paperwork drawn up."

"Did he actually agree to sell?" Sarah doodled furiously on her scratch pad. "Did he sign any documents?"

"No," Luke said slowly. "But he hasn't put a bean into this place in years."

Sarah wasn't surprised her father had neglected the station. He'd never given her mother a cent for Sarah's maintenance, either. "Burrinbilli belonged to my mother's family—she grew up there. I'd like to give it back to her."

"I didn't know that about your mother," Luke said. "Burrinbilli used to be one of the best properties in the area, but with the drought times have been tough. There are better stations around if you're looking for an investment."

"What exactly is the problem?"

"Cattle yards need repairing. Machinery needs replacing. We badly need a new bull. That's just for starters."

"And the homestead?" Sarah twined the phone cord around her finger.

"Bloody shame about the homestead."

Her heart sank, but only for a moment. Something in his voice didn't quite ring true. "If it's that bad you should be glad I'm willing to take it off your hands so you can buy one of those other stations you were talking about."

"Well," he said slowly, "I guess we won't bulldoze it just yet." After a pause, his voice deepened. "The truth is, I've invested ten years and my life savings in this place. I don't intend to sell."

"I'll pay you whatever you want." It was a stupid thing to say, but she might do it if she could raise the money.

"Be careful, I could take you up on that—except I know you're probably in shock over your father's death."

"There was no love lost between me and my father."

"Fair enough. But I don't want money. I want the land. And *I'll* only pay the market value."

Sarah popped a red Gummi Bear in her mouth and pondered her next move. He sounded like one determined dude, but everyone had a weak point. However, she wouldn't find out his on the telephone. She hated traveling but... "I guess I'd better come down and check it out."

"Do you have some notion of running this place yourself?" he asked warily.

"Goodness, no! I wouldn't have the first idea. My home is here in Seattle. Would you have room for me to stay at the homestead if I come for a brief visit?"

"Plenty. Just my daughter and I live here. But we're coming up to the annual cattle muster," he warned. "And we're late this year, so I'll have my hands full."

"I won't disturb you. Promise." She'd only bug him a little, just enough to get him to sell. "I'd better go for now. Sorry for waking you."

"No worries."

"I'll let you know my flight number."

"Hop a train from Brisbane, then take the bus from Longreach. We're at the end of the line."

The end of the line? Oh, God. "I'll see you soon."

"Right, then. Cheers."

Sarah hung up. Her gazed drifted back to the faded

photo of Burrinbilli. It seemed to call to her. Or was that Luke's voice echoing in her imagination?

LUKE RAN WATER into the kettle. Through the window above the sink the predawn sky was paling in the east. A new owner for Burrinbilli—he'd thought it would be him. Bloody oath, it *would* be him. He was thirty-three and too old to be moving on.

Becka appeared in the doorway in her nightgown, clutching her doll. "You woke me up. Why are you having breakfast in the middle of the night?"

Luke forced himself not to react to her accusing tone. Was this hostile nine-year-old really his daughter? Where was the loving child who used to swing on his knee? And when had the emotional distance between them, as vast as the desert, sprung into existence? Maybe he should have taken her to live with him right after Caroline died, instead of leaving her with Caroline's aunt Abby. But how could he have cared for a baby when he was out on the cattle run all day?

"Go back to bed," he told Becka. "I'll be in around nine for morning tea. I'll make you breakfast then."

"I don't want to go back to bed. I want breakfast now." She dropped into a wooden chair at the long jarrah-wood table in the middle of the kitchen and twined a finger through her sleep-tangled blond hair.

Luke exhaled through flared nostrils. It'd only been a week since he'd brought her here; things were bound to get better. Meantime, he didn't have a clue how to discipline her. So he turned his back and set about making breakfast, cracking half a dozen eggs into one pan and frying strips of lean steak in another.

"I don't see why I had to leave Aunt Abby's to live out here in the middle of nowhere," Becka whined. "I want to go home."

"*This* is your home now. Abby and I agreed when you were a baby that when you turned nine you'd be old enough to live out at the station."

He hadn't realized then that the move would be such a huge emotional wrench for all of them. For most of Becka's life their only contact had been the few days a month he could get away from the station to spend with her. Was it any wonder she didn't want to be here with him now?

But she was his daughter, his flesh and blood, and he loved her. If Caroline hadn't drowned when that rust bucket Thai ferry sank he might have convinced her to marry him and move out to the station. They could have been a family.

Luke placed a plateful of steak and eggs in front of Becka and sat opposite. She stared at it, then at him, silent and incredulous.

He motioned to her plate with his fork. "Eat."

"I can't eat that! Why did you give me steak? Aunt Abby never cooks steak for breakfast."

"You're not at Aunt Abby's anymore. Better get used to it." He'd never liked Abby overly much; she was fussy and irritating and spoiled the girl something chronic. Although, to her credit, she loved Becka and had given the child the time and attention that Luke couldn't have.

His harsh tone made Becka's face crumple. She turned to the doll still cradled in her arms. "Don't worry, Suzy, we'll visit Aunt Abby soon."

Ah, hell. Luke laid a gentle hand on her arm. "Sorry if I sound a bit rough, possum. I'm not used to having a lady in the house. I'll have to learn to mind my manners."

"I want Coco Pops."

He pulled back his hand, muscles tense. "Next time we go into Longreach for supplies we'll get Coco Pops. Till then, eat up."

Still holding her doll, Becka picked up a fork and poked at the fried egg. "Couldn't I have stayed in Murrum at least until school ended?"

"The bus runs right by here. I'll drive you down to the road every morning."

"What about during the Wet when the road floods and I can't get to school? And I'll never be able to play with my friends on the weekends. Station life sucks."

Luke rapped the butt of his knife on the table. "Watch your mouth." Then he made an effort to soften his tone. "Summer holidays are coming up in December. You can have a friend out to stay."

Becka sullenly began to eat. A minute later she started in on him again. "You're out with the cattle all day. What am I going to do by myself? Who will help me with my lessons?"

"We'll sort something out. I'll help you in the evenings."

The situation was rough on her, he had to admit, moving away from town and the aunt she loved to the isolated station. Probably he should have let her finish the school year in town, but he hadn't thought, didn't have the experience to know, these things were so important to kids.

"You can come out on the motorbike with me this morning to check the water bores."

Her miserable glance of disdain told him what she thought of that idea. Luke carried his dishes to the sink, his love for his daughter like a knot of pain in his chest.

"Station life isn't so bad," he said, rinsing off his plate. "You can ride Smokey whenever you want."

"Aunt Abby was going to get me a puppy."

"We've got Wal, the Wonder Dog." In the corner by the stove, Wal raised his speckled black-and-white head and thumped his tail.

"He's not *mine*."

Luke had had enough of trying to appease her for one morning. "Listen, miss, your attitude had better change. We're going to have a guest shortly. The other part owner of the station is coming from America to see the property. I expect you to be polite and cheerful around her."

"Why would she want to come to this dump? If I were her I'd rather stay in America."

"She wants to bring her mother down here to live."

"Oh, great. Does that mean we'll have strangers living with us?"

Luke stopped short. He hadn't had time to consider all the implications. If he couldn't persuade Sarah Templestowe to sell her half of the station to him the situation could be tricky. "It might mean we'll move into the manager's cottage."

Her face fell. "Not that awful place."

"We'll soldier on, Becka, even if it means living in the jackaroo's quarters. Now, when you're finished your breakfast you can get dressed and help me feed the chooks.''

Luke went through the sliding glass doors onto the veranda. The rising sun had gilded the silvery limbs of the river gums down by the dry creek bed. From their towering branches, a flock of white corellas lifted, screeching as they flapped noisily away, their snowy crests spread against the deep-blue sky.

He loved Burrinbilli as much as if *he* had grown up here. And he'd been *that* close to having all of it.

He took his battered Akubra hat off the peg beside the door, clapped it on his head and headed toward the milking shed, whistling for Wal. Soldier on.

SARAH PUSHED THROUGH the door of her mother's import store, setting the brass bell to tinkling. The scent of ylang-ylang wafted from the oil burner on the windowsill beneath colored crystals and ornaments of stained glass. Anne was seated on a stool behind the counter, head bowed, as she entered accounts by hand into a ledger. Wisps of short auburn hair curled around her temples and a pair of half glasses sat midway down her nose.

''Hi, Mom.''

Anne glanced up and smiled. ''Sarah, darling, what brings you out on this awful day?''

''I had a meeting with the executor of Warren's estate last night.'' She dropped her briefcase on the floor and shed her wet coat onto the horns of a carved wooden rhinoceros. ''I've been trying to call you all day. Where've you been?''

''The phone was off the hook,'' Anne said, folding shut the ledger. ''It was hidden under a pile of papers and I didn't notice until a little while ago.''

Sarah laughed. "Only you would do something like that. Anyway, I'm glad you didn't have to be there. The way he swindled you out of Burrinbilli after your divorce was so unfair."

Anne adjusted the dark purple shawl draped over her black turtleneck sweater, her oval face expressing her resignation. "Let it go, darl', it's in the past. Anyway, he didn't swindle me out of it. I sold it to him."

Sarah tilted her head impatiently. "For a song."

"It allowed me to buy this shop, which was all I wanted back then—a place where I could work and care for you at the same time."

"But he left you with nothing."

"He left me you."

"Oh, Mom," Sarah said, her voice softening, and she stepped behind the counter to hug her mother. "I will never understand how anyone could walk out on you."

Anne's gaze shifted uncomfortably. "Since I wouldn't have met and married Dennis otherwise, I consider myself lucky your father and I split up. As for Burrinbilli, I always regretted letting it go, but...I've made my peace with the loss."

Sarah smiled, hugging her secret to herself a few minutes longer. "But you'd go back if you could, right?"

Anne got down from her stool and walked to the window to gaze out at the rain streaming down on the gray city streets. "I still dream about Burrinbilli," she said in her faintly accented voice. "The sun, the heat, the wonderful open country of the Downs—" her voice caught "—the homestead my great-grandfather built after he came out from England.'' She sighed and pulled her shawl tighter. ''What's that saying—'You can't go home again'?''

Sarah laughed, unable to contain herself any longer. ''But you can! Warren did one decent thing before he died. He left Burrinbilli to me.''

Anne turned, surprise and delight widening her dark brown eyes. ''You mean he still had it? I never would have thought he'd keep it all these years. That's wonderful!''

''Don't get too excited,'' Sarah cautioned. ''I don't own it completely. Apparently Warren ran into financial difficulties a few years ago and sold half to the station manager.''

''Oh, dear.'' Anne came back to the counter. ''And now it's too late to buy him out.''

''He wants it, too. I'm going down to Australia to convince him to sell me his half. And when the place is entirely fixed up you can retire and move back there.''

''I beg your pardon?'' Anne's voice sounded strangled.

''You can move to Burrinbilli,'' Sarah repeated. Her voice softened and she took her mother's hand. ''Dennis has passed on. You can go home. You've always said how much you missed Australia.''

''Yes, well…'' Anne pulled her hand away to run her slender fingers over a string of colored beads from Nepal. ''Are you actually traveling all the way to Burrinbilli?''

''You make it sound like the end of the earth. Not that that would worry *you*.'' Every year Anne practically begged her, in vain, to come along on her yearly buying trips to Third World countries.

Sarah moved the bead display to one side and

hoisted her briefcase onto the counter. "Wait till you see what I've got for us."

"Not another electronic gadget, I hope. I still haven't figured out the clock radio-cum-coffeemaker you gave me last Christmas."

"Oh, Mom." Sarah handed her an instruction booklet. "How are you doing with the laptop?"

"Don't ask."

"It would make your business so much more efficient if you'd only let it."

"I'm a Luddite, I'll admit. But I don't have room in my brain for programming instructions for a dozen different machines." Anne flipped through the pages of the booklet. "What's this, now?"

Sarah pulled two identical cellular phones from her briefcase. "Aren't they great? They also do fax and e-mail. We'll be able to communicate at all times."

Anne took one and gingerly turned it over in her hands. "When someone invents a device that facilitates genuine communication between people it'll be worth a fortune."

"*Mom.* Don't go all airy-fairy on me. Now watch. You press this button to make a phone call. That one to send a fax, and that and that for e-mail. Don't worry about the Internet connection. I've hooked you up to my server."

"I'll never use it."

"Try it," she urged. "You'll be surprised."

Anne put the cell phone down and held up her desk phone. "You can call me on this. And you've already got a cell phone. Why do you need another?"

"I thought it would be fun. This is an updated model that's compatible with Australia and Japan.

The new digital system spans the Pacific. Cool, huh?''

''Amazing.''

Sarah ignored her mother's dry tone and packed her phone back in her briefcase. ''Why don't you come with me to Queensland? It would be so much more fun going together.''

The bell over the door tinkled. Two teenage girls entered, smiled a greeting to Anne and disappeared behind a rack of cotton dresses from Ghana.

''I can't leave the shop just now, darl'.'' Anne gestured around her at the displays of colorful bric-a-brac.

To Sarah the store looked just as it always did— cluttered and colorful and a little too retro for her taste, but not desperate for attention. ''Your friend Mandy would take care of the place for you.''

''She left last night for two weeks in Mexico.'' Anne, her face suddenly troubled, reached out to stroke the hair away from Sarah's cheek. ''You're the sweetest girl in the world, but are you sure you want to do this?''

Sarah gave her a tight smile. ''Not entirely. I'd really miss you if you moved back there.''

''Then why don't you sell your half of the station and buy the apartment you have your heart set on?''

Sarah dismissed that with a wave of her hand. ''What would I want with an apartment? I'm too young to settle down.''

''What about what's-his-name, Quincy—?''

''Quentin.'' Sarah rolled her eyes. ''He gets a rash every time the word *marriage* is mentioned and rushes off to phone his analyst.''

''I thought *he* was an analyst.''

"He is, but apparently Physician Heal Thyself doesn't apply to shrinks. Anyway, I've decided I can't marry him. I want a *real* man."

Anne laughed. "And what is that, darl'?"

"I don't know exactly, but it's not Quentin." She glanced at her watch. "I'm on my way to the travel agent. Are you sure you don't want to come? I could book us two seats. You've never been back except for Pop's funeral, then Nana's, and that was years ago. We could have so much fun together."

Anne's eyes clouded. "There are too many ghosts, darl', living and dead."

Sarah studied her mother's face, totally not understanding her reluctance and certain it was time those ghosts were laid to rest. "Mom, all my life you've sacrificed for me. At last I have a chance to do something really special for you."

"I appreciate the thought more than I can say. You have a good time in Oz. You can tell me all about it when you get back. If nothing else you'll have a break from work. It's been what—two years since you've had a holiday?"

"Something like that. I'm looking forward to this trip. You know, discovering my roots and all."

A tiny smile curled Anne's mouth. "Maybe *you'll* decide to stay."

Sarah laughed. "Not a chance."

"Make sure you pack lightweight clothing. It's heading toward summer down there and it gets hot."

"I'm going shopping right after I arrange for my ticket."

"Take care, darl'," Anne said, hugging Sarah close. "If you run into Len Johnson, tell him..." She trailed off, her cheeks tinged with pink.

Sarah didn't think she'd ever seen her mother blush before. "Tell him what? Who's Len Johnson?"

The teenage girls came up to the counter with an armload of scented candles. Anne nodded to them before replying, "Just someone I used to...know. On second thought, you don't need to tell him anything."

Sarah moved aside so the girls could lay their purchases on the counter. "This is going to be so cool," she said. "Seeing your old stomping grounds, meeting your old friends..."

"Don't expect too much," Anne warned. "Compared with Seattle, Murrum is just a dusty little town in the back of beyond."

"I'm going to love it! Anyway, it's only for two weeks. I'll be back before you know it."

CHAPTER TWO

SARAH SHIFTED uncomfortably on the bus seat. The hem of her skirt had ridden up and her bare thighs were sticking to the vinyl. She'd been traveling for over thirty six hours and she felt grimy and hot and sweaty. She couldn't remember the last time she'd brushed her teeth.

The air-conditioning had broken down hours ago. The second-last passenger got out not long after. The sun was a yellow glare in a frighteningly immense blue-white sky. The flat red earth, sparsely covered with dry grass and dotted with cattle, spread to a distant horizon. With a shudder she pulled her gaze back inside the bus. Outside was too big, too empty, to look at.

Australians might affectionately call their country Oz, she thought moodily, *but out here the yellow brick road was a dusty red track across hundreds of miles of nothing and it led* away *from Seattle, the Emerald City, not to it.*

Out of the heat haze appeared the silhouettes of houses and stores. Oh, thank heavens, a town. Like the other towns she'd passed through, the shops had false fronts, wide streets and broad wooden awnings that shaded the sidewalk. They looked a little like towns of the Old West except for the occasional palm tree, which destroyed the illusion. The bus passed a tiny wooden church and a big, ornate hotel with a second-story veranda before slowing to a halt beside a boarded-up train station.

Murrumburrumgurrandah. The town's moniker rattled along the sign above the platform like an old man's phlegmy cough.

Shielding her eyes from the blinding sun, Sarah stepped off the bus onto the hard-packed red dirt beside the road. The heat hit her like a dry sauna, sucking the moisture from her skin and turning her ivory linen skirt and top as soft as dishrags.

While the driver retrieved her luggage Sarah stood in the shade of the corrugated-iron bus shelter and fanned herself with the magazine she'd bought in Sydney. It kept the flies off but didn't provide much of a breeze. If she didn't get to someplace cool *right now* she was going to expire of heat exhaustion.

"Someone meeting you?" The driver set her bags at her feet, then wiped the sweat off his forehead, smearing his skin with red dust.

"Yes, at least I think so. Is there a taxi service into the town center?" Second on her priority list was a long cool drink followed by a double latte with a generous sprinkling of cinnamon.

The driver tipped back his hat to scratch his head. "This *is* the center of town."

That was what she'd been afraid of.

"Where is everybody?"

He shrugged. "Middle of the day, most folks stay out of the sun."

"Do you know if there's a telephone booth?" The batteries on her cell phone were flat from hours of talking to her mother in the airport and on the train trip.

"You can call from the petrol station up the road."

"Thanks."

The driver got back in his bus, made a U-turn in the middle of the wide empty street and pulled away in a cloud of red dust. When the pall had cleared Sarah gazed around her for anyone who might be Luke Sampson. There was no one in sight but a lone sheep chewing the stubble beside the road, its fleece as red and dusty as the dirt. Could this deserted place really be the bustling town of her mother's child-hood?

Panic fluttered in her breast. Spooky music echoed in her brain. She'd entered the twilight zone.

And not a drive-through coffee stall in sight.

Stop it, she told herself. *Think.* Petrol was gasoline. So the petrol station would be that low-slung build-ing up ahead with the pumps. Looking closer, she saw that in the dappled shade of a gum tree, two men sat on a bench, drinking soda from bottles and watch-ing her.

With the sun crisping the skin on her nose and the sweat dripping down the back of her neck, Sarah hitched up her bags, quashed her misgivings and set forth across the baking tarmac. Her spirits picked up a little when she saw the men wave. At least the locals were friendly. Her hands were full and she couldn't wave back, so she smiled, instead. The men kept waving languidly. Sarah kept smiling. She smiled and smiled.

Until a fly buzzed around her nose and she shook her head to send it away. Another fly came and landed on her chin. Half a dozen more lit on her arms and on her hands, still wrapped around the suitcase handles. One landed on her upper lip and tried to fly up her nostril. *Eeeuuww.* She dropped her bags in the middle of the road and batted at the cloud of flies buzzing around her head.

The men weren't being friendly—they were waving away the damn flies!

A once white Land Cruiser, now red with caked-on dust, motored around the corner and pulled in at the service station. A man in beige pants and a light-brown shirt with the sleeves rolled up got out. He lifted his broad-brimmed hat, revealing wheat-colored hair streaked with gold and ocher. "G'day. Sarah Templestowe?"

The voice from the telephone. "Luke. Hi."

A large sun-browned hand enclosed hers in a callused grip. "Bus must've been on time for once."

She shrugged and smiled, too hot and weary to make small talk. But not too tired to notice his piercing blue eyes.

He picked up her bags. "If you don't need anything in town we'll save the Cook's tour for another day and head straight to Burrinbilli."

"Fine." She doubted there was a single thing in this godforsaken town she wanted. As for tourist attractions, the concept made her want to laugh. Which was maybe his intention, though it was hard to tell from that dry-as-dust tone.

They went past the men on the bench. The younger man, deeply tanned and not more than twenty, wore a large sheathed knife strapped to the belt of his dusty shorts, and an open shirt with the sleeves cut out. Around his neck was a choker of some carnivore's teeth. He raised a smoothly muscled brown arm to tip back a leather hat with a feather stuck in the band. "Luke. How ya goin', mate?"

"Could be worse." Luke gestured to Sarah. "This is Sarah, from Seattle. She's the new part owner of Burrinbilli. This is Bazza." He indicated the young man. "And this is Len," he added, nodding at the older man. "Len's the mayor of Murrum and he owns the general store."

Len. Sarah eyed him curiously. He looked about Anne's age, and under his broad-brimmed hat his face was kindly and intelligent. A hearing aid was tucked discreetly behind one ear. He wore a blue cotton shirt with the sleeves rolled up and navy twill pants. He was studying her, too.

She smiled at them both. "Hi. Nice to meet you."

"I'll be mustering in a week or so," Luke said to Bazza. "Interested?"

"Yep. I reckon Gus and Kev'll be interested, as well." Bazza pulled out tobacco and rolling papers and leisurely prepared a cigarette. He glanced at Sarah. "You been to Hollywood?"

"Uh, no," she said, caught off guard. "Although my mother took me to Disneyland on my tenth birthday."

"I was in a movie some American blokes filmed out here last year." He lit his rollie and squinted through a puff of blue smoke. "*Outback Ordeal.* Ever heard of it?"

Bazza's drawl and thick accent forced her to listen hard to understand his words. Aware of Luke standing slightly behind her, waiting, she searched for a tactful remark. "I don't get to a lot of movies."

Len spoke. "You're Anne Hafford's daughter."

"Yes," she said, happily seizing on a link with

reality. "Mom told me about you. Well, she didn't actually *tell* me *anything*. Just that I should say hello if I saw you. It's so cool to meet someone from her childhood. Did you know her very well?"

He smiled blandly. "A little. For a while."

She couldn't read his face so she just babbled on. "She'll be so pleased I met you. And on my very first day, too. I'll tell her you said hello, shall I?"

There was a long pause. "If you like."

Behind her, Luke cleared his throat. She glanced back and he nodded toward the four-wheel-drive. *Sure,* Sarah thought, as she turned to follow him, *why waste words?* She'd used enough for all four of them. "Nice meeting you," she said again over her shoulder to Bazza and Len.

When she was a few steps away she heard Bazza say in a low voice obviously not meant for her ears, "Not hard on the old peepers, but a bit of a dag, don't you reckon?"

Sarah couldn't make out Len's softly spoken reply. *Dag?* she thought, and strode after Luke. What the heck was a dag? Or had he said *dog?* She'd never been called a dog before.

Luke was placing her bags in the back of the Land Cruiser. "Is he for real?" she asked.

"Bazza?" Luke smiled. "Ever since he got a bit part in that movie he's been waiting for a call from Spielberg. Thinks he's bloody Crocodile Dundee. Don't pay any attention."

"He doesn't bother me," she said. It was Len she found unsettling. She'd give anything to know what had gone on between him and her mother.

She climbed in on the passenger side and strapped herself in, noticing with dismay that her top and skirt were dusted with fine red earth. So much for first impressions. She tried to brush the earth off and it smeared, staining the pale fabric. Perfect.

She caught Luke staring at her. "It's okay. Rust is my color. What's a dag?"

One corner of his mouth lifted. "Don't worry about it."

He started the vehicle and drove through town— a trip that took all of ten seconds.

Sarah flipped down the sunshade to reduce the glare and kept her gaze firmly fixed on the truck's interior. Her discomfort at being surrounded by the wide-open spaces was increasing instead of easing. After this, Burrinbilli had better be good.

Be positive, she chided herself. *Be the little Aussie battler your mother taught you to be.*

After this, Burrinbilli would be *damn* good.

LUKE DROVE in silence, thinking about poor Wal, who'd been left at home in case Sarah Templestowe was afraid of dogs, and how pathetic his life must be if he felt less comfortable with a woman seated beside him instead of Wal. He rubbed his jaw, unused to being smooth-shaven in the middle of the day.

"Mustering is like a roundup, right?" Sarah asked.

Damn, he'd forgotten to put up the notice in Len's store advertising for a muster cook. "That's right. Normally we muster during winter, when it's cooler. Cattle don't like working in this heat."

"Why the delay?"

"I broke my leg in a tractor accident a couple months back. Took a while to heal."

"Oh, I'm sorry. What kind of cows do you—*we*— own?"

"Santa Gertrudis."

"Oh."

He glanced sideways and caught her mild frown. No doubt cows were like cars to a city-bred woman—identified by color rather than breed or model. "They're the solid reddish-brown ones. Originated in Texas."

"Oh. And the cattle yards you mentioned on the phone are…?"

"Where we hold the cattle after we bring them in from the run—for branding, drenching, cutting out the yearling bulls—whatever needs doing." He realized she was actually listening. Maybe she *was* interested in the station. Well, it would justify her father's hanging on to it all these years, but it didn't bode well for him buying her out. "Do you ride?"

She hesitated, casting a lightning-swift glance out the window. "Er, once or twice at summer camp. I don't suppose that counts."

"I could find you a gentle mount."

"You don't have to worry about entertaining me," she added quickly. "I'm only here for a short time and I'm sure I'll have way too much to do to be a tourist."

"Fine." It was all he could do just taking care of the station and dealing with Becka.

"How far is it to Burrinbilli?" she asked.

"Eighty kilometers or thereabouts. This grassy plains country we're driving through is called the Downs." His gaze slipped sideways again, to see her lightly freckled nose wrinkle as she engaged in mental calculations. Her cheek was smeared with dust and her clothes a disaster. Her auburn hair was twisted up at the back, but the ends sprayed out in a spiky arc from the plastic thing that clamped it in place.

He smiled. Bazza was right. She *did* look a bit of a dag. Still, clean her up and she'd be bonza—tall, with long, strong limbs. He liked a woman who didn't look as if she might snap in a stiff breeze. She had the warm coloring that went with auburn hair and the clearest green eyes he'd ever seen.

"Why, that's...fifty miles!" she exclaimed. She whipped her head around to look through the rear window at the road down which they'd come. "Please don't tell me Murrum is the nearest town."

"Didn't you know that?"

"I knew it was a long way from Burrinbilli to the town, but from what my mother said, Murrum was a bustling place."

"Things have changed since your mother's day." He couldn't keep the trace of bitterness out of his voice. "First the train stopped coming through. Then the banks pulled out. Then we lost the post office and the government offices were relocated. Wasn't much left after that except the pub, the petrol station and the general store. Oh, and the church. They share that around the various religions."

She shook her head sympathetically. "Economic rationalism strikes again."

She was right, but something in him didn't want her feeling sorry for the place he called home. "Some folks say Murrum's picking up again. Tourism and such."

There was the briefest pause. "I'm sure it is."

Luke had spent enough time in cities to know what she must be thinking: why would anyone live out here? It wasn't something city folk understood. Not many people who came from the "big smoke" stayed long to discover the attraction. Rose had stayed. But Rose had married Tony, the owner of the pub. Luke couldn't see someone like Sarah settling down with anyone around here.

"How long did you say you were here for?"

"I've taken my two weeks' annual leave. I've also got a few weeks' worth of flextime owing me, but I'm hoping to be home before the end of the month."

He reckoned she'd be long gone before that. Bazza and Len each had five dollars on the departure date. They'd wanted to cut him in, but seeing as she was staying at his house, he didn't think it right to participate.

But it wasn't just his house, he realized. *Their house?* That didn't sound right. He and Warren had never felt the need to clarify who had rights to the homestead.

They passed a small wooden cottage set back from the road. Luke pointed it out with a nod. "That's where my daughter's great-aunt Abby lives. Becka's visiting her this afternoon after school."

"How old is your daughter?"

"Nine."

"You didn't mention a wife. Are you divorced?"

She inquired with such innocent directness he found it hard to take offense. But some people needed to understand that other people didn't like to talk about their personal lives. He told her part of the truth. "I've never been married."

"Oh."

He could tell she wanted to know more, but this time she just nodded and pressed her lips together. There was nothing shameful about his relationship with Caroline. She just hadn't wanted to get married, not even after she'd gotten pregnant. She'd said she didn't want to marry anybody, but she'd died before it could be proven one way or the other.

"Are you going to have to go all the way back for Becka?" Sarah asked.

Luke shook his head. "Abby's bringing her out later."

Silence fell over the truck. She must be thinking up more questions, Luke thought. He stared straight ahead, not wanting to disturb the peace, and wondered if the fencing materials he'd ordered would arrive tomorrow. Halfway to the station turnoff the bitumen ended and they continued on a hard-packed red dirt road. A road that developed deep pockets of fine dust called bulldust in the Dry and became a red bog—and often a lake—in the Wet. When they *had* a decent Wet.

"I can't wait to go for a swim," Sarah said, plucking her damp top away from her chest.

He gave a short laugh. "Swim?"

"Yes, in Lake Burrinbilli." Sarah leaned back with a dreamy smile. "When I was a little girl Mom told me how she and her brother, Robby, used to swim there. With this heat I can see why it's important to have water nearby."

"Your mother told you she swam in a lake?" He wanted to laugh, but it wouldn't be nice.

"Everything sounded beautiful, the way she described it—the old Victorian homestead set among ghost gums, and out the back, not far away, Lake Burrinbilli. I am *so* hot and that water is going to feel *so* good."

Ah, that *lake*. Luke wished he'd placed a bet with

Bazza and Len after all. He would have cut Bazza's estimate of four days in half. "The, ah, water level's down a little. Not too good for swimming."

Her mouth drooped, but only for a moment. "Oh, well, splashing around will cool me off."

"There might be a water hole in the creek that hasn't dried up."

Her eyes widened. "But…?"

He caught sight of the old refrigerator they used as a mailbox and geared down. "Here we are."

"Where?" She gazed around at the featureless landscape. He could swear he saw her shudder.

"The driveway," Luke said, and turned off onto a rutted dirt track.

Sarah took another glance outside and this time he was positive about the look of revulsion.

"The driveway?" she repeated, aghast.

"Yep. Only thirty kilometers to the homestead from here."

Sarah heard this with a sinking heart. By now she knew every detail of the dashboard as well as she knew the keyboard of her computer. She watched the digital speedometer with glazed eyes. Anything to take her mind off the weird feeling that stopped her from looking out the window. She'd never experienced anything like it before. But then, she'd spent all her life nestled between the mountains and the sea, swaddled in cozy enveloping clouds that lowered the sky and brought the horizon in close.

Just when she thought she couldn't stand it another minute, she saw in the distance a stand of smooth white-limbed trees and the sloping roof of the homestead, half-buried among their leafy branches.

Burrinbilli at last.

She'd never been here and the landscape was completely foreign, but she'd heard so many stories that she felt a strange sense of homecoming. Here, her mother had lived as a child. Here, her grandmother had given birth to her mother. Here, her great-great-grandparents had built the homestead and run cattle.

Luke lived here now. Had for ten years. It probably felt like home to him, too, and for more tangible reasons than hers. She glanced sideways at him, wondering what he really felt about her visiting. His chiseled profile gave nothing away.

"Have you given any more consideration to my offer to buy you out?" she asked.

Luke stopped in front of a wire gate across the road and put the truck in neutral. "Only how I might convince you to sell, instead. I was a signature away from owning it all."

"I've brought back your deposit." She rummaged in her purse for an envelope and held it out to him.

Ignoring it, Luke swiveled on the bench seat to face her, one elbow resting on the seat back, the other on the steering wheel. "I would have thought you'd honor your father's intent."

Luke was a big man, Sarah realized, tall, broad shouldered and well muscled. But being tall herself she wasn't intimidated by size. "I don't know my father's intent. Anyway, I owe him nothing."

Luke pushed a hand through his hair, sweat dampened at the temples from his hat. "How can that be?"

"After he and my mother split up he bought Burrinbilli from her for a pittance. Not long after that he remarried and moved to the east coast," Sarah added bitterly. As good a father as Dennis had been to her, it still hurt that her real father had cared so little about her.

"I'm surprised your mother didn't return to Australia after her marriage broke up."

"Her father died fighting a bushfire not long after she came to America. Her brother had been killed in Vietnam the year before. With no men left to run Burrinbilli, my grandmother passed it on to Mom, thinking she and Warren would come back. Nana went to live on the coast, where she died when I was about ten. So even though Mom owned the station, none of her family lived there anymore. I guess she didn't feel she had much to come back to."

Sarah paused to take a breath. The glazed look on Luke's face suggested he already knew more than he ever wanted to about her family history. But she wanted to get it all over at once. "Also, Mom thought I should be raised near my father. The trouble was, his second wife didn't want him to have anything to do with us. By the time Mom realized Warren wasn't going to go against her to see me, she'd met my stepfather, Dennis, who had an established business in Seattle. So, she stayed."

"I see." Luke eyed her warily a moment, as if to make sure she'd really stopped. Then he yanked on the hand brake and jumped out of the truck to stride toward the gate.

Sarah sat where she was, her stomach churning as it always did when she thought about her father. Watching Luke walk back to the Land Cruiser, she recalled the old Mills and Boon romances by Lucy Walker, which were set in the outback and which she used to sneak from her mother's cache of books as a young girl. It was the passenger's job to open and close the gates.

Luke got back in and drove through the gate. "I'll shut it," Sarah said when he stopped on the other side.

She jogged back to the gate through the searing heat. The metal latch burned her fingertips as she pushed it shut. Then she made the mistake of glancing over the top of the gate. The land was so huge, so open. Nothing for her eyes to fasten on except the haze of heat that shimmered over the dusty track. To her surprise, a wave of panic quivered through her. Oh, no...

Her chest tightened until she was literally gasping for breath. Black spots appeared before her eyes and she doubled over, wrapping her arms around her waist. Beads of cold sweat popped out on her forehead. She was going to pass out...

Strong hands gripped her shoulders. "Keep your head down. Breathe deeply."

She did as he said and after a minute she was breathing easier. "Thanks," she said shakily, and struggled upright.

Luke's eyes searched her face. "What happened? You went as white as a ghost gum."

Sarah smiled feebly. "I felt...a little...faint. It must be the heat."

He regarded her dubiously but said nothing as he helped her back to the vehicle.

Sarah was quiet the rest of the way. The heat, although a fierce contrast to autumn rains in Seattle, hadn't caused that panic attack. She knew that was what it was because of Quentin, even though she'd never experienced one before.

Finally they topped a low rise and her worry fled as she got her first close-up view of Burrinbilli. The homestead was a long single-story building bordered by two stocky palm trees. Built of creamy sandstone blocks, it had a sloping roof of sage-green corrugated iron and a wide wraparound veranda. Tall narrow windows flanked by shutters were set into the walls at intervals. The iron pillars supporting the veranda were lush with a tangle of purple bougainvillea that almost obscured the intricate iron filigree trim.

"Vines are overgrown," Luke said, braking to a halt.

"It's beautiful," Sarah declared from the edge of her seat.

A speckled black-and-white dog with pointy ears and stubby legs rose from the veranda, barked once and wagged his nether regions furiously as Luke got out of the truck.

"How ya goin', mate?" He bent to rub the dog behind the ears, then presented him to Sarah. "Wal, the Wonder Dog."

"Hello, Wal. Aren't you gorgeous." She crouched to let him sniff her hand. "Wonder Dog? Does he do tricks?"

"Nah, he's a blue heeler, a working cattle dog. I call him Wonder Dog just to make him feel good."

Sarah rose and gazed around. A hundred yards away to the left of the homestead gardens was a me-andering line of huge gum trees. They must mark the path of the creek, she thought excitedly. To the right was a field dotted with horses. A glossy chestnut trot-ted along the fence toward them, arching its muscular neck and tossing its mane.

Sarah noted the spring in its step and briefly regretted her lie about not knowing how to ride. "Summer camp" had been a series of intensive courses in advanced equitation. The lie had come on impulse, an instinctive denial so she wouldn't be expected to ride in the open country.

She would have to get over this phobia. That was all there was to it.

She climbed the single shallow step onto the shady veranda, her sandals sounding dull on the wooden flooring as she crossed to the entrance. A fanlight topped the door and on either side were panels of engraved glass. Sarah traced the roughened surface of a Scotch thistle twined with roses and shamrocks. Her mother had an antique silver-and-garnet brooch in the same pattern.

She'd known none of Warren's family background and precious little of her mother's. Here at last was her heritage. She hadn't missed it until this moment, but now the smidgen she glimpsed left her wanting more.

She heard a step behind her and turned to find Luke with her suitcases in hand. "Thanks. Sorry, I should have helped bring those in. I was just so excited at seeing the house. I never thought it would affect me this much. Suddenly I'm reliving all sorts of memories—my mother's memories, really—stories she's told me through the years. I feel I know Burrinbilli almost as well as if I'd lived here myself."

Luke gave her a dry glance and gestured her inside. "Make yourself at home."

Oops, her pride of ownership was showing. Sarah stepped into the large entrance hall, her gaze rising to the high, ornate plaster ceiling before alighting on an impressive glass-encased display of butterflies.

"Of course, I couldn't ever *live* here," she assured him. "I'm an urban girl through and through. Bright lights, skyscrapers, the sound of traffic in the streets. To tell you the truth, all this quiet makes me nervous. Give me an apartment, a café and a view of the city over Puget Sound and I'm at home. Speaking of water, will you show me the lake?"

Luke hung his hat on a peg beside the door. "Okay. But like I said, it's not what you're expecting."

CHAPTER THREE

HE LED THE WAY to the other side of the house, through the biggest country kitchen Sarah had ever seen. She just caught sight of a stone fireplace you could stand up in enclosing a modern stainless-steel stove before Luke pushed open the sliding doors to the back veranda.

This section of the veranda was enclosed with fly screen and clearly used as an extension of the living space. At one end stood a child's school desk and bookshelves, while at the other end wicker chairs padded with cushions were grouped around an outdoor table.

She gazed eagerly through the screen, past the sheds and the clothesline and the tall trees whose spreading boughs shaded the yard to— *Huh?* Where the lake should have been was nothing but a broad dent in the dry red earth. Tufts of salt grass grew here and there.

"That's it?" Although he'd warned her, seeing the empty lake bed made her feel like crying. Anticipation of Lake Burrinbilli had sustained her through the long hours of the journey and now... It simply didn't exist. "When did it last have water in it?"

"Three, maybe four years ago. It's not really a lake, just a depression that holds water when it floods. It's been six years since it was deep enough to paddle in.''

Sarah pressed two fingers to her closed eyelids and felt moisture seep beneath her lashes. Fatigue was sending her emotions up and down like a yo-yo. She was dying for a coffee, but even more than that she wanted to be alone with her disappointment. ''I think I'll take a shower and lie down.''

''It's a different world when the rains come,'' Luke said, as if he hadn't heard her. ''Green shooting up over the Downs, thousands of wildflowers. Frogs seem to spring right out of the mud. Flocks of birds so large they darken the sky.''

Sarah opened her eyes. He was gazing across the dry lake bed, looking into the past. Or maybe it was the future.

''I wish I could see that,'' she said, blinking at the sun-bleached landscape. Faced with reality, she numbly realized that even her mother's memories failed her.

''Life will flourish here again.'' His eyes, locked briefly with hers, seemed to add, *For those who stay.*

He led her back through the kitchen and down a long hall. ''This is my room. Becka's room.'' He gestured to closed doors. ''Loungeroom's out the front. Bathroom's in there. And this—'' he pushed open a door and stood aside ''—is your room.''

Sarah stepped past him into a square room with faded floral wallpaper. The matching curtains were clean but frayed around the edges. A white coverlet lay across the iron single bed. On the opposite wall sat a dresser made of distressed pine that her antique-collecting friends in Seattle would pay big money for. In one corner stood a matching old-fashioned wardrobe. Overhead a ceiling fan whirred quietly.

Luke set her bags down beside the bed and returned to the doorway. "I was going to move out of the main bedroom while you're here, but—"

"I wouldn't want to put you out."

"I reckon this was your mother's room."

"My mother's room?" she said, glancing around with new interest. "What makes you think so?"

He nodded toward the dresser and a notebook lying on top. "I found her diary tucked under a loose floorboard beside the bed. Must have been there for years. I told your father about it, but he didn't mention returning it. Don't know why, but I kept it instead of throwing it out."

Sarah moved across the room to pick up the notebook. Scrawled in a loopy, slanted hand on the front of the faded red cover were the words *Anne's Diary. Private. Keep Out. This means you!*

Sarah smiled. The handwriting was more rounded and immature than nowadays, but it was definitely Anne's. "Did you read it?"

Luke looked offended she would even ask. "Says right on the cover that it's private. Anyway, I don't have time to read girls' diaries."

Sarah flipped through the closely written pages and found herself tempted. *Don't even think it.* She returned the diary to the dresser. "I'll take it to her. She might find it amusing after all these years."

"Right. Well, I'll let you get settled." He backed out of the room and shut the door.

Sarah put her clothes away, then flopped on the bed with her cell phone. She replaced the old batteries with the spares from her suitcase and dialed her mother's number.

"Hi, Mom," she said, disappointed when she got the answering machine. "I'm here. My God, what a trip! It's *so* hot. How come you never mentioned the flies? *And the lake that's not a lake.* But the homestead is beautiful. By the way, Luke found your old diary. Oh, and I've already met Len. What's the deal with him? I'm going to rest now, but I'll call you later. Love you. Bye."

LUKE PACED the front veranda, his frowning gaze on the dirt track that cut across the Downs toward Murrum. The wide western sky was bloodred with the setting sun, yet still no cloud of dust heralded Abby and Becka's arrival.

"Where do you suppose they are, Wal?"

The dog, who was never far from Luke's side, pressed his cold nose against his master's palm.

Luke heard a movement behind him and turned to see Sarah standing in the doorway. She'd put on a sleeveless cotton-knit dress, which hugged her curves and showed plenty of leg. Her damp auburn hair fell in long wispy spikes around her bare shoulders. His dormant libido stirred like a bear after a long winter, ravenous and on the prowl.

"Is something wrong?" She came forward, bringing with her the subtle fruity scent of her shampoo.

"It's almost seven o'clock. Abby hasn't brought Becka back yet." *Back in your cave, Sampson.*

Sarah stooped to pat Wal. "Maybe she's on her way."

"Abby won't drive out here in the dark. It's too

easy to stray from the track and get lost. She said she'd have Becka back in time for tea.''

''Tea? Oh, you mean dinner.'' Sarah glanced down the track and stepped behind the screen of bougainvillea, her fingers brushing the glossy dark green leaves. ''Maybe her car broke down or she got caught up in something.''

Luke strode back into the house to ring Abby again, realizing belatedly that he'd just walked off without a word. He wasn't used to informing others of his movements. First Becka, and now Sarah.

''Hello?'' Abby sounded pleasant, unconcerned.

''Why aren't you here?'' he demanded. ''Is Becka okay?''

Outside the kitchen window, dozens of snowy white corellas screeched as they flapped home to roost in the river gums.

He listened to Abby's excuses— ''Low on petrol, the station's closed for the night, tried to call you earlier.'' She was unapologetic, unrepentant, plausible. He wanted to rant and rave and tell her how worried he'd been, but that would be overreacting.

''Okay. Okay,'' he said, reassuring himself rather than her. ''I'll pick Becka up tomorrow.'' He wasn't taking any chances on more excuses.

He found Sarah on the side veranda, watching the corellas perform acrobatics in the branches, swinging upside down and cracking gum nuts between their strong hooked beaks as they squabbled among themselves. Luke's attention, though, was drawn to the curve of Sarah's neck, lengthened by her upturned face and repeated in her wide smile as she turned her delighted gaze upon him. ''Aren't they gorgeous!''

''Yeah,'' he grunted. ''Want something to eat?''

"Yes, please." She followed him back inside. "Did you get hold of Abby?"

Luke smoothed his face into an expressionless mask. "Becka's staying overnight. I'll pick her up tomorrow."

Sarah's green eyes probed his. "Are you all right with that?"

No, he was not "all right" with that. He'd barely had his daughter with him a week before she was back at Abby's. What really rankled was that he'd had no choice but to let Becka stay, unless he wanted to make the long trip back into Murrum. Abby must have known he'd be reluctant to do that on Sarah's first night. He felt bamboozled by Abby and oddly uneasy about leaving Becka.

"She'll be okay," he assured Sarah, but the catch-all phrase was meaningless in the present context. "Come and have some tucker. Hope you like steak and potatoes."

"Steak! I haven't had a steak since 1989."

"We eat the odd one around here. You a vegetarian?" He was amused that the owner of a cattle station might not like beef.

"No, I just don't usually eat big chunks of meat."

"I reckon we can find you a knife." But first he opened the bottle of cabernet sauvignon he'd been saving for a special occasion. He twisted the cork off, not even wanting to think about what was prompting him to serve his best wine.

"That's an interesting corkscrew," Sarah said, examining the implement. The handle was fashioned out of a cow's horn, with a large nail driven through and twisted into a tight spiral.

"My grandfather made it. He made or grew just

about everything he owned and used. He was so self-sufficient he even made his own coffin and dug his own grave.''

She grinned. ''And this is something you aspire to?''

''Self-sufficiency, yes, but I'm not turning the sod just yet.'' His answering smile felt rusty through disuse. He hadn't exactly wanted her to come here, but at least she was taking his mind off Abby and Becka.

After dinner they carried their coffee out to the side veranda. Luke settled into a creaking slung canvas squatter's chair. Before Sarah's arrival he'd wondered what kind of a person she would be and what arguments he could use to convince her to sell him her half of the station. It had never occurred to him that he might find himself attracted to her. He propped his booted feet high against the pillar and tried not to dwell on it. She wasn't even that pretty, he told himself. Her nose had a slight bump and her jaw was a touch strong....

Sarah remained standing, her hands wrapped around her cup. ''It sure is quiet.''

''You think so? Sounds pretty noisy to me, what with the cicadas down by the creek and the possums crashing around in the gums....''

''Doesn't it get lonely out here all by yourselves?''

Only at night, going to a solitary bed.

''There's a difference between being alone and being lonely,'' he said. ''Anyway, we get plenty of visitors passing through. I catch up with friends at race meetings or dances.''

Luke rubbed a thumb around the rim of his cup. Compared with town, it *was* isolated. He was used to it, but Becka wasn't. If only she were an outdoor sort of kid she might be happier at spending time with him out on the cattle run. Abby had turned her into a townie.

He glanced up to see Sarah sip her coffee and grimace. "Coffee okay?"

"Fine." She smiled brightly. "Just fine."

Like hell, he thought, but it was the best he had. Suddenly he wished he had something better to offer. But she was a townie; probably nothing would seem good enough. "What do you do back in Seattle?"

"I'm a computer programmer. I design educational software for a large company. Are you on the Internet?"

Luke snorted. "I'd rather cross the Simpson Desert than venture into cyberspace."

"Really?" Sarah paced down the veranda. "I don't know how you stand all this emptiness."

"It's not empty. It's full of life if you know where to look. I'd go off my nut cooped up in a city."

She wandered back and leaned against a pillar, gazing down at him. "What did you do before you came to Burrinbilli?"

"I was a stockman in far north Queensland on a station owned by a large pastoral company."

"And before that?"

"Did some traveling. Before that I was a jackaroo on my uncle's station near Hughenden. That's where I grew up." In the deep dusk of the gum trees a kookaburra made its laughing call. Another chimed in, and another. *You don't hear that in the city.* "I had a friend as a kid, an aboriginal from the local community. He and I would go out in the desert. His grandfather taught him how to track and find water and hunt. And he taught me."

Her eyes widened. "Did you, like, eat grubs and things?"

"That's right." He couldn't resist teasing her. "Moreton Bay bugs are my favorite. We'll have them sometime while you're here." He smiled, knowing it was too dark for her to see the twinkle in his eyes.

She shuddered. "Ugh. I guess I'd eat bugs if I were starving, but only then."

He laughed. Then drained his coffee and got to his feet. "Reckon I'll turn in. Sunrise comes pretty early." He paused at the doorway. "You planning on staying up awhile?"

"Well..."

"Because if you go for a stroll at night, mind you take a torch. Brown snakes usually go to sleep at sundown, but death adders and mulgas are out and about."

"Death adders? Mulgas? Those are poisonous, right?"

"Most snakes in Australia are."

Sarah scrambled to her feet. "Actually, I'm feeling pretty tired after my long trip."

"Thought you might be."

As she went past him into the house the overhead light illuminated her bare freckled shoulder and the scent of her warm skin reached his nostrils, reminding him it had been a long time since he'd held a woman in his arms.

It would be a while longer, he thought, sliding the door shut behind him.

And it wouldn't be this woman, tempting though she was.

Pity.

LATE THE FOLLOWING afternoon Sarah was in her room, going over the list of items she wanted to buy for the house. Now that she was part owner she ought to do her bit to take care of the place—if Luke let her. Real money needed to go toward machinery or a bull, but fresh paint and new fabric could make a big difference for relatively little expense. She'd found an old sewing machine on the floor of the linen closet and although she was no seamstress she could manage curtains and cushion covers.

She heard the sliding door to the kitchen open and checked her watch. Five o'clock. Luke was in from the cattle run to go and get Becka. He'd asked Sarah this morning if she wanted to go with him and look over the property. Maybe tomorrow, she'd answered, not meeting his eye.

Sarah went down the hall and paused in the kitchen doorway. Luke had stripped off his shirt and was bent over the kitchen sink, sluicing hot soapy water over his head and arms. She'd never been one for westerns, and the popular appeal of cowboys escaped her, but the sheer physicality of his broad shoulders, lean muscled back and strong arms left her blinking like a cursor on a blank screen.

He reached blindly for a towel and blotted the water from his face and hair. Opening his eyes, he saw her and for an instant froze, towel clutched against his chest. "G'day."

"Hi." She folded and refolded her list. "Are you going to get Becka?"

He nodded and reached for his shirt, bunching it in his fist. "Want to come?"

"No. Thanks." She noted the odd, intense light in his eyes and wondered if it was obvious she found him attractive. "I thought I'd make dinner if you would show me how to work the woodstove."

"Nothing wrong with the electric stove."

"Let's just say the woodstove inspires me. Mind if I raid the pantry?"

One corner of his mouth lifted as he slicked back his damp sun-streaked hair. "Go for your life."

LUKE PULLED INTO Abby's driveway and jumped out of the car. Doors were never locked in Murrum and friends and family didn't wait for a formal invitation, so he knocked once on the front door and went in. "Abby? Becka?"

No answer.

He wandered through the kitchen and looked out the window into the backyard. Becka and Abby were on their knees in the vegetable patch, staking up tomatoes. Stepping out the back door, he called, "G'day."

Abby glanced up and pushed a strand of gray hair off her forehead. "Hello, Luke. We're almost done."

He glanced eagerly at Becka, ashamed at how much he longed for her to run to him the way she used to. *Daddy, Daddy, see what I did.*

Now she only glanced up without smiling before going back to the tomatoes. Any encouragement at all and he would have given them a hand. But he might as well not have been there for all the notice they took of him.

"Don't mind me," he muttered, and retreated into the house.

He helped himself to a glass of water from the tap and sat at the kitchen table. There was the usual clutter: a stack of paid bills, Becka's hair ribbons, a half-done crossword puzzle. At the end of the table, above the salt and pepper shakers and the tomato sauce bottle, hung one of Caroline's watercolors of a desert landscape. A mutual love of the desert had brought them together, but it hadn't been enough to bind them. Nor had his love.

The painting reminded him that this house had been hers before she'd died. Abby had taken it over, as she'd taken Becka over.

Idly, he flipped open the photo album. There were Caroline and her parents, Caroline and Abby... He turned the page to see old photos of Abby as a young woman. She wasn't unattractive really, although her one brown eye and one blue eye were disconcerting. Too bad she'd never married and had children of her own since she loved them so much. He seemed to recall Caroline's saying something about her being in love with Len and never getting over it.

He flipped the pages. Caroline painting. Caroline pregnant. They hadn't planned to have a baby, but when she'd gotten pregnant he'd thought they would be a family. Turned out she'd wanted to travel, not settle down.

Luke flipped another page, to find an unsealed envelope tucked into the crack. He slipped out the photo that was inside—one taken of Caroline in the hospital after she'd had Becka. He frowned. Something was odd about this. He peered closer, hardly believing his eyes.

Caroline's face had been cut out of the photo and a picture of Abby inserted in its place.

Oh, God. He dropped the photo and jumped to his feet. Though the room was stifling, a chill swept over his body. He couldn't seem to catch his breath.

Unbelievable. Impossible.

He looked again.

It was true. He thought he was going to be sick right here on Abby's kitchen floor.

Voices at the door. He crammed the photo back in the envelope and slammed the album shut.

Abby came through, smiling, scraping the red earth from her feet. "All done. Time for a cuppa before you go?"

His mouth was dry. He couldn't say a word. Abby, humming, ran water into the electric kettle. She was so familiar, yet suddenly a stranger.

Becka. His baby. All blond ponytail and coltish legs under her shorts. What lies had Abby told her?

"Becka, get your things. It's time to go."

"Relax, Luke," Abby said. "You've got a couple hours of light left." She hovered over the girl. "Wash your hands, dear. Use the nailbrush. A little more soap. That's right."

"Sarah's making dinner." He struggled to keep his voice normal, unaffected by the rage building inside. "Becka—now, please."

She turned away from the sink, wearing her aggrieved-princess look. "Do I have to?"

"*Yes.*" He waited for her to dry her hands and leave the room. Gave her another five seconds to get to the far end of the house. "Abby—" he began.

"So Sarah Templestowe is making dinner, is she?" Abby's voice turned coy, her mismatched eyes watching him. "That sounds cozy."

Luke refused to be sidetracked by Abby's sly remarks. She was always digging for information, making something out of nothing, then seeming oddly pleased when there really was nothing. Nothing lasting, at any rate.

"I looked at your photo album."

She smiled pleasantly and reached into the cupboard for cups. "Did you hear Sandy Ronstad had her baby?"

"Abby." His hands clenched. "Why did you cut out Caroline's photo and replace it with your own?"

Her body gave a kind of jolt, but she didn't answer right away. The cups trembled in their saucers as she set them on the table. "Whatever are you talking about?"

He flipped open the album and waved the envelope at her. "Did you show this to Becka?" If she had, so help him, he'd—

"I'm not surprised Sarah Templestowe would move in fast on a handsome bachelor," Abby continued, her voice wavering but still sounding determined. "Look at her mother. Taking off with that American after only a few weeks. Poor Len. She broke his heart."

Luke gripped her shoulders, stopping just short of shaking her. *"Did you tell Becka you're her mother?"* he demanded in a fierce whisper.

"Of course not." Abby pressed her fingers to her temples. "That would be crazy."

"Then why did you put your photo in Caroline's place?" Abby covered her ears with her hands. "Answer me," he ordered harshly.

"She's all I've got, Luke. Don't make me give her up."

"It's time, Abby. We agreed after Caroline died that Becka would come to live with me when she turned nine."

"Nine was just an arbitrary number. She still needs a mother—" she quailed under his fierce scowl "—figure."

"She needs her father, too," Luke said, hardening himself to her beseeching gaze. He couldn't get the image of the defaced photograph out of his mind.

"Dad!" Becka called from her old room. "I need help."

Luke glared at Abby and strode down the hall to Becka. She was struggling with her overnight bag and two shopping bags full of clothes.

"What's all this?" he asked.

"Aunt Abby bought me some dresses and stuff."

Luke pulled out a handful of slippery blue fabric with spaghetti straps. "Is this a nightgown?"

"It's a party dress. Isn't it cool?"

"You're only nine. You're not going to parties dressed like this. Leave it."

"Da-a-a-d."

Abby appeared in the doorway. "Let her have them, Luke. She should have something fun and pretty in her wardrobe."

He turned on her. "You shouldn't have done this, Abby. Not without asking me."

"Rubbish! Men have no idea how to shop for young girls. Do they, Becka?" She stroked Becka's hair and the girl smiled up at her.

"Take...them...back. She doesn't need party clothes out at the station. She needs jeans and T-shirts and boots." Luke tossed the shopping bags on the bed as though they were contaminated.

"I was only trying to help. In case you hadn't noticed, Luke Sampson, your little girl is growing up."

Luke had noticed, all right. And he hated it. He'd already missed too much of her life. "You're making her grow up too soon. These are for a much older girl."

"You're out of touch with what children are into these days," Abby said. "It's not surprising, living way out on that station. I've been caring for her almost all her life. I know what she needs. Anyway, she's grown out of practically all her old clothes."

"If she needs new clothes *I'll* buy them for her."

Tears burst from Becka's eyes. "I hate you!" she screamed at Luke, and ran out of the room, her overnight bag banging against the doorjamb.

Abby gazed at him reproachfully. "I really think you could have handled that better, Luke. But then, you haven't had much practice being a father, have you?"

His jaw clenched so hard it hurt. "We won't be seeing you for a while. Becka's going to be busy out at the station."

From the front porch, Abby watched them drive off, the wheels of the Land Cruiser spinning in the dirt before hitting the bitumen and squealing away. She gripped the wooden railing till a splinter pierced her skin, raising a bright red drop of blood. She didn't notice. The pain was nothing compared with the pain in her heart. Becka was all she had and Luke had taken her away. Just as Anne Hafford had taken Len away from her all those years ago.

Don't worry, Becka, my darling. We'll be together again soon—somehow.

"Ouch!" Sarah snatched her blistered finger back from the hot cast iron of the wood-fired oven and thrust it under cold water. Wood-fired oven be damned. It didn't turn out the savory masterpieces the one at Alfredo's Bistro did. Her pizza was burned around the edges, pale and gloopy in the center. Maybe if she switched on the electric stove and put the pizza under the broiler...

Irritably, she wiped a smudge of flour from her nose and blew the hair off her forehead with an exasperated sigh. Canned tomatoes were no substitute for sun-dried, even drained through a sieve. And the closest she could get to paper-thin parma ham was a thick rasher of bacon complete with rind and little bones.

But the burned dinner was a mere annoyance. The thing that set her teeth on edge and had her jumping out of her skin was the total absence of decent coffee. The instant stuff Luke made last night was okay once or twice, but she needed something more. She needed full flavor and rich aroma. She needed concentrated caffeine and lots of it. It was humiliating to admit, but she was addicted. Throwing down the hand towel, she strode down the hall to her room.

She snatched up her cell phone, jabbed in her mother's home number, and almost wept with relief when Anne answered the phone. "Mom! Thank goodness you're still up."

"Darling, what is it? Is something wrong?"

"I need coffee. Real coffee. Beans, freshly ground, covered with briskly boiling water. Frothy, steaming milk. Espresso, French roast, cinnamon hazelnut, cappuccino, café latte—"

"Sarah, Sarah, are you all right?"

"What was that noise?" Sarah demanded as she

paced back to the kitchen. "I heard a slurping sound. Are you drinking something?"

"Just a cup of herbal tea. Really, darl', get a grip."

"I can't. You've got to send me some coffee."

"I know Murrum isn't exactly the center of the civilized world, but they do have coffee."

"*Instant* coffee. At least that's all Luke has." Sarah checked the broiler to see if it was hot and slid one of the pizzas under it. "Mother, *please.*"

"Consider it done." There was an odd hint of laughter in Anne's voice. "How is the homestead? I've been thinking about you all day. Have you been down to the creek yet?"

"Er, no. There's so much to do in the house I haven't had a chance to get out." Sarah wrapped her free arm around her waist. She wasn't going to tell her mother she was *afraid* to go outside the yard. It was too ridiculous.

"So is it very run-down?" Anne sounded wistful.

"A little shabby. Don't worry, I'll have it looking fabulous in no time. But Luke may not be as amenable to selling his half as I'd hoped. He's really dug in here."

"Well, he's been there long enough. What's he like, do you think, as a manager? Would you say he's trustworthy?"

She pictured Luke—squinting into the sun, bare chested at the sink, grinning in the dark of the veranda at some private joke. "He doesn't say much, but he looks you in the eye when he says it. I went over the photocopies of the station accounts before I left Seattle. They seem perfectly okay. In fact, I don't know how the place survived on what they've pulled in the past couple of years."

"It's a tough life." Anne paused. "You said you met Len."

"He remembered you right away, but when I told him I'd give you his regards, he clammed up."

"Oh, well, it was all a very long time ago. No point in dredging up ancient history."

Sarah listened for disappointment, but Anne's voice was neutral—too neutral. "I'll bet he was a babe and a half in his day."

"I believe he's married, darl'. Er, about that old notebook of mine…tuck it away somewhere safe, will you? There's nothing of interest in it. Just the typical angsty ramblings of a teenage girl—"

"Don't worry, Mom. I won't read it." Sarah paused to check the broiler. Yikes! The pizza was done, all right. The surface looked as though it had been charred with a blowtorch. On the plus side, the tomatoes were definitely dry.

"I'd better go," she said. "Dinner's…uh, ready. I'll call you tomorrow."

Sarah heard the Land Cruiser drive up and put the pizza on the table, trying in vain to hide it behind the salad and the garlic bread. Surely it didn't look *too bad*.

A stony-faced Luke strode into the kitchen, trailed by a sullen young girl with blond braids who dragged her overnight bag on the floor.

"Sarah, this is Becka. Say hello, Becka."

"H'llo."

"Hi, Becka. Nice to meet you." Sarah smiled, hiding her shock at the girl's swollen, red-rimmed eyes and the tears staining her freckled cheeks. There was an awkward pause before Sarah said brightly, "Dinner's ready."

Luke sat down. After a second, so did Becka with a loud scrape of her chair on the slate floor. Her face was set mutinously and she wouldn't look at her father.

Sarah took her seat and tried to keep the conversation rolling as she dished up the pizza. "It's not exactly a gourmet delight, but there's salad, too. And with the leftover dough I made garlic bread."

Luke took a big bite of burned pizza. He chewed and swallowed without seeming to notice what he was eating.

"How is it?" she asked.

"Good."

Now she knew he hadn't tasted it. She turned to Becka. "What do you think?"

Becka shrugged and picked off the tomatoes.

Sarah ate salad and wished she could show Luke there were things she could do really well. Why, she could work the bugs out of a software program in the blink of an eye. She was a good manager, too. She organized a team of six and oversaw all technical aspects of their designs—

She stabbed a piece of red pepper and crunched it down. What was she thinking? The things she was good at meant nothing to a man like Luke. Why should she care what he thought, anyway?

"Did you have a good time at your aunt's house?" she asked Becka.

Tears flooded from the girl's eyes. Instead of answering Sarah's question, she turned to Luke and shouted, "Why can't I see Aunt Abby again? *Why?* You hate me, don't you?"

"Becka, you know that's not true—" Luke began.

"It *is* true! You said I can't go back to Aunt Abby's, but you won't even tell me why." Blinking ferociously, Becka pushed away from the table and went through the sliding doors onto the veranda.

Sarah turned to Luke. "Oh, dear. What happened?"

"Kids," he said with a dark scowl, and took another bite of charred pizza.

Sarah put down her fork. Clearly, more was going on than he was prepared to tell her. "Is there some reason I shouldn't mention Becka's aunt to her?"

Luke's forearm flexed as he gripped his water glass in his fist. "Don't mention her to *me*."

"Okay," Sarah said carefully. "*You're* angry with the aunt but don't want to talk about it. Becka is upset about whatever it was that happened and *can't* talk about it. *I'm* completely in the dark but should mind my own business because I'm a stranger here. Have I got it right?"

Frowning, Luke nodded. "Nothing personal."

She glanced out at Becka, who was leaning morosely against a pillar. Wal came up and tried to lick her face, but the girl pushed him away. "You *are* going to talk to your daughter, I hope?"

His scowl deepened. "I've said all I'm going to say."

He got up and stalked out of the room instead of going out to comfort his child. Or explain what was obviously incomprehensible to her, too.

Sarah watched him go, shocked and saddened. It really was none of her business. But she'd had a father who'd never been there for her as a child or as an adult. And now he was dead and there was no possibility of reconciliation.

Sarah knew she shouldn't project her feelings of rejection onto the little girl who was crying on the veranda, but her heart ached for Becka. Although Sarah didn't know a lot about kids, she remembered how much it hurt to think her father didn't care about her. She'd seen the worry on Luke's face last night when his daughter hadn't been brought home on time. He loved Becka, but for some reason he couldn't express it. Whether it was any of her business or not, Sarah knew she wouldn't rest until she discovered what was wrong between Luke and his daughter.

And fixed it.

CHAPTER FOUR

THE NEXT MORNING Sarah put on a skinny sleeveless top and short skirt and slathered sunscreen over her arms and legs and as much of her chest and back as she could reach. She wanted to see the creek where Mom had caught the yabbies.

Jet lag had awakened her in the wee hours, but she'd fallen asleep again at last and now the clock over the kitchen stove said it was nearly ten o'clock. She felt the kettle. Still warm. Luke must have come in for morning coffee and gone out again on the cattle run. Becka was still in her room if the sound of the radio behind the closed door was any indication.

After a quick breakfast of toast and coffee, Sarah stepped outside onto the back veranda. The air was warm and dry and smelled exotically of eucalyptus. Her cross-trainers raised puffs of red dust as she stepped off the veranda and rounded the galvanized steel tank used to collect rainwater.

She headed in the direction of the creek, her mother's reminiscences ringing in her head. *Once a yabby pinched Robby's big toe and wouldn't let go. I never laughed so hard.*

Sarah could almost hear the sound of children's laughter coming from the dappled shade near the creek. A few more steps took her out of the comforting shadow cast by the house and into an open stretch of ground. Then it happened again.

Beneath the relentless sun, Sarah began to shiver. Her heart pounded and she struggled to take a breath. She tried to take another step and couldn't. Her gaze crept involuntarily to the open land on her left that reached into the distance. Her stomach floated; her head felt light.

With an effort she dragged her gaze back to the trees. Suddenly the distance between her and them seemed a vast, untraversable expanse. In her mind the sound of children's laughter turned mocking.

With her heart thumping so hard she thought it would burst, she spun on her heel and race-walked back to the veranda. There she clutched an iron pillar for support before dragging herself across the planks to sink into a wicker chair, her eyes shutting in sick relief.

What was happening to her? Was she dying? Going crazy?

Gradually her heart slowed to normal and she got her breath back. She stood up, walked the length of the veranda and turned the corner to pace the perimeter of the house. At the front of the homestead she quickly averted her eyes from the view of the open Downs and hurried on around the next corner. She was beginning to feel like a tiger exploring the confines of her cage. Tomorrow. She would overcome her fear tomorrow.

Right now she could use some company. She went in search of Becka, and found her sitting on the floor of her room amid boxes of unpacked toys and books, playing quietly with her doll. Her long blond hair had been pulled into a clumsy braid and she wore a frilly, flowered sundress that matched her doll's outfit but didn't suit her tomboyish looks.

Sarah leaned on the doorjamb. "Hi, Becka. What are you doing?"

Becka glanced up, her oval face grave. "Playing."

"May I come in?" Becka nodded listlessly, so Sarah moved into the room to sit on the bed. She eyed the windows. "I'm going to sew new curtains. What color would you like?"

Becka shrugged. "Whatever."

"I always think your surroundings make a lot of difference to the way you feel, don't you? For instance, if we replace those brown curtains with yellow ones—maybe a sunflower pattern—this room would be a lot cheerier. What do you think?"

"Fine."

"Is something wrong, Becka?"

Becka's small chin lifted defiantly. "No."

"I can see you're unhappy about something," Sarah said cautiously. "Your dad's really worried about you."

Becka snorted. "My dad doesn't care about me."

Sarah leaned forward on the bed, her elbows on her knees. "Your dad loves you a lot. Even I can see that."

"Then why is he keeping me prisoner?" Becka demanded, sullen and defiant. "He won't even talk to me."

Sarah's heart went out to the girl. Behind the defiance lurked fear and uncertainty. "I guess you miss your aunt."

Becka bit her lip and combed her doll's hair with a tiny pink comb. "I hate it here. It's the middle of nowhere."

"It feels strange to me, too—" She broke off. That was no way to talk around the child. "Hey, I noticed a brand-new superdeluxe computer in the office."

"Dad bought it so I could use it for school. He tried to teach me, but he doesn't know how to work it." Becka's mouth pursed disapprovingly. "He said a swear word."

"I can show you how to use it," Sarah said, suppressing a smile. Surely it would be more fun than dolls at Becka's age.

Interest sparked in the young girl's eyes and for a moment Sarah thought she would say yes. Then her shoulder's drooped as she remembered her role as the unjustly imprisoned. "Nah," she said, turning back to her doll. "I'll just stay here."

"Let me know if you change your mind," Sarah said, rising from the bed. "Would you mind if I tried it out?"

Becka shrugged, presumably in the affirmative. Then as Sarah was leaving she said so softly it was almost a whisper, "Thanks, anyway."

Sarah slowly shut the door. Poor kid.

She walked back down the hall to the little room off the living room—or the loungeroom, as Luke called it—that served as an office. Sarah skimmed the titles in the bookshelves lining one wall. Among the volumes on cattle breeding and animal husbandry were a surprising number of books on the geology, botany, zoology and natural history of Queensland.

Along another wall stood a tall wooden chest with many narrow drawers. *What was in Luke's drawers?* She grinned at her own pun, but although she was curious about what the chest might contain, the lure of the computer was stronger.

She booted it up, admiring the speed at which it went through its paces. The PC was state-of-the-art and loaded with software. In spite of Luke's disavowal of the Internet there was even a modem. Regardless of his financial constraints, he'd spared no expense for Becka's link with the world. For that Sarah thought he deserved a medal. And if he'd learn how to use it himself, he would surely see there were benefits for the station, as well.

But Luke wasn't kidding when he said he hadn't ventured into cyberspace. Tsk, tsk. A modem and no Internet connection. She searched the cluttered desk beside the computer, found a phone book and rang up the nearest service provider. She paid for a year's connection with her credit card and asked for the software to be couriered care of Murrum general delivery. Aside from helping Luke and Becka, if she could get on the Internet she could look up agoraphobia and hopefully find out how to help herself.

Satisfied with her morning's work, she shut the computer down and repaired to the kitchen for another blah cup of coffee. The phone rang while she was waiting for the water to boil. "Hello?"

"Good morning," said a cultured masculine voice. "This is Professor Winter, from Australia National University in Canberra. May I speak with Luke?"

"He's not in at the moment," Sarah replied. Now, why would a professor be calling Luke? "Can I take a message?"

"Please ask him to call me back on this number...."

Sarah wrote the number down on a pad of paper beside the phone. She'd barely hung up, when she heard boots on the veranda. Luke came in, glanced at her and hung his hat on a row of pegs that already held a bridle, a rope and a coiled, short-handled stock whip as well as several other beat-up felt hats. "Two rules about hats," he said. "Never wear them in the house. And never go outside without one."

"I'll remember that. Oh, a Professor Winter just called. His number's on the notepad."

"Thanks. I'll ring him later." He crossed to the sink and scrubbed his hands.

She eyed him, mildly frustrated. He not only had no intention of satisfying her curiosity about Professor Winter, he wasn't even aware she was suffering from it. Heck, he barely seemed aware of her existence. She sighed. It was probably just as well, since there was no possibility of anything but a business relationship between them. "Do you have ground coffee, by any chance?"

"Not worth the bother to make real coffee for one."

Huh? Coffee was always worth bothering about. Then again, she wasn't looking after forty thousand acres and fifteen hundred head of cattle single-handedly.

"That's an excellent computer you've got there. I've signed you up for the Internet."

Luke, at the open fridge door, glanced over his shoulder so quickly a lock of sun-streaked hair fell over one eye. "What's that going to cost?"

"Don't worry, it's my treat."

His jaw stiffened. "I'll pay you back."

"No, you won't," she replied cheerfully, and poured water over the instant coffee she'd spooned into two cups. Before he could protest further, she added, "I'd like to contribute somehow to the running of the station."

Luke rummaged in the fridge and returned to the table bearing a plate of cold roast beef, a container of leftover salad and jars of mustard and mayonnaise. "There *is* something you can do if you don't mind."

"Sure. Anything."

"With the muster coming up we need a cook."

Anything but that.

On the other hand, how could she *not* cook if that was what was required? She placed a cup in front of Luke and loaded her own with cream and sugar. She had a responsibility to the station, too.

"No problem," she said, curving her lips in a smile both firm and cheerful. Sacrifice was her middle name.

Luke looked up from the piece of bread he was spreading with mayonnaise. "Beg your pardon?"

"I'll be the cook. It'll be...fun." Even as she said it, her resolve wavered. Was she capable of producing three large *edible* meals a day for a gang of hungry men? "How many did you say will be in the muster crew?"

"Four, including me. But that's not the favor. All I want is you to drive into Murrum and put a notice on the board outside Len's store, advertising the position. I meant to do it yesterday and forgot."

Oh, no. The next time she faced a long journey through the Downs it would be on the bus out of here. Just the thought of going out there made her tense in case panic struck again when she was alone, away from help. "Truly, I'd be *happy* to cook."

Luke began to carve thick slices off the roast beef.

"Stockmen like their tucker. It's got to be good and it's got to be plentiful or they'll shoot through."

"You really can't go by the pizzas."

One dark-gold eyebrow rose above a skeptical blue eye. "The garlic bread wasn't bad. If you really want to help, you could make bread. Homemade beats store-bought anytime."

"Bread?" she repeated, trying to picture herself up to her elbows in dough. "Uh, sure. But about going to town—"

"I'd bake myself, but you have to do something with the dough every couple of hours or it's ruined."

"Like children." Oh, dear. She hadn't meant to say that, but now that it was out she wasn't sorry. His eyebrows drew together in a scowl as he silently layered his roast beef with tomatoes, lettuce and sliced beetroot. *Beetroot?*

"I know it's not as if you have a lot of choices," she said, sipping her coffee and trying not to grimace. "And I'm sure you have a really excellent reason for not wanting Becka to be with her aunt—"

His fierce glance stopped her, but only momentarily.

"You *need* to talk to her," Sarah insisted. "She's upset and confused. She thinks you don't care about her."

Luke carefully laid another slice of bread atop the massive sandwich. "Did she tell you that?"

"It's obvious."

"That's ridiculous. She—"

Becka burst into the room, calling, "Sarah!" She saw her father and her steps slowed.

"G'day, Becka," he said. His gaze followed her as she went silently past him and up to Sarah.

"Will you show me how to use the computer now?"

Sarah looked helplessly at Luke. Whatever their differences, it wasn't right for Becka to ignore her father.

"Sarah's going into town for me," Luke said. Then he added more gently, "You can go, too, and show her the way. Get yourself a treat at the store."

"Can I go see Aunt Abby?" Becka asked eagerly. His scowl returned. "You can visit a school friend."

"That sounds like fun," Sarah interjected quickly. "Who's your best friend, Becka?"

Becka kicked at the table leg with her bare foot. "Lucy. I guess that'd be okay."

"Great!" *Yeah, perfect,* she thought with a sinking feeling as Becka ran off to get ready. Now there was no way out of making the drive into town.

"Hang on a tick," Luke said when Sarah reluctantly started back to her room for her purse. "I'll give you the advertisement I made up."

"Isn't this kind of short notice for hiring a cook?" she asked, following him to the office.

"I had one lined up, but she quit at the last minute when her boyfriend got a job up north." He fished in the desk drawer for a piece of paper, then scanned the hand-printed sheet.

Sarah peered over his shoulder and her attention wavered from the advertisement to him. Up close, Luke's skin, tanned and faintly glistening with sweat beneath his open shirtfront, gave off a clean, earthy scent. The only men Sarah knew who raised a sweat did so at the gym.

"Why did you write this by hand?" she asked. "I

could have designed an ad on the computer with borders and clip art and printed out a dozen copies.''

''No call for anything fancy,'' Luke said, handing the paper to her with barely a sideways glance.

Did Luke notice *her* at *all?* ''If we don't return by dark, send out a search party,'' she joked.

''Just remember the cardinal rule of the outback,'' Luke replied without a hint of a smile. ''If you break down, stay with the vehicle. Oh, and don't leave the lights or the radio on when the engine's not running. The battery's getting low.''

''Maybe I should pack emergency supplies,'' she said, still not taking his comments seriously.

''There's a five-gallon container of water in the back.'' He wrote out a short list of groceries to buy on another piece of paper. ''So can I leave the hiring to you?''

''Sure. Any specific requirements you're looking for?''

He handed her the list. ''No, just as long as the person has had experience and doesn't drink too much. Alcohol seems to be an occupational hazard with station cooks. Drive safely and stay out of the bulldust.''

SARAH DIDN'T KNOW how safe it was to drive a vehicle and not watch the road for more than fifty yards in front of her. Once again, just the thought of another panic attack made her heart palpitate. She probably shouldn't be driving Becka under the circumstances. And she should have said so to Luke, but she'd been too embarrassed.

''So, Becka, what's bulldust?'' she asked in an

attempt to keep her mind off the open land, which seemed to stretch to infinity on all sides.

In the passenger seat beside her, Becka was playing with some small plastic figurines of a popular kids' TV show. "It's the stuff by the side of the road. You can get bogged in it."

To Sarah the fine red dust looked innocuous enough, but what did she know? Everything was foreign, from the pale greeny-gray and silver of the scrubby bushes to the glare of the relentless sun. She squinted behind her dark glasses. Was that cloud of dust in the distance another car?

The dust cloud grew slowly larger as it came closer, and from its height Sarah deduced a truck must be creating it. She tightened her grip on a steering wheel already slippery with nervous sweat. Then suddenly the truck was upon her in a towering whirlwind of red dust, its horn blaring and engine roaring.

Sarah swerved as the enormously long truck—one, two, *three* semitrailer lengths—thundered past. A back wheel of the Land Cruiser dragged in the thick soft bulldust. Sarah pressed the accelerator to the floor and the vehicle fishtailed back onto the hard dirt road.

"What was *that?*" she exclaimed, staring into the rearview mirror.

Unfazed, Becka didn't even glance up. "Road train. No big deal."

Maybe not to outback Queenslanders, but Sarah didn't feel safe until they reached Murrum and the security of buildings and trees and people. As they passed the house Luke had pointed out as belonging to Becka's aunt Abby, a woman bent over the garden bed in the front yard looked up and waved. She was too far away for Sarah to see clearly, but the little cry that came from Becka left no doubt she was Becka's aunt.

Becka turned to Sarah. "Could I—" she pleaded.

"Not a chance." Sarah cut her off firmly. She herself might disagree with Luke's attitude toward his daughter, but she was a guest in his house and she wasn't going to interfere in how he raised his child. "How do I get to Lucy's place?"

Becka directed her to a house on the other side of town, a two-story structure built on stilts, with a wraparound veranda on the second floor. A palm tree rose high above the house. Swinging on the front gate was a brown-haired girl Becka's age. Sarah dropped Becka off, telling Lucy's mother she'd return in about an hour.

She found her way back to the wide main street and pulled in perpendicular to the curb in front of Len's store. Across the open doorway hung a fly curtain made of long strips of colored plastic. She pushed through into air-conditioned coolness. The store appeared deserted.

Len stocked goods of all sorts—food, newspapers and magazines, assorted hardware and small appliances. A sign above the checkout advised that this was an Australia Post outlet and the long wooden counter was crammed with jars of candies, pickled eggs and displays of chewing gum.

Sarah picked up a shopping basket from a stack near the door and moved down the aisles containing dry goods. Consulting her list, she tossed a box of salt into her basket and tried to decide whether Luke preferred his baked beans with pork or tomato sauce.

Len came out of a back room, carrying a box of

tinned goods. "G'day, Sarah. A package arrived for you this morning."

"Hi, Len. A package? Nobody knows I'm here."

He cleared his throat. "I believe it's from your mother. Came by courier this morning."

"Oh, wow. That was fast. May I have it, please?"

Len set the box of tins on the floor and disappeared again, to return a few seconds later with a large package. He handed it across and gave her a paper to sign.

Sarah put her nose to the box, breathing deeply. Ahh. Even through the cardboard she could smell the delicious aroma of real coffee. Len slit the tape with a penknife and she eagerly bent back the flaps.

A note was tucked between two large bags of flavored coffee beans. "Thought you might appreciate some good coffee right about now. Love, Mum."

Sarah glanced at the date on the note. The package had been sent the day she'd left Seattle, two days before she'd begged Anne for this very substance. Half laughing, half growling at her mother for letting her sweat it out, Sarah pulled out a packet of Hawaiian hazelnut and one of mocha almond.

"Anne always did have a taste for the exotic."

Sarah glanced at Len curiously. Had he been her mother's boyfriend in high school? She was on the point of asking, when he nodded at the window display of assorted small appliances.

"Will you be wanting a coffee grinder with that? I know Luke only buys instant."

"Oh, yes." Sarah drifted over to the display. These old-fashioned stores might lack selection, but they made up for it in convenience. Where else could you get tuna and a toaster without reparking? Besides wholesale warehouses, that is, and she hated the line-ups in those places.

She picked up a coffee grinder and was about to turn back to the checkout, when her gaze fell upon a bread maker. She'd always wanted one. They had a menu for different bread types, she knew, and timers that could be programmed so that the baking would finish at whatever hour people hauled themselves out of bed in the morning. She was a sucker for a good timer. If Luke wanted homemade bread, she'd give it to him the easy way. Once she was gone, he could make his own.

"I'll take this, too," she said, tugging the bulky box over to the counter. "You accept Visa, don't you?"

"Sure do. Yeast is in aisle three, right above the flour."

"Thanks." Humming, she whizzed through the rest of the store, picking up the items Luke had requested as well as yeast and whole wheat flour. While Len bagged her purchases, she dug in her purse for Luke's ad. "Is it all right if I put this on your notice board?"

"Wanting another cook, is he?"

Sarah glanced at him in surprise. "How did you know?"

"Not many secrets in a town this size." Len smiled, and suddenly Sarah saw what her mother might have seen in him.

"Everyone knows about Rachel running after the Calhoun boy," he added. "She'll come to grief before it's over." He spoke with surprising vehemence before he stopped abruptly and seemed to collect himself. "Go ahead, put your notice up. I'll mention it to a few people who might be interested."

"Thanks." She hesitated, then decided to plunge right in. "Were you in love with her? My mother, I mean."

Len's lean, lined face tightened. "We went together during high school," he said tersely, taking Sarah's credit card to run off an imprint. "Murrum just wasn't big enough for her."

"She still likes to travel. She has an import store and goes on buying trips a couple times a year."

He said casually, "Is she still with Warren?"

"They split up when I was a baby. She remarried a couple of years later to my stepfather. He died two years ago." She leaned over to sign the credit card receipt. "Did you marry?"

He nodded. "Margaret passed on five years ago. We had a good life and a couple of fine boys." He paused to rip off her copy of the receipt. "Think your mother will ever come back here?"

Sarah studied his face, but it was unreadable. "I hope—" She was going to say she hoped her mother would one day be resident owner at Burrinbilli, then realized it wasn't fair to Luke to tell him so at this point. "I hope she will," Sarah finished lamely. "Maybe we could get together for a barbecue."

Len nodded noncommittally. Sarah picked up her bag of groceries. "Nice talking to you. See you later."

She put her things in the Land Cruiser and went back to the notice board. Reading the various notices kept her busy for a good five minutes. A local horse race was coming up, someone had a hay baler for sale and someone else wanted work as a jackaroo.

Sarah found a spot for Luke's ad near the center of the board and was pinning it up, when a small blue sedan parked beside her vehicle and a woman with short-cropped gray hair and a matronly figure encased in a lilac print dress stepped out.

"Oh, something new at last," she said in a friendly tone, and peered over Sarah's shoulder. "Luke wants a muster cook! Well, now, isn't that a coincidence? I myself was looking for a position as a cook." She drew back, her inquisitive gaze darting over Sarah from head to toe. "You're new in the district."

"I'm Sarah," she said, putting out her hand. "I'm just here for a couple of weeks."

"Sarah...Anne Hafford's daughter? You must be. You're the spitting image of her. I heard you were in town."

"Did you know my mother?" Sarah asked excitedly.

The woman laughed. "We went to school together."

"This is fantastic. And are you really a cook? I can't believe my luck. I've barely tacked the notice up and already I have an applicant. I guess I ought to ask if you have any qualifications."

"I worked for many years as a short order cook in a restaurant in Brisbane. Since I retired, I usually do a stint somewhere during mustering. I'll dig out my references if you want."

Sarah took in her open honest face and pleasant smile. She appeared both homey and competent, as if she belonged in a country kitchen, whipping up big beefy meals for hungry jackaroos. If Sarah hired her, she wouldn't have to make the drive into town again to interview prospective cooks. To clinch the matter, the woman was a friend of her mother.

Yet she'd better not forget she was acting for Luke. "I hate to get personal, but I have to ask...do you drink much?"

"Oh, no, I'm a teetotaler."

"Wonderful. Why don't you drive out to the station tomorrow," she said, removing the notice from the board. "You can meet Luke and we can finalize the arrangement." She extended her hand. "What's your name?"

"Er..." The woman faltered briefly, then took Sarah's hand and shook firmly. "Gail. My name's Gail. I'll come out in the afternoon—I imagine he'll be on the cattle run most of the day. I'll bring my things to stay, since it's such a long way back. I have no doubt I'm just what you're looking for."

Sarah had no doubt, either. She congratulated herself all the way home, listening with only half an ear to Becka's chatter. Gail was such a friendly, nice woman—although there was something about her eyes that seemed odd, something Sarah couldn't quite put a finger on. Never mind. She was perfect. Luke would be so pleased. And wait till she let her mother know she'd met another old friend.

Sarah told Luke about the new cook that night over dinner. He was relieved she'd found someone so quickly, though he spent some time puzzling over who the woman might be, as he was unacquainted with anyone named "Gail" in Murrum.

About the bread maker he was more skeptical, until the kitchen gradually filled with the delicious smell of baking bread. By the time the first loaf was ready at nine o'clock he was pacing the floor in anticipation. And after he'd eaten half the loaf spread thickly with fresh butter he agreed it was damn near as good as bread made from scratch.

Sarah was mixing the ingredients for a third loaf the next afternoon when Gail showed up armed with references and suitcases.

"Come in," Sarah said, leading her to the kitchen. She glanced at her watch. "Luke's late getting back. He and his daughter went out on horseback after she got home from school. Would you like some coffee?"

"Thank you, I would," Gail said, and insisted on bringing out the cups and cream and sugar herself. "You just finish what you're doing. Does Luke's daughter like to ride?"

"She hasn't done much so far, I gather, but I'm sure she'll love it. She's just the right age." In truth, Becka had been reluctant to go, but out of Luke's hearing Sarah had bribed her with a promise of the latest computer game. It was obvious Luke and Becka hardly knew each other, even though they were father and daughter. Sarah felt sure all they needed was time together and a little two-way communication.

A few minutes later Sarah and Gail were sitting over steaming cups of fresh Hawaiian hazelnut coffee. Sarah skimmed through the glowing references Gail had provided. Abigail was her full name. Abigail McCrae. Sarah frowned. Was there some reason that name should ring a bell?

"My, this is wonderful coffee," Gail said.

Sarah warmed to her. "Your references look just fine, Gail. I don't see why we can't sign this standard contract, which Luke drew up, right now." She was a teensy bit worried at closing the deal without Luke's final approval, but he *had* given her the go-ahead.

"Certainly," Gail agreed, reaching for the contract and a pen. "There's no need to bother Luke with details." She put pen to paper and then pushed the contract over to Sarah, who happily added her signature to the document.

Sarah was pouring them another cup of coffee when two pairs of boots clattered across the back veranda. A moment later Luke entered the kitchen with Becka right behind him.

"Luke," Sarah said proudly, getting up from her chair. "Meet your new cook, Gail—"

She broke off as Luke's deeply tanned face turned pale.

"Abby!" he exclaimed in a hoarse whisper. "What the hell are you doing here?"

"Aunt Abby!" Becka cried in joy, and flung herself across the room and into her aunt's arms.

CHAPTER FIVE

BLOODY OATH! Luke spun on his heel, his hands clenched into fists. He strode back through the sliding doors, across the veranda and into the yard. He had to get away and cool down or his hands would end up around someone's neck; Abby's or Sarah's, he wasn't sure which.

His long legs ate up the ground as he headed toward the machine shed, Wal trotting faithfully at his side. "Abby's got her nerve, eh, Wal?" he growled. "Sitting in my kitchen drinking coffee, smug as you please. And why did Sarah go against me to hire Abby when she *knew* I didn't want Becka having anything to do with her aunt?"

He'd finally coaxed Becka out on a ride with him—they'd even had a conversation of sorts. And now Abby was back.

Luke stopped short in the middle of the dusty yard. "I'm damned if I'll put up with that. C'mon, Wal."

He turned and stalked back to the house. Wal gave a tiny questioning yip and fell in at heel.

From the kitchen window Sarah watched Luke march across the yard like a storm cloud advancing across the horizon. She didn't blame him for being mad.

"Gail?" she said, turning around. The woman was gazing fondly after Becka, who had dashed off to get something. "*Abby*. Why didn't you tell me you knew Luke? Or that you were Becka's great-aunt?"

Abby's mismatched eyes avoided hers. "I miss Becka so much. I raised her from a baby. Now he's taken her away from me to live at the station. I don't think he's *deliberately* trying to turn her against me, but…" She got up and started to clear away the cups. "I'll just quickly wash these."

"Leave them." Sarah didn't know what to say to Abby's accusation; there was no denying Luke's antipathy toward the woman. "The situation is a difficult one," she said cautiously.

"It's terrible. Just terrible." Abby pulled out a handkerchief and blew her nose.

"Would it help if I talked to him?"

"Thank you, but I'd better do it myself."

Becka returned with her plastic figurines. Abby, still sniffing, gave her a hug. "I'll be right back, love," she said, and went outside.

"What's wrong with Aunt Abby?" Becka asked worriedly.

"She's just going to talk to your dad."

While Becka arranged her toys on the table Sarah went back to the window to watch the exchange between Luke and Abby. Abby had one hand on Luke's forearm as if to hold him in place and was talking at length while Luke listened in stony silence. Wal, ears pricked, sat beside Luke's dusty boots, eyeing first one face, then the other.

"You're in need of a cook and I've had plenty of experience at it," Abby insisted, calmly persuasive.

"That's not why you're really here."

"Maybe I've decided to take you up on your offer

to live at the station," she said, still even tempered. "I'll earn my keep as cook and housekeeper."

"That offer was made years ago. It's closed." He turned and walked away.

Abby hurried after him. "It's not right for Becka and me to be separated. If you don't want me here, then let me take Becka back to town. It's what Caroline would have wanted."

Luke stopped abruptly. "Caroline's dead. I'm Becka's father. It's what *I* want now."

"You should want what's best for Becka," Abby argued, her voice becoming sharp and hectoring. "Living in town close to school and her friends is where she'll be happiest."

"We don't know that. She's never given the station a proper go. Besides…" He tried to think of a tactful way of expressing his deeper concerns.

"Besides what?" Abby asked, but the sudden fearful look in her eyes told him she knew he was thinking about the photo.

"You and Becka need time apart. *You* need to talk to someone. A doctor."

Abby wrung her hands. "You're wrong. It—it's just the change. It's got me all emotional. But I'm not crazy."

"That photo with your face in place of Caroline's. It's…" He wanted to say "sick," but that seemed too close to the bone. "It's not…healthy."

Abby choked on a sorrowful laugh, her eyes misting. "Oh, Luke, it was only a game I played sometimes—that I was her mother and she, my daughter. A rather sad game, perhaps, but only make-believe. You know I always wanted a child of my own. I won't do it again, I promise."

Luke tried to gauge the sincerity in her mismatched eyes. Her abrupt mood transitions threw him off balance, and although her explanation mollified him somewhat, he still didn't trust her completely. Where Becka was concerned he couldn't be too careful. He didn't think for a minute Abby would hurt the girl, physically or emotionally, but...

He faced his true fear—with Abby around, Becka would never regain her affection for him.

With a groan, Luke rubbed the back of his neck. Nothing was simple when it came to people and their emotions. He couldn't allow his fears to get the better of him. And although he was ashamed to admit it, he knew he'd win points with Becka if he let Abby remain, whereas if he sent her away he'd lose what little ground he'd gained.

"All right," he said planting his hands on his hips. "You can stay and cook for the muster on one condition."

Abby's eyes gleamed. "Anything."

"You don't take Becka off the station." He could just see her spiriting Becka away to her house in town and keeping her there with excuse after excuse. He would only have a short time with Becka in the evenings and he wanted to make the most of their time together.

"Yes. Thank you, Luke!" Abby clapped her hands. "I'll tell the others."

"Wait a minute. You don't need to tell Sarah any of the background on this." Sarah was a stranger who had no ties to him or his daughter. Abby at least was kin of a sort.

She looked affronted. "Of course not."

Luke watched her scurry back to the house. "What do you reckon, Wal—can we trust her?"

Wal licked Luke's hand and kept his opinion to himself.

LATE THE NEXT afternoon, when the shadows of the river gums stretched across the dry creek bed, Sarah took one of the battered Akubras from the hat peg and ventured back outside. Abby and Becka were baking pies and Luke was out on the run with Bazza, who'd come to help repair the cattle yards in preparation for the muster. Now was the time to try for the creek again, since there was no one around to see her fail.

It'll be easy, she told herself. She wouldn't even look at the open land stretching west of the homestead. All she had to do was keep her eyes on the river gums and think of something, *anything*, else. She stepped away from the house. *One times one is one, one times two is two…* Flies buzzed around her head and her scalp began to sweat under the heat of the afternoon sun. One foot in front of the other, she kept going. *Six times eight is…*

A shadow fell across her forehead. She glanced up. And found herself standing under the smooth broad limbs of a towering gum tree. She'd done it!

Now that she was in the shelter of the trees, her anxiety abated somewhat. She scrambled down the slope to the dry creek bed and followed its meandering path through the trees. Overhead, rainbow lorikeets chattered noisily. Sarah was so pleased to be out of the house that she didn't care how far she walked. She was just wondering what happened to the yabbies during a drought, when a rustling in the grass ahead made her freeze on the spot. *Snakes.*

Heart thumping, she picked up a big stick and slowly continued, bolstering her courage with a silent chant, *Mulgas and adders and browns... Oh, no! Mulgas and adders and—*

She broke off as, glancing up, she spied a feather curving from the top of a leather hat just visible over the long grass beyond the stand of gums. She knew that feather. She scrambled up the slight incline, to see Bazza lying on his stomach in the grass, squinting down the sight of his rifle at some invisible target.

"What are you doing?" she said, coming up from behind.

Blam! Bazza's arm jerked and the rifle went off uselessly in the air. A string of curses Sarah mercifully couldn't decipher for the broad accent filled the air. Bazza got to his feet, his hat knocked askew. "Don't *ever* sneak up on a man with a gun in his hand!"

"Sorry. What are you doing?" she asked again.

"Clearing your land of vermin."

Sarah noticed with distaste the cluster of dead rabbits dangling from his belt. "I don't want you shooting poor defenseless little bunnies on my land."

"If you don't shoot 'em they breed like—like bloody rabbits," he explained in his drawl. "Then in their multitudes they chew the grass to the roots, leaving nothing for the cattle to eat. The dirt dries up and blows away."

"I see. Well, I'd still rather you didn't shoot them."

"Pardon me, ma'am, but you don't bloody know

what you're talking about.'' He shucked the spent cartridges on the ground and reloaded his rifle.

''Where's Luke?'' she asked, noticing Bazza's motorbike parked beside the dirt track.

''In the south paddock, checking on a weaner calf with a sore hoof. He'll be along any time.''

''So you want to be in movies?'' If she kept him talking, it might distract him from shooting rabbits.

''Yep.'' He squinted into the middle distance, presumably searching for moving bits of brown fur against the dry grass.

''Do you…have an agent?''

''Course I do, over in Sydney.''

''Sydney? Not Los Angeles?''

''She's back and forth to America all the time. Why, every time I call, her secretary tells me she's in L.A. If that's not dedication to my career, I don't know what it is.'' He raised his gun to his shoulder, sighting along the barrel.

Sarah tripped accidentally on purpose and knocked his elbow. ''Sorry.''

He glared at her. She swatted at the flies and moved to put Bazza between her and the Downs. She was getting that queasy feeling in her stomach again. ''Have you always worked with cattle? I mean when you're not in the movies or shooting rabbits.''

His scowl transformed into a cocky grin. ''I've done practically everything. Hunted wild boar, wrestled salties in Darwin, crossed the Sturt Desert on camel—''

''Salties?''

''Saltwater crocs. Mean buggers, them salties. Get you in a death roll and *ssst.*'' Bazza drew a finger across his neck.

"My, it sounds…exciting."

"Beats shoving peas up your nose. I reckon Hollywood could do an adventure series set in the outback about a bloke who goes around rescuing people and getting into danger."

Sarah bit back a smile. "Starring you."

"Naturally." Bazza lifted his gun to his shoulder.

Sarah took a step closer, prepared to bump into him.

He lowered his gun. "You going to keep doing that?"

She smiled and shrugged. "Yes."

With a heavy sigh he hoisted his rifle over his shoulder. "Reckon I've done enough shooting for today."

"Oh, good," she said, relieved.

"I'll check my traps, instead." He started to walk off along the rutted track that bordered the stand of gums.

"Wait!" she called, and hurried to catch up.

He stepped off the track into the long grass. "Beauty!"

Sarah gave a cry when she saw the tiny rabbit with its ear caught in the steel jaws of the trap. "It's only a baby. A poor little bunny." She pushed past Bazza to kneel in the grass. Blood was smeared over the rabbit's brown fur. Limp and panting, it stared up at her with a pleading look in its round black eyes. Or so it appeared to Sarah.

Bazza edged forward, his gun raised. "If you'll move out of the way, ma'am, I'll put it out of its misery."

"You'll do no such thing." Sarah flung a protective arm between the rabbit and Bazza.

A cloud of dust coming down the track caught her eye. It was Luke on his motorbike. His Akubra hat was pulled low on his head and the wind flattened his shirt against his chest. He slowed to a stop beside them and planted his long legs on either side to balance the bike. "What's going on?"

Sarah jumped up. "A baby rabbit. It's hurt."

"She won't let me shoot it," Bazza said in disgust.

Luke tipped his hat back on his tanned forehead. He squinted first at Bazza, then at Sarah, then slowly got off the motorbike.

Sarah held her breath. "Its ear is hurt."

"Rabbits are a pest," Luke told her. "Graziers shoot them. It's a fact of life."

She knew he was right. Her attitude was that of a city slicker with no knowledge or understanding of what it took to survive in this harsh environment. But she couldn't stop herself from pleading for the rabbit. "It's only a baby."

Luke spoke in an aside to Bazza. "You know what women are like. They've got soft hearts."

"Soft in the head, you mean," Bazza muttered.

Luke silenced him with a look. He turned to Sarah. "What would you do with it?"

"I—I'd nurse it back to health," she said wildly. She hadn't thought about what would happen *after* she saved the rabbit's life, only that she'd probably have nightmares if she witnessed the blowing out of bunny brains. "I'd keep it as a pet. It wouldn't eat much, only kitchen scraps—"

"And when you go back to Seattle?"

"Uh…a pet for Becka?"

"It's a wild animal."

Sarah glanced down at the rabbit. Its leg spasmed and she gave an involuntary cry of distress.

Luke heaved a sigh and shrugged. "Keep it."

"Oh, for crikey's sake!" Bazza exclaimed, and took off back to his motorbike.

"Thank you, thank you, thank you," Sarah said joyfully, and threw her arms around Luke.

"Steady on!" Her embrace knocked his hat sideways and he stepped back in haste. From a safe distance he regarded her sternly. "If that animal gets into the kitchen garden…"

"Don't worry, I'll make sure it stays locked up in—in—the cage I'll build for it." *Build a rabbit cage, Sarah? You've never even built a house out of Lego.*

"Fair enough." Luke knelt and pried open the jaws of the trap. Sarah crouched beside him and held out her hands for the weakly struggling rabbit.

"Careful," he said. "Their nails are sharp. Give me your hat."

She took it off and Luke nestled the rabbit inside, then folded the brim over tightly. "You'd better ride behind me back to the house," he said.

She glanced at the track, which veered away from the sheltering gums in a direct line across the Downs toward the homestead, and felt her body grow tense with apprehension. Then she glanced back at the creek. It would be a long walk with a struggling, injured rabbit in her arms.

Suddenly she had to smile at herself and the situation. This was almost like living a Lucy Walker novel where the station owner helped the lost heroine back to the homestead after she'd wandered away. How midsixties could you get?

"Well?" Luke said.

"Why aren't you riding a horse?" she asked, focusing on the bit of whimsy rather than mentioning her fears. To be authentic Mills and Boon she and Luke should be on the back of a tall and spirited horse.

"For general maintenance work around the station I can go farther, faster, on the bike," he explained, plainly puzzled by her question but willing to answer. "I ride a horse for the muster, though. Helicopters and motorbikes have their place, but for the fine, cutting-out work, you can't beat a good stock horse."

"I'd love to see a muster." She'd love to see him ride.

He unstrapped a helmet from the back of the bike and placed it on her head. "Come out with us."

Out there on the open Downs, where she could have a panic attack in front of everyone? "I don't think so."

"You could ride Becka's horse, Smokey. He's perfect for beginners."

She was acutely conscious of his warm fingers brushing her jaw as he adjusted the chin strap. "No. No, thanks."

His eyes met hers, very close and slightly suspicious. "What is it you're afraid of?"

"Afraid? Me? What is there to be afraid of? Besides snakes, spiders and sunstroke, that is." She held up the hat. "Where'll we put the bunny?"

Luke threw a leg over the bike and started the engine with a kick of his foot. "Tuck it between us and hold on tight to me."

Sarah climbed on behind, cradling the hat with the

rabbit in it between her stomach and Luke's back. With her arms tightly around Luke she shut her eyes against the Downs. All she needed to do was hang on.

And was he ever something to hang on to. Solid, like the trunk of an iron gum. An anchor against that mysterious force in this wide empty land that left her light-headed and breathless, as though she might fly away and be lost in the vast bowl of blue sky, or tumbled along the grassy plains for hundreds of miles until she was a dust speck in the desert.

The warm breeze lifted her hair and whipped it around her chin as he accelerated toward the home-stead. She pressed her cheek against Luke's back, breathing in the oddly comforting scent of warm cotton, sweat and dust. Maybe Lucy Walker wasn't so out-of-date. Some things were timeless.

She was almost sorry when he pulled up outside a shed made of solid round timbers, with a low roof of corrugated iron. Wal, alerted by the sound of Luke's motorbike, rose from his shady spot beneath the water tank and trotted over. The blue heeler raised himself on his hind legs to sniff the hat.

Sarah lifted the hat. "No, Wal. The sound of your heavy breathing is going to give poor Dorothy a heart attack."

"*Dorothy?*" Luke's eyebrows rose. "You'd better hope it's not a she." But he spoke sharply to Wal and the dog sat with a plaintive whine.

Sarah followed Luke into the shed. It had large benches for welding and woodwork and the walls were hung with tools, some obviously antiques. Propped against the back wall were gas cylinders, along with compressors, tires, motors and various power tools and machines. In one corner was a rack stacked with timber and beside it rolls of chicken wire, baling wire and an assortment of pipes and tubing.

"Your great-great-grandfather probably built this shed a hundred and fifty years ago," Luke said. "Some of those old tools would have been his. I found them in a corner here and cleaned them up."

"Do you use all this stuff?"

"It's not just for show. I maintain and repair the station vehicles, pumps and machinery, shoe the horses, you name it. Let's put Dorothy in the stable for now."

The stable was a nearby stone building fitted out with box stalls, a tack room and wooden bins having hinged lids, which Sarah deduced contained oats and other feed. Luke lifted the lid on an empty one and dropped the rabbit inside.

From one of the stalls came a soft nicker as Luke's chestnut gelding greeted his master. "He's a wonderful animal," Sarah said, going over to stroke the smooth powerful neck. "He looks like a Thoroughbred, only smaller. What is he—about fourteen and a half hands high?"

"Exactly fourteen and a half hands," Luke said, resting his arms on the top of the stall. "Kimba is a registered Australian stock horse." He turned to gaze at her. "You said you don't know much about horses, yet you correctly estimated his height in hands. How is that?"

"Lucky guess?" Sarah flashed him a guilty smile and avoided his skeptical gaze. "Does 'Kimba' mean something?"

"It's aboriginal for bushfire." Luke let the animal nuzzle his open hand. "He can move faster than fire through mulga scrub after cattle." He gave the horse a final slap on the neck and moved away from the stall. "Let's see what we can find to do up that cage."

Back in the workshop he took Sarah to the rack stacked with odds and ends of timber. "You choose some pieces to make a frame while I get my tools."

Sarah gazed at the timber in frustration. Without a plan to work from, how was she supposed to know what she needed? If she was at home, she could download a design from the Internet, modify it graphically and print up detailed instructions from the manufacturer's Web site.

But she wasn't at home. She was in the middle of nowhere, with no idea of how to go about constructing a simple rabbit hutch. Finally she pulled out half a dozen two-by-fours of roughly the same length.

"What should I do first?" she asked when Luke came back with a toolbox and a handsaw. Wal found himself a ringside seat and settled in for the show.

"Maybe I'd better just build it."

"No," she insisted. "I wanted the rabbit—I'll make the cage. Just give me a few pointers." Luke opened his mouth to say something and she held up a hand to stop him. "Don't even suggest I'm being just like a female, because this isn't about gender at all."

"Of course it isn't," he said, running a tape measure along the wood she'd chosen. "It's about you being a townie and lacking certain essential skills.

These two are the same length. You can start by nailing them together at the corners.''

A townie. He said it as if she were from outer space. Crouching awkwardly on the wooden floor, she picked up a handful of nails and stuffed them in her mouth the way she'd seen them do on those home improvement shows on TV.

Luke took hold of the nails and removed them. ''I'd hate to see you swallow those.'' He handed her one back. ''Didn't he ever visit you?''

Carefully she positioned the nail and raised the hammer. ''Who?''

''Your father.''

Her arm tensed and the hammer came down on her thumb. *Damn.* ''A few times,'' she said testily, sucking and blowing on her thumb. ''But like I said, his new wife didn't want him to have anything to do with Mom and me. And then, of course, he moved to the east coast.''

Luke ignored her throbbing thumb and realigned the lengths of wood. ''Try bracing the wood with your foot. That's better.'' He turned to his dog. ''Wal, bring me the saw.''

To Sarah's amazement, Wal got up and dragged the saw over to Luke with his teeth. She banged in a nail. It only bent a little.

Luke measured and marked two more pieces of wood and began to saw them into the same length as the first two. ''I can't imagine having a child and letting someone else tell me I couldn't see her.''

''He sent birthday cards and Christmas presents,'' she said, starting to feel defensive, even if Warren didn't deserve it. ''And he left me this station.''

"A white elephant where you're concerned."

"You're just saying that because you want it."

"I'm surprised your mother didn't insist on more contact, for your sake."

"She would have died before she'd ask him for anything. Even for me." She stopped hammering. "Look, Mom remarried and I had a great stepfather who loved me a lot. Can we change the subject?"

"Okay. What would you do with Burrinbilli if I did sell my half to you?"

"My mother—"

"Your mother didn't come back here when she inherited—" he paused to give her a swift perusal "—twenty-five plus years ago. Why would she come now?"

"I'm twenty-nine," she said, answering his unspoken question. "I'd like my mother to have the opportunity to return to her childhood home." The truth was, this was starting to be less about Anne and more about herself. She knew she couldn't live at Burrinbilli, but she felt a connection to the property and didn't want it to go out of the family. "What would you do with the station?"

"My dream is to make it totally self-sufficient. Grow all my own food, generate my own energy, and what I can't produce myself I'd buy with the proceeds from the cattle."

"You can't do all that on your own, surely."

"No, I'd need a partner, a wife, who'd want the same thing." A fierce yearning flashed in his eyes, and as if he realized it, he bent his head to fit another piece of wood against the frame of the cage.

What would it be like to be such a woman? Sarah wondered. "Did Caroline want that, too?"

He snorted. "No. That's why she wasn't my wife. She refused to live on the station."

He spoke with such bitterness Sarah felt his pain. Yet as a fellow townie, she understood where Caroline was coming from. "Maybe we can compromise and split the station in two. Naturally I'd pay extra to keep the homestead, since it belongs in my mother's family."

"Half of this station isn't big enough to run a mob of cattle large enough to see a profit. Nor can I afford to build a new house." Luke put down the saw. "Suppose I did sell you my half. Has your mother said she'd come back here to live?"

"Not exactly. She's so used to giving to *me* she finds it hard to accept in return. Especially when she knows that if it were just me I'd use the money for something different."

He gazed at her. "What is it Sarah Templestowe wants?"

"*You'll* think it's silly, but there's this penthouse suite for sale in the building where I work." She shrugged and reached for another nail. "It's just a fantasy."

"Sometimes dreams are all that keep us going." He held the pieces of wood while she hammered them together. "What'll you do if your mother decides not to live here?"

She didn't want to think about that.

"Well?" he insisted.

"Why, I'd—I'd get someone to manage it and come here for holidays and..." She couldn't take his steady skeptical gaze, so she hammered away and made a lot of noise, only bending four out of five nails.

He handed her another piece of wood and pretended to inspect the box of nails. "I should warn you, we're down to the last five dozen."

"Ha, ha."

"Seriously, Sarah, don't you reckon you ought to have thought things through before you lobbed on down here and tried to buy me out?"

She winced and it had nothing to do with her throbbing thumb. "I *did* think. I just didn't think the right things. I knew this place wasn't like Seattle. I knew about the climate and the geography, the distances and the isolation. But until I experienced it I just didn't *comprehend* it. Do you know what I mean?"

He contemplated that. "Like when I traveled to Europe and encountered snow for the first time."

"Exactly. Now, imagine being naked in the snow at the mercy of the elements and you'll get an idea of what I feel."

At the word *naked* his eyes met hers and the sudden intense heat that rose between Luke and her made her cheeks burn. Maybe he did notice her after all.

But if he was attracted he seemed determined not to show it. He rose to his feet and unrolled the chicken wire, then handed her the wire cutters.

Why, oh, why, had she made such an issue of being able to make a rabbit hutch? Laboriously she clipped her way along the wire, gathering scratches from the sharp edges. She guessed she couldn't blame him for not acknowledging whatever was happening between them. She was so not what he wanted.

"Let's suppose I *did* own Burrinbilli outright and my mother *did* move down here. Would you stay on as manager? We could renovate the manager's cottage. All mod cons, etc."

He shook his head. "I'm after land of my own. But don't worry, you'd have no trouble finding a new manager. Plenty of stockmen about who wouldn't say no to the job."

She had no doubt there were hordes of stockmen roaming the outback just desperate for a low-paying job on an isolated station. "But they wouldn't know the place as well as you. Or care about it as much."

"I care so much because it's half-mine. Because through my efforts to improve the land I can pass on a better property to my daughter."

"What if Becka decides she doesn't want it?" Sarah asked. "She's not too thrilled to be here at the moment."

"She'll get used to it. It's a good life and one day she'll appreciate it. Maybe someday I'll have more children. If not, I'll work the station as long as I'm able. You see..." he paused to gaze at her "...I want Burrinbilli for *myself,* as well. That's the difference between you and me, and the reason *I* should own it."

"That doesn't follow at all," Sarah said, though she had a nasty feeling it did. But she wasn't going to admit that to Luke, at least not at this point. The only thing to do was change the subject.

"I don't want to pry, but don't you think you

should tell me what's going on with Abby and Becka? I mean, so I don't put my foot in it. I honestly didn't know who Abby was or I would have run it by you before I asked her out to the station."

"Yeah, I know." His eyebrows drew together. "Abby…"

"Yes?" She waited.

"Let's finish this hutch first." He helped her wrap the chicken wire around the frame, then picked up the staple gun and loaded it. "I'll handle the staple gun. These things can be dangerous."

"If you insist," she murmured, and stepped back to give him room. Some things she didn't feel compelled to prove.

Within minutes he'd stapled the wire to the frame and tacked the whole thing onto a wooden box, with a hinged lid for a door. Then he rocked back on his heels, inspecting his handiwork. *Their* handiwork, Sarah thought, proud to have contributed even a little to it. "Well?"

"Jerry-rigged, but it's only temporary so it'll do."

"I meant *Abby*."

Luke began putting away his tools. "After Caroline died, Abby and I agreed that when Becka turned nine she would come live here. Abby's finding it hard to give Becka up."

"But why would Abby lie to me to get here? And why did you have a fit when you saw her? I have the feeling there's more to the story than you're telling me. What has she done? Is it something I should know about?"

He gazed at her a long time. "Abby is—"

He paused again, so long that her nerves stretched to breaking point. "What? What is Abby?"

"A bloody good cook," he said, and got to his feet.

"You don't like to talk about anything personal, do you?"

He grunted and brushed the dust from his pants.

"Is that a gender thing or a cultural thing?"

He shot her a piercing glance. "It's just who I am. Let's see if Dorothy likes her new home."

His large hands cradled the baby rabbit with unbelievable tenderness, considering his attitude toward the "pest," while Sarah washed the blood off its ear with a clean rag. Then he dropped it into the cage and Sarah gave it a horse carrot before he closed the latch.

"Why did you do this?" she asked. "Why go to all this trouble for a rabbit?"

He shrugged. "You wanted it."

As if that were reason enough to do something he thought was not only inconvenient and a nuisance but downright wrong. "Is that like the creed of the bush, or something?"

He chuckled. "That's right. If a neighbor's property is threatened by bushfires, you fight the fire. If he needs a hand during shearing or muster, you bring your horses and equipment. If his vehicle breaks down, you try to fix it. If someone wants a rabbit hutch, you build it."

Sarah tried to imagine going to her neighbor's apartment to help fix the plumbing or clean up after a party. Then she tried to remember who her neighbors were and if she'd ever even met them. Helping people just because they needed help. What a radical concept. She gazed at Luke with growing admiration. What a guy.

"Then you don't think I'm a complete idiot for rescuing the bunny?"

"Of course I think you're an idiot." He gave a half grin as her face fell and added gruffly, "A bloody sweet idiot."

Sarah gazed into his smiling eyes and felt a jolt of adrenaline rush through her. Without thinking she took a step closer. Luke's smile slowly faded. His face drew nearer to hers—

"Daddy! Are you in here?"

CHAPTER SIX

"IN HERE, BECKA."

Luke spun away so quickly Sarah felt the breeze. No question who was Luke's best girl, she thought, without begrudging Becka that status.

The shed door creaked open and sunlight flooded the dim interior. Becka poked her head in. "Aunt Abby is going to Longreach for supplies for the muster tomorrow. Can I go with her?"

"You've got school."

"It's a curriculum day. Can I go?"

Luke frowned. "Did she ask you to go?"

"Not exactly, but I know she'd like me to come. She said if I wanted to I should ask you."

Standing next to him, Sarah could sense his body tighten as he replied, "I'm sorry, possum."

"But Da-a-ad—"

"Becka." His tone held a distinct warning.

"Come and see my bunny," Sarah said quickly. "Bazza caught it in a trap and your dad helped me rescue it."

"He did?" Becka said, as if that were the last thing she'd expect from her father. She crossed to the cage and knelt down beside it. "Oh, it's so cute."

"Dorothy's her name. I'm assuming she's a girl." Sarah dusted off her jeans and clapped the battered hat back on her head. "I'm going to the house. There are a couple of things I'd like Abby to pick up for me in Longreach. That's the town where I caught the bus to come here, right?" She remembered seeing a fabric store not far from the bus station.

Becka started to go with her, but Luke put a hand on her shoulder. "Wait a minute, Becka. I—" he glanced at Sarah "—I'd like to talk to you."

Sarah flashed him her most brilliant smile and tweaked Becka's braid as she turned to leave. Luke and Becka were going to talk!

The moment she stepped outside her stomach got all queasy again. She seemed to be okay among the trees and the outbuildings, but she didn't feel entirely comfortable never knowing if a full-blown panic attack was on the way. She had to get over this. If only because now she'd have to walk out here every day just to feed Dorothy.

The journey of a thousand miles… Yadda, yadda, yadda.

Fixing her gaze on the homestead, she put her right foot in front of her left.

LUKE PACED the straw-strewn wooden floor and wondered how to start. There was so much he wanted to say to Becka. How much he loved her, feared for her, longed to see her happy and fulfilled. How much he wanted her love and respect. Troubled emotions filled his chest, emotions he didn't know how to express.

Crouching beside her, Luke lifted a wisp of blond hair away from her forehead. "Abby's going to be here for the muster, but that's all."

"I just want to go with her to Longreach. Why can't I?"

"She shouldn't have let you ask me. She knows I don't want you off the station with her."

"I made my bed this morning and fed the chooks without being asked," Becka pleaded, hanging on to his hand with both of hers. "I'll do whatever chores you want. I'll even eat steak for breakfast. If you'll just let me go."

Was there anything harder to resist than the earnest entreaty of a much loved child? Luke's heart ached for her. "I'm sorry, Becka."

Tears burst forth and the spoiled Becka lashed out at him. "You're mean. Why are you so mean? I hate Burrinbilli and I hate you."

His chest tightened. Abby was right. If this desperate pain in his heart was what being a father was all about, he hadn't had much experience. If only he and station life could be enough for Becka. If only she could understand that by not telling her of his concerns over Abby he was trying to protect her, trying to preserve her affection for her aunt.

"Give it time, Becka. You'll see things differently."

God, he hoped he was right.

THE NEXT DAY Sarah waved Abby goodbye from the front veranda. She was just closing the door, when Luke appeared behind her in the hall.

"Has Abby gone already?" he asked.

Sarah nodded, still feeling slightly awkward after that near kiss in the barn. At least in *her* mind it was a near kiss; Luke seemed to have forgotten all about the incident. Maybe that was best. While tempting, romantic involvement with Luke was hardly appropriate.

"I meant to tell her the battery was low on the Land Cruiser. Never mind, I don't suppose she'll leave the lights on." He started back toward the kitchen. "I'm going to make coffee. Do you want something?"

"Thanks, but I'll help myself in a little while. I was just about to call my mother." She was dying to know how his talk with Becka yesterday had gone but was certain he'd clam up if she asked.

In her room, Sarah reached for her cell phone and dialed her mother's number. While she waited for Anne to pick up she traced the letters on the cover of the diary. What was it that was so intriguing about a diary? The prospect of discovering thoughts and feelings never before revealed? But she and her mother were close. Surely Anne had no secrets from her. Hmm, then again, there was Len.

"Good afternoon, Trade Winds Imports. May I help you?"

Sarah pictured her mother perched on her stool in the store, as cool and serene as an alpine lake. She plucked at her damp top, still not used to the heat. "Hi, Mom. It's me."

"Hello, darl'. What time is it?"

Sarah glanced at her watch. "Around noon on Wednesday. What time is it there?"

"Nearly 5:00 p.m., Tuesday. I was just about to shut up shop for the night."

"Thanks for the coffee. It was a really nice surprise."

"Let me know when you want some more."

"Len said he'd order it in from Sydney. Thanks, anyway."

"He always was nice." Anne's voice sounded unnaturally stilted.

Sarah walked across the room to rummage in her cosmetic bag for a bottle of nail polish and some cotton batting. "He's a widower now. He told me you two used to go out together. Have you ever thought what it would be like if you and he got together again? He spoke really well of you."

"Did he? I'm surprised."

"Why?" Sarah sat on the bed again and stuffed cotton between her toes.

Her mother sighed. "He and I didn't part on the best of terms, that's all. You can forget any romantic notions you may have about us getting back together."

"I met another friend of yours today," Sarah said, shaking the bottle of copper-colored nail polish. "Abby McCrae. She's Luke's little girl's greataunt."

"I remember her. Abby was a year younger and she wasn't exactly a close friend."

"Really? She seems nice enough, although she and Luke don't see eye to eye over Becka." Sarah didn't mention her feeling that there was something odd about Abby. It was probably nothing. She dipped the brush in the nail polish and smoothed metallic copper over her left big toenail.

"She had a pash on Len for years. It was embarrassing for the poor man. I thought she went away to Brisbane."

"She came back to look after Becka after Becka's mother died. She's staying here now, to cook for the muster."

"I expect she'll be good at that. She was always winning prizes for her baked goods at the Brisbane Show."

"Speaking of baking, have you ever thought about getting a bread maker? It's a really cool device."

"Sarah."

"Okay, okay. Oh, I went down to the creek today, but I haven't found the water hole where you and Robby used to catch yabbies." Sarah put more cotton batting between her toes and started on her right foot.

"Keep an eye out for snakes coming by for a drink."

"Trust me, I'm very aware of the possibility of snakes. Have you given any more thought to coming down?"

"I just don't know how I can get away, darl'. How are you adjusting to station life? It must seem lonely after the city and all your friends."

"Not really, there's so much to do. I helped build a rabbit hutch today and I've got the scars to prove it." She waggled her ten copper-tipped toes and set the bottle of polish aside. "Nights are a little uneventful. The sun goes down and a while later the lights go out and that's the end of everything till the rooster crows the next morning. I wouldn't mind a night on the town. Dress up, go out for dinner, maybe dancing…" She sighed. "I guess I'll get plenty of that once I'm home."

"Has Luke agreed to sell his half?"

Sarah hesitated. Her door wasn't shut firmly and

she'd thought she heard a noise in the hall. She rose from the bed and walked on her heels to the door. When she peeked out she saw Luke disappearing through the doorway into the kitchen.

"Getting him to part with his half of the station is going to be tougher than I thought," she said as she shut the door. "Am I wrong to want to keep Burrinbilli in our family?"

Anne hesitated. "It depends...."

"What do you want, really?"

"I have a strong sentimental attachment, but..."

"But what?"

"My feelings are mixed. Your going there has dredged up a lot of memories—not all of them pleasant."

Sarah was silent, eager for her mother to elaborate. When she didn't, Sarah said, "My only hope at the moment is that his daughter will persuade him to move into town."

"Is that likely?" Anne sounded skeptical.

"No," Sarah admitted. "Though not for lack of trying on her part. But he's stubborn."

"Outback men are a different breed. Some can be pretty macho."

Luke would be hard to beat for strength and stoicism, but saving a bunny rabbit didn't strike Sarah as macho. "He's an entity unto himself—I'll give you that." She turned and stretched. "I guess I'd better go. Will you at least think about coming for a visit?"

Anne hesitated. "Maybe you should read my diary after all. It'll explain a few things."

"Are you sure?" Sarah said, trying to sound casual. "I don't want to pry into your secret past or anything."

"I'm sure. Bye now, darl'. I'll talk to you soon."

After she hung up, Sarah propped herself on one elbow on the bed, arranged her feet so her toenails wouldn't smudge and opened the diary.

March 1, 1969. My sixteenth birthday party was really fab. Robby, my usually dumb brother, gave me the new Beatles album. Everybody came, even the Myers, and they're over five hours away. Dot Myer was Mum's best friend in school and Trina and I are like cousins. All the kids I invited from boarding school came, too. P.S. I think Len likes me.

Sarah smiled in happy anticipation and turned the page. She loved a good romance. So she was disappointed when Anne's diary entries over the next two months were mostly to do with her girlfriends and station life in general, until…

May 14, 1969. Len definitely likes me. He kept looking at me when he and his dad came over to help with the branding. We had a good clean muster this year, Dad says. Robby is talking about joining the army and going to Vietnam. Mum's freaked out. Dad's having a fit. I think Robby must be off his nut to want to go to war.

With a sigh Sarah glanced at her watch and closed the diary—for now. She washed her face and brushed her hair, but Luke had gone back out by the time she entered the kitchen. Becka was at the table, working on a drawing in her sketchpad. Ignoring a small stab of disappointment at missing Luke, Sarah made herself a sandwich.

"Where did this come from?" she said, spying a package with her name on it on the counter beside the phone.

"Bazza brought the mail in from Murrum this morning," Becka said. "What is it?"

Sarah ripped open the package. "It's the Internet starter kit I ordered. Cool."

She quickly read over the information, then took her sandwich and sat down to watch Becka. With watercolor pencils the little girl had colored in a gum tree crowded with rainbow lorikeets and pink-and-gray galahs and was now carefully brushing on water, transforming the picture into a watercolor.

"That's really good," Sarah said between bites of her cheese-and-tomato sandwich.

"Thanks." Becka dipped her brush and stroked a light wash over the gray-green of the gum leaves. "My mother was an artist."

"You've definitely got her talent."

"She drowned when I was a baby," Becka remarked matter-of-factly. "Abby's like my mum now."

"Er…" Sarah decided not to go there. "I'm sorry about your mom. Your dad's a pretty nice guy."

Becka shrugged and made no reply.

"He works awfully hard," Sarah continued. "I feel lucky he's been managing the station so well."

Becka raised curious blue eyes. "You seem to like my dad an awful lot. Are you going to stay here?"

"God, no!" Sarah blurted, then caught herself. She hadn't meant to sound so vehement, but Becka had totally misconstrued her interest in Luke. "I mean, this place is so different from what I'm used to."

"At least you know you're only going to be here for a little while." Becka put down her brush and pushed aside her finished picture. "I need to let this dry before I do the birds. Will you show me the computer now?"

"Sure! We can install the Web browser." Sarah brushed the crumbs from her fingers and carried her plate to the sink. "Are any of your friends in Murrum on the Internet?"

"Lucy is and Julie's getting on soon."

"I'll show you how to e-mail them. It's almost as good as talking on the phone."

They went down the hall to the office and Sarah configured the computer for the Internet service provider. As she tested the connection, she asked idly, "What's in those chests with all the drawers?"

"Oh, that's Dad's bug collection."

"Moreton Bay bugs?"

Becka giggled. "*No.* I'll show you." She got up and slid open the top drawer.

Sarah peered over her shoulder. Beetles. Big ones, little ones, fearsome ones and cute ones. Spotted, striped, iridescent and black matte. All neatly mounted and labeled with their Latin names in tiny hand-printed lettering.

The next drawer contained flying insects. Wasps, bees, moths, dragon flies and a whole fleet of airborne creatures she'd never seen or imagined.

Fascinated, she reached past Becka for the third drawer—and nearly shrieked at the sight of spiders in jars of alcohol. They were of every size and shape, some as big as her hand, some with eight eyes and huge fangs. She shut that drawer quickly and opened the next, to find a pair of stick insects so big they could have passed for chihuahuas if they'd had fur and a tail.

"Wow. Where did all these come from?"

"Dad collected them."

"Around here?" She wasn't sure she wanted to know that.

Becka nodded. "Any time we go for a picnic or a trip he takes nets and plant presses and snake tongs and specimen jars...I found this one," she said, pointing at a large green beetle.

"Lovely. Why does he do all this?"

"He likes it, I suppose. People are always ringing him up to ask him stuff."

"Professor Winter-type people?"

"Yes. Professors and scientists from the museum." She glanced at the computer. "Can we go on the Internet now?"

"Sure." While they'd been looking at the insect collection she'd heard the familiar electronic signal that indicated the modem was connected to the server in Longreach. They sat in front of the computer, Becka on the office chair and Sarah in a kitchen chair to one side. Sarah showed Becka how to send an e-mail and tested it by transmitting a message to her mother. Not much of a test, Sarah thought, since Anne was unlikely to check her Inbox.

When they'd spent an hour exploring the basics of

the World Wide Web Sarah disconnected. "It's an awful lot to take in all at once. Before we shut down I'll show you the word processing program."

"This is way cool," Becka said after Sarah had set up the computer so that Becka had her own directory for word processing and art files.

"You can put your essays and projects on here. Or you can write stories or keep a diary. Do you keep a diary?"

"Just at school. You know, stuff we do on the weekend."

"I was thinking of something more personal. Sometimes if you write down what you're going through it helps you understand and accept your feelings."

Becka pulled a face. "I know how I feel about my freckles. I hate them."

It wasn't the problem Sarah'd been thinking of, but she smiled sympathetically. "I never liked mine, either. In fact, *hate* is probably too mild a word to describe how I felt about freckles. I used to fade them with lemon juice."

"Did it work?"

"I thought so. Do you want to try it?"

"What do you have to do?"

"Let's shut down the computer and I'll show you. Have you got any lemons?"

"There's a tree out the back."

The lemon tree grew between the rotary clothes hoist and the fenced kitchen garden. "I've never used one of these before," she said to Becka as they passed the clothes hoist. "Maybe you can show me later."

"It's easy." Becka giggled and raced ahead. "Bazza calls this a gin-and-tonic tree. Look, there's a good one."

Sarah jumped and snatched at the lemon, bringing a shower of leaves down with it. "Let's go cut it in two."

A few minutes later they were sitting on the veranda and Sarah was rubbing the cut side of the lemon across Becka's freckled nose.

"You, too," Becka said.

Sarah shrugged and squeezed lemon juice over her face. "Now we sit in the sun and let it bleach out the spots."

"Without hats?" Becka looked dubious. "Dad wouldn't like that."

"A few minutes won't hurt."

Sarah set the timer for five minutes and they sat on the edge of the veranda, eyes shut, faces defiantly raised to the sun. Probably nothing much would happen, but she was enjoying Becka's company.

"Freckles often fade as you get older," Sarah said. "But you know, freckles aren't all that bad. I actually like mine now. They're a part of me so I figure I'd better. Your dad even has a few under his tan."

"Yeah, but he's a man."

"So?" Sarah wrinkled her nose as the lemon juice dried and tightened her skin.

"Do you *really* like your freckles?"

Sarah cast her a sideways glance. "I'm working on it."

A shadow came between them and the sun. "Looks to me like you're working on a case of melanoma."

Sarah opened her eyes to see Luke standing over them. Wal sniffed her face with his cold wet nose and started to lick. Laughing, she pushed him away and he moved on to Becka. "We've only been out here three minutes."

"Three minutes too long. What's this all about?" Becka eyed Sarah and giggled nervously.

"Becka?" Luke said sternly.

Sarah could see he wasn't really angry, but Becka didn't seem to know that. "Girl stuff," Sarah volunteered.

"I hate my freckles," Becka blurted. "Sarah said if you put lemon juice on them and sit in the sun they'll fade."

"That's right," Sarah said, hoping Luke would be sensitive to his daughter's budding feminine self-image.

Luke crouched beside Becka and stroked the end of one blond braid across the tip of her nose. "I'd like you to be happy just the way you are."

Becka regarded him soberly. "Freckles are ugly."

"Are you saying Sarah is ugly?"

"Oh, no!" Becka flashed a worried glance at Sarah. "I think she's beautiful."

Sarah felt herself start to flush, but Luke ignored the comment. "So it's *your* freckles you don't like."

"Well, *duh.*" She caught his eye. "I mean, yes, sir."

"I think you're the cutest girl in the whole world. And your freckles are cute, too."

Becka appeared startled, then a smile spread across her face at the compliment. Wal slurped his tongue over her cheeks and Luke put his arm around the dog to pull him away.

"You'd better go wash your face."

"It's only lemon juice," Becka said.

"Wal, here, had a horse pie sandwich for lunch."

"Eeeuuww! Gross!" Becka jumped up and ran shrieking into the house.

Luke glanced at Sarah and grinned, his teeth white against his tanned skin. Lines like miniature smiles radiated from the corners of his blue eyes.

Sarah smiled at him. "That was good. You made her feel attractive and special."

Luke absently ruffled Wal's fur with his long fingers. "She *is* special."

A bittersweet pang assailed Sarah. Her mother and Dennis had instilled in her a strong sense of self-worth, but Warren had never told her she was special. She told herself it didn't matter, that *Dennis* was her real father, but somehow it still hurt.

"So, do you really think freckles are cute?"

One corner of his mouth tilted up, counterpoint to the lift of the opposite eyebrow. "Freckles are cute on little girls...."

"Oh." She swallowed useless feelings of disappointment.

Tilting his hat back, Luke leaned closer, his voice low and soft. "On you, they're sexy."

"Oh." Her ear and neck tingled where his breath touched her skin. She gazed into crystalline-blue eyes and felt the heat of the day in every pore of her body.

He tipped his hat to her and followed Becka into

the house. Sarah sat where she was for five full minutes before she trusted her wobbly knees to carry her.

THE NEXT DAY while Becka was at school and Luke out on the run, Sarah typed in *agoraphobia* on the Internet Web browser and hit the search button. Seconds later she had a list of Web sites devoted to the subject. Agoraphobia, she was surprised to learn, was not in fact the fear of open spaces but the fear of losing control and having an anxiety attack in public.

The list of symptoms was huge and included those she'd experienced: palpitations, queasiness, light-headedness and gasping for breath. Apparently the attacks were caused by an underlying anxiety brought on by a stressful period or a traumatic event such as childbirth or the loss of a loved one.

Sarah sat back. Okay, so her biological father had died, but she'd hardly known him and for sure hadn't been traumatized by the event. Quentin would probably say she had unresolved issues, but what did he know?

She scrolled down to discover that certain locations could trigger an attack thereby causing the sufferer to avoid those locations. That made sense. In her case, it was open land.

…blah, blah, blah…important not to self-diagnose…

She would have to ignore that. She'd given Quentin a final farewell before she'd left Seattle and asking him for help now probably wouldn't go over very well. She thought about telling Luke, getting the name of a local therapist… No, too embarrassing.

Scrolling farther, she came to treatment options:

relaxation, cognitive behavior therapy, meditation, medication, breathing techniques…. Without a doctor's diagnosis medication was out of the question. She was already doing some of those other things, such as using the times tables to block out unwanted thoughts.

She sighed and shut down the computer. No easy fixes. She'd just have to tough things out on her own.

SARAH DIDN'T SEE much of Luke over the next few days as he was busy preparing the cattle yards for the muster. So she occupied herself with painting her room and then Becka's. Luke had kept the house structurally well maintained but through lack of time had neglected cosmetic details. Sarah would have liked to freshen the butter-yellow walls and cream trim in the kitchen, but that room had become Abby's domain.

"Take your coffee into the loungeroom," Abby said, busily stacking dirty dishes into a sink full of soapy water after dinner on Friday night. "I'll finish up."

"But—" Sarah began.

Abby removed the empty casserole dish from her hands with a firm smile and walked her to the door. "Don't worry about me. I'm just the hired help. Off you go and relax."

Abby might be the hired help, but she acted like the mistress of the house, Sarah grumbled as she was herded into the loungeroom. There, the brief détente between Luke and Becka had broken down and Luke was engaged in a defense of both life on the cattle station and the cattle industry in general to one skeptical little girl. Sarah took a chair in the corner of the room and listened unobtrusively.

"We're doing a really important job out here, Becka," Luke said. "If everyone lived in town, who would produce the beef and grow the wheat that feed the people of Australia? We'd have to depend on buying food from overseas."

Becka sat on the floor, playing with a collection of tiny stuffed horses. "What's wrong with that?"

"What others give, they can also withhold," Luke explained patiently. "Far better for a country to stand on its own, independent and self-sufficient. That way other nations can't take advantage of your need or exact a price that's too high."

There was more to his words than met the ear, Sarah thought, sipping her coffee. She detected a subtext to his argument, an unconscious justification for closing himself off from people. "What about the things we can't produce by ourselves?" she interjected. "For some things we have to rely on others."

"Like phosphate," Becka suggested.

"Pardon?" Sarah said, startled. She'd been thinking of things like love and companionship.

Becka twirled a braid. "My teacher says Australia has to import phosphate from the island of Nauru to make fertilizer because we don't have any phosphate of our own. On Nauru they mine phosphate from millions and millions of bird droppings."

Sarah looked to Luke. "So, what about phosphate?"

"Well," he said slowly, eyeing her. "I reckon you have to ask yourself, do I really need fertilizer or can I get by without it?"

"Maybe you could get by without, but how would that affect your quality of life?" Sarah replied. Luke knew what he was saying and what she was getting at.

Becka's forehead wrinkled as she looked from one to the other. "The wheat wouldn't grow as high?"

Luke smiled at his daughter. Then he said to Sarah, "We're used to doing for ourselves in the outback."

"I'd *still* rather live in Murrum," Becka said to him, going back to the real dispute. "You don't even care that I don't like it here."

Luke snapped open a magazine on cattle breeding, signaling the end of the discussion.

"You haven't given station life much of a chance," Sarah said to Becka, seeing that the girl felt she wasn't being heard. "You could learn to like it eventually."

"What if I don't?" Becka insisted unhappily.

Sarah fumed inwardly. *She* shouldn't be having this discussion with Becka. It was clear Luke hadn't resolved anything with his daughter during their conversation in the barn. Maybe if Sarah pushed him hard enough he'd jump in and take over. Becka needed to know he cared enough to at least talk to her about her feelings.

"I'm sure your father will find a way to compromise," she said recklessly. "Maybe if by the end of the Wet, you still don't like it—"

"Stop right there," Luke warned, firing a sharp glance her way.

"Then I can go back to Aunt Abby's to live?" Becka finished Sarah's thought excitedly. "Please,

Dad. If I'm really really good during the holidays, can I?''

''Absolutely not!'' Luke got to his feet just as Abby entered the room, humming. He threw down his magazine and glared at her. ''Don't *you* bloody start.'' Then he turned to Becka. ''It would help if you tried to be more cheerful about the situation.'' With that he stormed out of the room and seconds later they heard his boots echoing across the veranda.

''My word,'' Abby said. ''Luke is in a temper tonight.'' She came over to where Sarah sat and tidied away her half-finished cup of coffee.

Sarah started to protest, then let it go, watching irritably as Abby scoured the room for cups and crumbs, marking her territory with Pledge and a dust cloth. With a grunt of impatience Sarah got up and followed Luke out. Truth was, she was irritated with herself as well as him. She should never have opened her big mouth and butted in where it was none of her business.

She reached the veranda in time to see him striding across the darkened yard. Damn. He carried the flashlight from the kitchen and she didn't know where another was kept. One more minute and he'd be in the barn.

''Oh, don't be such a wuss,'' she scolded herself. She stepped through the screen door and into the yard, which her imagination had filled with more writhing poisonous snakes than Indiana Jones's worst nightmare.

''Luke,'' she called. He didn't even slow down. ''Luke!'' she called louder, and jogged toward him.

Impatiently he turned, hands on hips. "What is it?"

His anger banished her guilt and transformed her apology into a challenge. "Okay, so I shouldn't have interfered—"

"Damn right you shouldn't have. You know nothing about us or our life, yet you barge in here and fill Becka's head with nonsense."

"Why don't you explain exactly what the deal is with Abby and Becka? Then maybe I won't go blundering where I shouldn't. I can see you don't like Abby, but aside from some irritating habits I don't know why you think she's so bad for Becka. Neither does Becka." Sarah took a step closer and pushed on his chest lightly with her fingertips. "If you don't talk to her, you'll lose her."

Luke grasped her fingers and his voice sank to a hoarse whisper. "You don't understand. I'm going to lose her, anyway. There's no high school in Murrum. When Becka is twelve she'll go to Mount Isa to boarding school." He dropped her hand and looked away. "I've only got a few years left with her."

All the fight went out of Sarah. "I didn't know. I'm sorry." When he remained silent she went on. "It's just that I know how she feels out here, separated from the life she's used to. The difference is, I can go home."

Luke's gaze flashed back to hers. "Becka *is* home."

"That's not how she feels."

"I know how she feels."

"Maybe. But she doesn't know how *you* feel. Or why."

"We'll just have to see, won't we? Meantime, I'll thank you to not come between me and my daughter."

"That is so unfair." To her horror tears pricked her eyes. "I've been trying to bring you two together."

"I don't *need* your help."

"Excuse me, but it's painfully obvious you do." Stumbling, she turned to go back to the house.

Before she'd taken a dozen steps he was at her side, grasping her arm. "Sarah, wait. I—" his hand slid down her arm to hold hers "—I'm doing the best I can."

The hint of agonized entreaty in his voice touched her more than an apology would have. "I know," she said softly.

Luke was silent a moment, his hand lingering in hers. "Look, I overheard part of your conversation with your mother the other day," he said at last. "There's a bachelor and spinster ball coming up not this Saturday but next. It's not what you're used to, but it's a chance to have a bit of fun and you could get to know some people. Would you like to go?"

"Bachelor and spinster? Is this the outback version of a singles club?"

He chuckled. "I reckon you could call it that."

"Okay...thanks. That sounds fun." And a good way to wrap up her stay. It was hard to believe she'd been here almost one week already. "Is it dressy? What should I wear?"

"Bachelor and spinster balls are dressy, but you

could wear anything,'' he said as they walked back to the house.

"Spoken like a true man." Sarah casually dropped his hand—this was already sounding a little too much like a date. Yet part of her wished his warm fingers were still wrapped around hers. "Is the ball in Murrum?"

"Rowan. It's a couple hundred kilometers north of here."

"*What!* It'll take all night to get there and back."

He gave her a sideways glance. "We'll stay overnight, of course. Everybody does."

CHAPTER SEVEN

SARAH AWOKE before dawn the next morning. She lay in bed to read a few more pages of Anne's diary.

December 18, 1969. I finished Year 11 with flying colors! One more year and I'm done for good. Mum says I should think about university, but what I really want is to travel. London, Paris...the world!

January 1, 1970. New Year's. Len and I danced every dance last night at the hall. At midnight Neville Foster dimmed the lights and he kissed me on the lips. Len, that is. He's awfully nice. Robby's going to Vietnam. It's definite. Mum's been crying all day.

Robby, the gangly boy towering over Anne in her mother's old photo album. Sarah had never given much thought much to the young man who would have been her uncle. Suddenly she wished she'd had a chance to know him.

March 7, 1970. Robby's finished his training in Darwin and is flying to Saigon next week. He'll miss the muster this year. Dad's furious. Len will be here at least. He can't join the army because of his slight hearing problem. Abby makes such a fool of herself over him. But it's me he likes.

Sarah paused in her reading. So Abby and Mom had been rivals. Abby had only pretended to have been Anne's friend to get the job as muster cook and be near Becka.

August 30, 1970. The acacias are blooming. They're beautiful, but Mum's hay fever acts up. A few of the cattle have died. The vet suspects brucellosis and now the whole mob has to be quarantined. Len is coming over again today. I really like him and think about him all the time. Is this love?

Too weird, this voyeuristic glimpse into her teenage mother's life. But Sarah eagerly turned the page, not wanting to miss a single episode.

November 28, 1970. Robby is missing in action. I'm so scared. Len came over when he heard the news to see if there was anything he could do. He *is* kind. And he doesn't pressure me, if you know what I mean. We like all the same books and music, etc., but…oh, I don't know. He's stuck here, taking care of the station for his mother. He couldn't travel even if he wanted to.

It sounded to Sarah as if Anne didn't know a good thing when she had it. And that Len probably had a lot to do with her reluctance to return to Australia.

January 6, 1971. I'm finished school and home
for the summer. Beef prices are falling and the
bank is getting stroppy about extending our
loan. The Wet promises to be long this year—
30,000 acres under water and the cattle all on
high ground. I feel so cut off from everything.
Robby's still missing. Every night I pray for
him to come back.

The tear-stained page bore mute testament to her
mother's anguish of thirty-odd years ago. With a
sigh, Sarah flipped the diary shut and went to breakfast.

Abby bustled about the kitchen, washing dishes as
soon as they were emptied. Becka was working on
her second bowl of cereal and Luke was in for morning coffee, having already put in three or four hours'
work. Apparently Saturdays weren't holidays on a
cattle station.

Sarah sat across the breakfast table from him,
munching Coco Pops and trying *not* to recall that first
day when she'd seen him without a shirt. Her trouble
was she didn't have enough to occupy her mind.
Painting was all very well, but it involved many sol
itary hours and increasingly she used them to fanta-
size about Luke.

He had a strength and solidity about him that had
nothing to do with his physical self—although even
clothed, his physique was hard to ignore. Mentally
she scrolled down his body, admiring the way his
light blue shirt strained across his pecs and the dark
gold hairs curled from the open neckline. Funny,
Quentin had seemed perfect for her—similar background, interesting profession, suitable geographical

location—but he'd never inspired such dedicated preoccupation as did Luke.

The object of her attention took a sip of the mocha almond coffee she'd just made and grimaced. Oh, well. No one was perfect.

"Are you painting again today?" he said, pushing back his chair to stretch one long leg over the other.

Sarah clicked out of her imagination before it could drift below the tabletop. "I thought I'd take a break to see if I can find that water hole and try to catch some yabbies."

"It's along the creek in the opposite direction from where you found the rabbit. Becka could show you. That is, if she doesn't want to come with me." He glanced at his daughter, who shook her head. Frowning he poured more cream into his coffee and stirred so hard the spoon clattered against the side of the cup.

Becka seemed to sense she should soften her refusal. "I have to recite a poem for school on Monday. Would you listen to me, Dad? It's cheerful."

Luke nodded so Becka wiped her mouth and rose to stand, straight backed, arms rigid at her sides. "Okay, here goes.

'I want to be a glowworm
A glowworm's never glum
How can you be downhearted
When the sun shines out your—'

"Becka!" Abby exclaimed.

Luke snorted. Sarah laughed outright.

"I didn't make it up," Becka wailed in her own defense.

"That's no sort of poem to say at school." Abby wiped a speck of milk from the side of Becka's mouth with her thumb.

"You spoke slowly and enunciated clearly. I reckon that's the main thing," Luke said. "Will you show Sarah the water hole?"

"Becka was going to help me bake some cakes to freeze for the muster," Abby interjected.

Luke took another sip of coffee and gazed silently at Abby. Becka glanced anxiously from her father to her great-aunt. Sarah stuffed another spoonful of cereal in her mouth. She would *not* interfere, even though it was *so* unfair that Becka be tugged from all sides like this.

Eventually the tension proved too powerful to endure. "What would *you* like to do, Becka?" she asked.

Becka shrugged. "I don't know."

"If you help me you can lick the spoon," Abby offered.

"Let Becka decide for herself," Luke said sharply. He turned to Sarah. "There are traps in the toolshed. Take some meat scraps for bait."

"Thanks. Maybe Becka could help Abby in the morning and come for a walk with me in the afternoon," Sarah suggested. "I ought to sew curtains, anyway."

"I appreciate your efforts on the house," Luke said. "But you don't need to spend all your time here working."

"She doesn't need to bother at all. I've already cut out the fabric and pinned it," Abby said, whisking away Sarah's bowl just as she was about to take her last bite.

"When did you do that?" Sarah asked, amazed and annoyed. There weren't many ways she could contribute and now Abby had usurped one of the main tasks Sarah had set herself.

"The other night, while you and Luke were walking in the garden." Humming, Abby went to the sink with her dishes. Under her breath she said, "Like mother, like daughter."

"What do you mean by that?" Sarah demanded, dumbfounded. She heard the scrape of Luke's chair on the slate floor and glanced over. He'd slapped his hat on his head and was halfway out the sliding door.

Abby came back to wipe the table with a wet dishcloth. "Just a little *fast*," she said in a low voice with a meaningful look at Becka.

"If by *fast* you mean *loose*, then you're very much mistaken—about my mother *and* me," Sarah said, rising, not sure whether to laugh at Abby's insinuations or belt her one. Keeping a rein on her temper, she turned to Becka. "Since I have nothing to do, how about going yabbying this morning?"

"But what about the cakes?"

Sarah smiled sweetly. "Your aunt Abby is so incredibly efficient I'm sure she'll manage just fine on her own."

Abby spun around, mouth open to protest, but it was too late. Becka had filled her pockets with something off the counter and was running out the door. "I'll get the traps."

"Thanks, Abby," Sarah said airily. "See you later."

"You take good care of Becka." Abby followed her to the door. "You don't know the bush. It can be dangerous."

"Don't worry, I carry a big stick in case of snakes."

Abby twisted the cloth in her hands. "A stick is no good if you miss. You see a snake, you'd better run."

"Yes, all right." Sarah brushed her off rather than be outright rude to the woman. "Hey, Becka, wait up."

Sarah and Becka found the traps, fed and watered the chickens and Dorothy, then set off for the creek just as Luke was heading out on his motorbike, a roll of fencing wire strung over his shoulder.

He slowed to a halt beside them and planted a foot on the ground for balance. "What about the cakes?"

Sarah rolled her eyes. "Don't ask." Then, because she didn't want Luke to think *she* was thinking along Abby's lines with regard to their walk in the moonlight, she leaned over to speak in his ear. "That woman is nuts."

He gave her the oddest glance, before he roared off down the dusty track that led to the grassy plains of the Downs, a place where she couldn't follow.

"Oh, no, we forgot the bait," Sarah said, dismayed at the prospect of going back to the house.

Becka pulled a wadded-up paper napkin out of her pocket. "I got the fat from the bacon."

"Smart girl," she said, and they resumed walking. "You're obviously an old hand at this."

"Dad took me a couple of times when I was little."

"My mother described it to me so often I feel I've done it before myself. Between the two of us we should be able to figure it out."

They walked along the dry creek bed. The height

of the banks testified to past Wets when the creek had been in full flood. Now not even a trickle of water flowed and the creek bed was fissured. The air was hot and very still, thick with the scent of eucalyptus. Even the birds were quiet and there was little sound from the dead leaves underfoot. Sweat dripped down Sarah's neck and into the hollow between her breasts. She shifted the traps to her other hand and scanned the track ahead of the small blond head bobbing in front of her.

After thirty minutes of walking, Sarah noticed that the trees grew denser. She and Becka came around a bend into deeper shade, where ferns grew beside the water hole—a dark pool of water that had formed where the creek twisted around on itself.

"Oh, boy." Becka dropped her yabby traps and slipped off her shoes to wade in.

"Be careful," Sarah called, and quickly followed suit, kicking off her cross-trainers without undoing the laces.

"We should have brought our bathers," Becka said, splashing water onto her heated face.

"There's no one around—we can swim in our undies," Sarah replied, and stripped down to her lilac-colored bra and panties. With the innate modesty of a nine-year-old Becka removed her shorts but left her tank top on.

"I hate to think what's down there," Sarah muttered, picking her way through the opaque reddish-brown water to dunk herself to the shoulders. Oh, heaven to be cool!

"Yabbies," Becka said. "They live in the mud under fallen branches and overhanging banks."

"We've probably scared them into their hidey-holes with all this splashing around. They'll never come out now.''

"They will if they're hungry.'' Becka waded back to the bank and began baiting the traps.

"So what do we do once the traps are in place?'' Sarah said a few minutes later as she submerged a trap beneath a section of overhanging bank. "How long do we have to wait for the yabbies to go in? Mom never mentioned that part.''

"Dad usually leaves the traps in overnight and comes back the next day,'' Becka replied.

"That's all right. When we return to empty them we'll get another swim.''

"I'm going to take a couple traps to the other side of that log,'' Becka said. She scrambled up the bank and disappeared behind a fallen tree that lay across the water hole.

"Okay.'' Sarah concentrated on stuffing strips of bacon fat into the mesh funnels of the remaining traps. When she'd baited and set them all she glanced up, realizing she hadn't heard a peep from Becka for a good five minutes.

"Becka?''

Into the silence a distant magpie warbled.

"Becka, where are you?'' Sarah waded out of the water and pulled herself up the creek bank. How could the girl have disappeared so quickly? "Becka?''

With a whoosh of relief that made her realize her heart was pounding, she saw the back of a blond head on the far side of the water hole. "Becka!''

Slowly, Becka turned her head. Her eyes were wide with terror and her face was deathly white.

"Oh, my God. Becka, what is it?'' Sarah started

to run toward her down the narrow path that bordered the creek.

"Stop, Sarah." Becka's voice was reed thin. Her limbs seemed frozen in place. "Don't run."

"Why—?" Sarah began, and in that instant *saw* why.

A six-foot brown snake lay on a patch of bare earth in front of Becka. Its upper half was reared up, and it was ready to strike.

Oh, God, Becka. Oh, God. Oh, God. Sarah stopped dead. Her legs turned to jelly and her stomach felt as though she were traveling upside down on a roller coaster.

The snake wavered in the air, its tongue flicking in and out. Tears streamed down Becka's face.

If you see a snake you'd better run.

"Don't worry, Becka. I'm coming." Cautiously, Sarah stepped off the path, hoping like hell there weren't other snakes curled up in the dead leaves. Twigs scratched at her bare legs as she circled the snake in slow careful steps. For one heart-stopping moment it swayed in her direction. She froze. Her one thought had been to get to Becka, but now she realized she had to do something once she got there.

The girl, too frightened to speak, trembled all over.

By this time Sarah was abreast of the snake. Its jaws were parted slightly and she could see the tiny but deadly fangs. She whispered a quick prayer and made a dash for Becka.

"No, Sarah," Becka screamed. "Don't run!"

Sarah ignored her warning. Barely pausing, she scooped the girl up in her arms—

A line of brown lashed out, as quick as a stock whip, and she felt fangs pierce her thigh.

She ran, stumbling and terrified, with Becka clinging to her neck and crying. Jagged thoughts flashed through her mind. House. Doctor. Luke.

Finally the sound of Becka's pleading voice penetrated. "Stop. You've got to stop. Please."

Sarah sagged to her knees, exhausted. Her hair was a damp tangle around her face and her body, unprotected by clothing, was scratched and bruised. On her right thigh, a few inches above her knee, were two pinpricks and a drop of dried blood. The area was starting to swell and redden.

She was going to die.

Becka was sobbing and pushing on her shoulders, forcing her to lie down on the path. "You must keep very still. Don't move. I'll be right back."

"Where are you going?" Sarah struggled to sit up as Becka started toward the water hole.

"I'm going back for our clothes to make bandages. *Don't move.* Or the poison will go through you faster."

Dazed, Sarah lay still and stared up at the layers of branches and leaves and high above, the blue sky.

Abby had said to run.

She tossed her head to the side. She must have heard wrong. She'd been angry and upset and not paying proper attention.

Becka came racing back and dropped to her knees beside Sarah, breathing hard and still crying. Her small hands, inefficient and fumbling, wrapped Sarah's T-shirt tightly around her upper leg. "It's too short to make a proper bandage," she moaned. "The whole leg should be wrapped. If only we'd worn long pants."

If only she'd never come to Australia, Sarah

thought. Her head ached and the leaves overhead were getting blurry. This was it then. "Goodbye, Becka."

"What! No, don't say that." Becka cupped one palm against Sarah's cheek and peered into her eyes. "I'm going to get help. Promise me you won't move."

Sarah smiled weakly. Tears ran down the side of her face and trickled into her ears. "I promise."

She listened to Becka's footsteps pound down the path, recede in the distance and then fade into silence.

Silence but for her thudding heart pumping the venom through her body. She might be lying perfectly still, but her tensed-up muscles were still in flight mode. She had to relax. What about that mantra Mom had taught her, but she'd never found the time to practice? Closing her eyes, she mentally intoned the meaningless two-syllable word over and over. Miraculously she felt her pulse slow, and gradually her mind drifted into limbo....

Or was this death? The thought made her eyes snap open and her heart pound all over again.

No, no, no. Relax, be calm. Mantra. Mantra. Again her pulse slowed and this time she fell into a deep meditative trance. Her body felt as though it were floating. She couldn't feel her fingers or her toes. Drowsy...she was getting drowsy....

The next thing she knew Luke was bending over her and she was looking straight into his crystal-blue eyes.

He brushed a lock of hair off her forehead. "You've got yourself in a bit of a pickle, Ms. Templestowe."

"Am I going to die?"

"Someday." As he spoke he calmly unrolled a long bandage. "Do you always run about the bush half-naked?"

She lifted her head to glance down at herself. Oh, God. She'd forgotten she had nothing on but a bra and panties. The nausea in her stomach made it hard for her to care.

"We were swimming." Becka had spoken and now Sarah noticed the ashen-faced girl standing off to one side, biting the knuckles of her clasped hands.

Luke removed the T-shirt Becka had tied around her leg. He glanced at his daughter and said quietly, "Good job." Swiftly and competently he bandaged Sarah's leg from her groin to her ankle. Then he strapped a splint to the outside of the leg and wrapped that around and around with another bandage.

Sarah lay in the dust and the dead leaves while sweat collected in the hollows of her body. She felt dizzy and faint and her stomach and bowels were rebelling against the snake venom. Fighting for control, she babbled to take her mind off the terror that was only a thought away.

"Did you call the Flying Doctor? If I have to be mortally ill my demise might at least be thrilling."

His lips twitched in the merest suggestion of a smile. "We only get him out for serious cases. I called the ambulance. We'll drive out to meet it and it'll take you into Murrum to the Bush Nursing Hospital."

"How long do I have before I…?"

"Plenty of time." He tied off the splint bandage.

"How long?"

"A good two hours."

Two hours. She glanced at his watch. Perhaps twenty minutes had passed since Becka had run for help. It took over an hour to get to town—providing there were no breakdowns. She closed her eyes. This was cutting it too close.

Luke handed his first aid kit across to Becka. "You carry this. I'll get Sarah." He slid his hands beneath her back and upper thighs to lift her.

"This is no time to cop a feel," Sarah joked feebly. All she needed was the adrenaline rush that came whenever he was close to speed the poison through her body.

"The less you move the better. That includes your mouth."

"Ha, ha." Thankfully, for once her body seemed to know a response would be inappropriate. All she felt in his arms was safe.

But as he hoisted her against his chest, he had to grip her leg hard and she winced. His eyes flickered to hers and tension arced around them, and in that split second she glimpsed his fear on her behalf. Then he drew his inner strength on as one would the mask in a suit of armor and carried her through the bush with steady strides to where the Land Cruiser waited. Becka ran ahead and opened the door.

"Have you got plenty of petrol?" Sarah asked with a nervous grin. "It'd be a hell of a time to run out of gas."

"I topped it up this morning." Gently he laid her across the seat and arranged a blanket over her. Then he touched her cheek with his fingertips. "You'll be right."

For the first time since she felt the fangs sink into her leg, she thought that just might be true.

SARAH WAS GIVEN a shot of antivenin and pronounced a "very lucky young woman" by the elderly Dr. Murchison. The snake's fangs hadn't sunk deep and it had bitten only once. Even so she was tucked up in the women's ward of the tiny bush nursing hospital and there she stayed for three long days.

Becka had thoughtfully packed her cellular phone in with a few clothes and she was able to chat to her mother every day. Sarah debated whether to tell her mother about her snake bite and decided not to worry her.

Except for the elderly gentleman in for observation, Sarah was alone in the six-bed hospital and the nursing sisters made a fuss of her. When they discovered she was a computer expert they bombarded her with questions. As soon as she was able, she was out of bed and in front of the hospital computer, troubleshooting various software problems.

Sarah was glad to help and gladder still to take her mind off Luke. She knew he was superbusy and he couldn't take time to make the long drive in order to visit. But deprived of his company for a few days, she missed him. So when the day came for her to leave the hospital she was eager to see him, though shy about expressing her pleasure.

She sat in the lobby, her overnight bag by her side, her gaze fixed on the narrow windows flanking the outer door. At last she glimpsed the dusty Land Cruiser roll by. Her hand went to her hair to make sure it wasn't sticking up—just in case he noticed.

Then the door opened and Abby came through, her

soft-soled leather shoes scuffing across the tile floor. "Oh, you poor dear," she gushed. "What an ordeal."

"I'm all right." Sarah quelled her disappointment and picked up her bag. Abby grabbed for it at the same time and they had a little tug-of-war until Sarah felt ridiculous and let her take it.

"You almost *died*," Abby insisted. "Now you know why I don't think Becka's safe out at the station."

Sarah glanced at the matron, who sat head down at the desk, ears pricked. "Hey, I'm the one who got bitten. Becka knew what to do. I guess Luke made sure of that."

"Humph, well, he may have. Come along if you're ready." She led the way out and loaded Sarah's suitcase in the back.

Sarah sat in the passenger seat and turned her face to the window, her eyes purposely glazed so she wouldn't have to see the landscape. Her mind went over and over her dilemma. How could she ask Abby if what she was thinking was true?

How could she not?

"Not feeling well, I expect." Abby's voice oozed sympathy, but Sarah imagined an underlying trickle of satisfaction.

She twisted in her seat so she could watch Abby's face. "Before I left the house that morning, you told me, 'If you see a snake you'd better run.'"

"No, I didn't," Abby said quickly. She turned to stare at Sarah. "Did I?"

"Yes. Why did you do that? I'd have thought every Australian would know you're supposed to stay still. Especially someone who grew up in the country.''

Abby faced forward, both hands gripping the wheel. "I'm sure you must be mistaken. I wouldn't give you such advice. You must not have heard right.''

Sarah didn't know what to say to Abby's blank denial. It was a moot point, anyway, since Sarah had survived. "Never mind,'' she said, and turned back to the window to practice focusing on the Downs for brief intervals. She was up to six seconds now before the uncomfortable feeling in her stomach came on.

"Your mother used to wander down by that creek, too,'' Abby said after several minutes of silence.

"So she told me many times.'' Sarah cupped her chin in her palm and rested her elbow on the window frame.

"I'll bet she didn't tell you everything.''

Sarah didn't for one minute believe the image Abby painted of her mother, but she couldn't help asking, "What do you mean?''

"That's where it happened,'' Abby replied.

Len, she must be talking about. Well, so what? Sarah felt herself flush with anger. Abby was just jealous.

"They were doing it on the bank, right in plain view.''

"Plain view if you were standing in the bush or along the creek yourself. How did you happen to see them, Abby?''

"I was leaving the homestead after dropping off some dress patterns for Anne's mother. I saw their horses grazing at the edge of the treed area.''

"You spied on them.''

"I wanted to talk to Anne about something," Abby said defensively. "It was the end of summer holidays and we were leaving for boarding school in another week."

Sarah shook her head in disbelief. "So you parked and walked down to the creek. Did you call out, let them know you were there?"

"Why are you cross-examining *me?*" Abby said, suddenly taking umbrage. "*I* didn't do anything wrong."

Sarah didn't bother to reply and Abby made no further attempts at conversation. Once they got home Sarah thanked her politely for the ride and went straight to her room. Becka was at school, Luke out on the run and she'd had enough of Abby for a while. She shut her door and collapsed on her bed with her mother's diary.

March 1, 1971. It's my eighteenth birthday and I'm stuck on the station for life. Len gave me a ring. I put it on my right hand, but he shook his head and put it on my ring finger. It was very solemn and dramatic. I'm so confused. I didn't say anything, but I didn't change it back. Have I agreed to marry him? We still haven't done "it." Abby shot daggers at me with her weird eyes.

June 15, 1971. Dad's delaying the muster as long as he can, hoping Robby will magically reappear. Mum waits by the mailbox every day for word of Robby. I'm so afraid for him. Afraid for us. Robby, please, come home.

June 27, 1971. An official letter came from Canberra today. I thought Mum was going to faint when she opened it. Robby didn't make it.

Tears filled Sarah's eyes. Her fingertips touched the sheet of paper dimpled with her mother's long-ago tears. With a deep sigh, she read on:

July 6, 1971. Len keeps asking me to set a wedding date. Dad wants him and me to eventually take over the station now that Robby's gone and Len's mum had to sell their station. When I was ten I believed I'd never want to live anywhere else. Now I feel I'll go mad if I have to stay here for another week.

Sarah closed the diary and reached for her cell phone to dial her mother's number. "Hello, Mom?"

"Sarah, darling, how are you?"

Sarah hadn't even been thinking about the snake, but Anne's warm greeting loosened a floodgate and suddenly her eyes were filling with tears and aftershock. "I was bitten by a brown snake. Down by the creek. Becka and I were yabbying. I got to the hospital just in time. If it hadn't been for Luke..." She paused to gulp in a breath.

"My goodness, darl', why didn't you tell me sooner? I'll shut up the shop and come right down."

"You don't have to," Sarah assured her. "I'm fine now."

"How did it happen? Tell me all about it."

Sarah breathed deeply once again. "It was Saturday afternoon," she said, and went on to relate the whole story. "I've just come out of the Bush Nursing Hospital."

"Well, thank goodness you're safe. Are you sure you don't want me to come down?"

"I want you to come, Mom, though not because of the snake. I feel lousy, but I don't need to be nursed back to health."

"With Luke out with the cattle all day who's there in case you need help?"

Sarah sighed. "Abby, I guess." She paused. "Mom, I've been reading your diary. I'm sorry about Robby."

"Thank you," Anne said quietly. "So am I."

THE NEXT DAY Sarah still felt lousy and out of sorts. She spent the morning lying in bed but dragged herself up for lunch rather than have Abby fuss over her. Afterward she left Abby in the kitchen cutting up a side of beef and took her coffee and a book out to the veranda. She was too well to be in bed but not well enough to do anything useful.

She was drowsing in her chair, when she heard the soft slap of bare feet on the wood slats and Luke dropped into the seat beside her. Wal wandered over from his spot beneath the water tank to settle at his master's feet.

Sarah straightened and pushed the hair off her face, taking in his damp hair and clean clothes. If Luke had already showered and changed it must be late. "I must have fallen asleep."

"How do you feel?"

"Not up to a marathon but basically okay." Their time apart had given her an even greater appreciation of him. He really was handsome, with that broad forehead, straight nose and long slanting jaw. Streaky blond hair grew away from one corner of his forehead and fell in fine waves over ears that stuck out just the teeniest bit at the top. Endearing ears. The thought made her smile. The absence of dust made him look shiny and new. Kissable.

"Maybe you should give the ball a miss on Saturday," he said.

She laid her book on the wicker table. "Oh, no, I'll be raring to go by then."

"Are you sure?"

"Absolutely." She wasn't sure at all, although if anything kept her home it would be fear of another anxiety attack. But she'd spent too many hours daydreaming about dancing the night away in his arms to give up that prospect now. It was a harmless fantasy—just as long as she remembered it was a fantasy.

"All right. We'll take it real easy. And Sarah—" he leaned forward, elbows on his knees "—I want to thank you for trying to save Becka."

"Please," Sarah interrupted, embarrassed. "I behaved like a total idiot."

Luke reached for her hand and smoothed it between his two palms. Sarah felt a response deep in her center and wondered if modern women ever swooned with pleasure.

But Luke's mind was not on seduction. "You deliberately risked your life for her." His gaze dropped, his jaw working. "I don't know what I'd do if anything happened to her."

Sarah folded her other hand on top of his, as if by doing so she could capture this rare display of emotion. "She loves you Luke."

"She doesn't act like it."

"Maybe she's afraid she won't measure up." Or was that herself she was thinking of? People in the outback were strong, resourceful and courageous. How could she ever be one of them? Not that she wanted to, of course.

Luke's gaze flickered over her face. "Sometimes people don't know what they can do till they try."

"That is so true," she said gently but pointedly. "Especially when it comes to opening up."

He leaned back, disentangling their hands. "I've tried talking to her. It's just…everything circles back to Abby."

"What do you mean?" she asked.

He glanced over his shoulder at the house. "Sometimes I feel Abby is trying to turn her against me. You probably think that's paranoid."

Sarah shook her head. She was tempted to air her own grievances against Abby, but Luke was finally talking about his worries over Becka and who knows, maybe she *had* misinterpreted what Abby said. "Abby's taken care of Becka all these years and now she's losing her. It's natural for her to cling and for you to fear that sharing will mean you'll come second. But for Becka's sake, share you must."

His eyes silently searched hers, tormented and wary. There was something more he wasn't telling her and she'd give anything to know what it was.

"Getting her the horse was a good idea," she continued, trying to think of ways he could connect with his daughter. "Abby doesn't ride and you can spend time alone with Becka."

"Pity *you* don't ride."

Avoiding his steady gaze, Sarah got up and went

to the edge of the veranda. "Yes, isn't it? Then maybe I wouldn't be wandering around where snakes can get me." She shivered at the memory. "I've never been that scared."

He came to stand beside her. "Nor I," he said quietly.

His hand felt warm on her bare shoulder. She glanced up, surprised to see his mouth descend to hers. And then she was lost in the delicious sensations aroused by the touch of his lips on hers and the warmth radiating from his body.

The kiss was chaste as kisses go. But the contact made her head swim and chaste might have become unchaste in short order had not Sarah retained enough presence of mind to pull back before things got too steamy.

Dazed, she peered into his eyes. *Oh, my.* If this was chemistry she was ready for the main experiment.

Luke knew he ought to say something, but his brain was badly overheated. He'd kissed Sarah out of gratitude and relief and growing affection. And okay, desire. But who'd have thought a simple meeting of mouths would have such an effect on his ability to think straight?

He was still grappling with the question of whether the kiss was a good thing or a bad thing and whether he should apologize or do it again when Abby appeared through the sliding doors from the kitchen. Knowingly she took in his arm around Sarah's waist and her pink cheeks.

"Soon you won't need *me* around here," she said, whisking past them with the bloody remains of the beef carcass. And away she went, humming "The Wedding March."

Sarah flushed crimson and turned away.

Luke drew her face around to his and blurted out what he'd wanted to tell her for days. "Abby's unbalanced."

Sarah stared at him for one horrified moment before struggling out of his grasp. "I get the picture. Excuse me," she said, pushing past him. "I've got to go...do something."

Luke scratched his head as he watched her run into the house. "What do you reckon, Wal?" he said. "Are women just naturally barmy or am I doing something wrong?"

Wal rumbled out a partisan growl.

"Thanks, mate. I knew it couldn't be me," he said, heavy on the irony.

CHAPTER EIGHT

WHEN THE SLIDING glass doors had shut on Sarah, Luke strode across the yard to inspect the jackaroo's quarters, where Bazza, Bazza's brother, Gus, and Kev, the aboriginal ringer, would shortly take up residence.

Luke could have kicked himself for that statement about Abby. Not only was it disloyal to family but Sarah might not feel good about sharing a house with a woman with a 'roo loose in the top paddock. Not that Abby was dangerous, just a little...strange. She created tension in the house, between him and Sarah, between him and Becka.

Luke ducked his head to enter the low mud-brick building built a century earlier. Abby had gotten it ready for his inspection. Four iron cots lined the whitewashed walls of the main room. A doorway led to a small washroom, where clean towels were stacked on a shelf. Basic but adequate. It didn't seem that long ago that he'd inhabited similar accommodation. After a long dusty day in the saddle he'd lie on his swag and dream about having his own station, working side by side with a woman who loved this way of life as much as he did.

With a sigh, he ducked out and headed across to the shed. Fifteen years later it was all still a dream.

"I should never have kissed her, Wal," he said as he went to work on a broken bore pump.

Wal whined and cocked his head to one side.

"Yes, she's a fine woman and I like her a lot, but she's a townie." As much as she tried to hide it, she hated the very sight of the wide brown land that supported his family and nourished his soul. "I know what you're thinking, Wal. No one around here, no one *suitable,* has gotten me so stirred up since Caroline. But what about the long haul? A man has to think of the future and there's no future for me with Sarah Templestowe.

"Pass me the small wrench will you, mate?"

Luke took the wrench from Wal and deliberately put Sarah out of his thoughts to concentrate on getting the pump working again. An hour later, his stomach told him it was dinnertime, so he flipped off the welding mask, put away the blowtorch and headed back to the homestead.

"Something smells good," he said, hanging his hat on a peg. He washed his hands and sat at the table.

Sarah placed a knife and fork beside his plate and continued laying cutlery around the table. "Abby won't tell us what she's cooking, but the aroma of garlic is unmistakable. And I saw half a bottle of red wine disappear into the pot."

"She wouldn't even let *me* into the kitchen," Becka confirmed as she filled water glasses from a jug. "It's a secret."

Abby bustled over to the table, carrying a covered serving dish between pot holders. "My friend Mary brought me back a cookbook from her trip to France last year. I wanted to make something special before the camp cooking starts. You know how unimaginative those boys are when it comes to food.''

She set the dish on the table and lifted the lid, loosing a cloud of steam redolent with wine and garlic and rosemary. "Ta-da.''

Arranged on the platter were steaming joints of braised meat. Luke leaned closer. The meat didn't look quite like chicken, but the pieces were too small to come from any animal much bigger. And then he noticed that at the ends of the ''drumsticks'' were the tips of brown furry paws. Oh, Lord.

"Mmm, it smells heavenly,'' Sarah said, laying the last of the knives and forks. "What is it, Abby?''

"Lapin au vin," she said proudly.

"Lapin?" Sarah repeated. "Isn't that—?''

"Rabbit,'' Luke said in a voice as dead as dinner.

"Rabbit?" Sarah spotted the intact paws and clapped a hand over her mouth, muffling a shriek.

Luke pushed violently away from the table and strode out the door. "I'll be right back.''

Halfway across the yard he heard Sarah running after him and then her hand clutched his sleeve. "She wouldn't, would she?''

His jaw was clenched so tight he could hardly speak. "She bloody well better not have.''

"The sight of those paws on the platter...'' Sarah's shoulders moved in a fierce shiver. "I felt like Joan Crawford when Bette Davis served up her pet bird for lunch.''

Their pace picked up as they approached the stable. The hutch was on the other side, in the shade of a lean-to. Luke took Sarah's hand and together they rounded the corner—

Dorothy was alive and well and calmly gnawing

on a carrot. Luke heard Sarah sigh, and as his arms went around her in a brief embrace he felt the tension melt from her body. Dorothy stamped her hind feet and raced back and forth in the confines of the cage.

Sarah eased away to pull up a clump of dried grass and poke it through the wire mesh. "Oh, Dorothy. I'm so glad you're *having* dinner instead of *being* dinner."

"Better not fatten her up," Luke said when Sarah reached for another handful of grass.

Sarah got to her feet. "How do we explain running out to check on Dorothy? I know Abby's a little odd, but she'll be so hurt."

"The same thought occurred to us both." Luke reminded her.

But Sarah was right. Abby's bewildered gaze silently reproached them as they trooped back into the kitchen. "You surely didn't think I would cook Sarah's rabbit!"

"Aunt Abby would never eat a pet," Becka told them indignantly.

"I know. Sorry." Sarah sat down at the table, but she seemed to have lost her appetite. Ignoring the *lapin au vin,* she reached for the dish of steamed vegetables.

Luke refused to appear shamefaced. "Rabbit's a pretty unusual choice for a country cook in Australia, Abby. Where did you get it?"

"That new butcher in Longreach. I thought it would be a treat." Abby's bosom heaved with distress. "If I'd known it would upset anyone I would never have cooked the dish. You like it, don't you Becka?"

"Oh, yes, Aunt Abby." Becka laid a small comforting hand on Abby's forearm. "It's delicious."

Luke took a bite of rabbit. It *was* tasty. But he was still irritated by what appeared to him to be a deliberate dig at Sarah. "Why did you leave the paws on?"

Abby shrugged helplessly. "I just followed the recipe. The book explained it's an old custom, done so no one accuses the cook of serving cat."

Luke reached for another piece of rabbit and Sarah gave him a how-could-you glare. "That could be Dorothy's cousin," she said.

"This is dinner and I'm hungry," he replied as gently as he could. "Dorothy's cousin or not, I'm eating."

"It *is* good," he admitted grudgingly to Abby. "But next time, stick to chops."

THAT NIGHT Sarah went to bed early so she could enjoy another installment of Anne's diary before the generator went off and the lights went out.

July 10, 1971. Big excitement in Murrum. An American soldier is staying at the pub. He was a pilot in Vietnam. Trina says he's not half-bad. I think I'll go into town with Mum this week and see for myself.

July 15, 1971. He's *gorgeous*. His name is Warren. And he's going to work the muster at Burrinbilli!

Sarah felt a thrill of excitement go through her. This was her father. Mom had never said much about how they'd gotten together and now she was going to find out. But how would poor Len take this development? She read on.

Len is furious...

I'll bet, Sarah thought. Poor Len.

...but with so many men away we need the help. Warren is like a gift from Heaven. Len's just jealous because the army rejected him.

August 29, 1971. The calves are all branded, dehorned and cut, and the fats are off to market. Muster's over, but Warren's staying to help with the fences! He has the most beautiful green eyes.

September 16, 1971. I showed Warren the water hole where we go yabbying. He kissed me and I could hardly breathe I was that excited. I've got the hugest pash on him. He's handsome and charming and he's been all over the world—so different from poor old Len. Dear Len. I'll have to give him back his ring.

Sarah lay back on the pillow, her fingertips brushing her lips where Luke's mouth had pressed. He'd been grateful over Becka; that's the only reason he'd done it. Even if he was attracted, she knew he didn't *want* to want her. And that was probably worse than not wanting her at all.

"SEE YOU TOMORROW, Becka. Have a good time with Lucy." Sarah leaned down from the Land Cruiser to give her a hug.

She and Luke were dropping Becka off at her friend's house to stay overnight before going on to the bachelor and spinster ball in Rowan. Abby hadn't been pleased at being left on her own, but she could hardly deny her great-niece the opportunity to spend time with the best friend she now rarely saw outside school hours.

Luke took Becka to the door, then walked back to the truck, immaculate in his black tuxedo pants and white dress shirt. Hanging in the back of the Land Cruiser was the tux jacket and a black bow tie.

"I feel underdressed," Sarah said as he slid back behind the wheel. She gazed discontentedly down at her simple cotton sundress. Who'd have thought she'd need an evening gown in the outback?

"An hour into a bachelor and spinster ball and no one will even notice what you're wearing," Luke assured her.

"Oh, thanks," she said with a laugh. "Did you honestly think that would make me feel better?"

He smiled. "You look great. Beautiful."

She didn't want to feel so good about his approval, but his warm gaze brought heat to her cheeks. "I wasn't fishing."

"I know." He threw the truck into gear.

They headed out of town on a road so straight it seemed to disappear into infinity. Grassy plains, unbroken by tree or building, extended on either side of the road as far as the eye could see. That is, if the eye could be persuaded to look. Sarah took out a nail file and studiously scraped and shaped, studied and pondered and filed some more.

"You'll end up sharpening your knucklebones in a minute," Luke observed over the twang of a country song on the radio.

She shrugged and let her gaze rest on the hand draped negligently over the wheel rather than meet his eyes and allow him to spot her discomfort. Between the shiny calluses on his palm fine red dust was ingrained in the minute crevices of his skin. He was part of the land and the land was part of him. She, on the other hand, barely touched down.

"What's eating you, Sarah?" Luke asked as the music faded and the disk jockey came on to plug an upcoming country music festival in some place called Tambo.

Sarah raised a finger to her lips and blew nail dust into the interior of the cab. "I don't know what you mean."

"You're toeyer than a chook caught in a swag."

She rolled her eyes. "I still don't know what you mean."

"We're driving through some of the finest grazing land in Australia, really beaut country, and you don't even look out the window!"

"I do so look out." To prove it, she leaned forward and stared through the windshield. They'd just come over an incline so slight she hadn't noticed it and suddenly she could see fifty miles instead of fifteen. Heat haze danced above the road. Spots appeared before her eyes. She started to get that choking feeling. She tried the times tables, but that didn't work. She tried her mother's mantra, but it was too late for that. With a gasp, she dropped her head between her knees while her heart threatened to beat its way out of her chest.

When the dizziness passed and her heart had slowed, she glanced up, to find Luke gazing at her, seriously concerned. She tried to think of an excuse, then decided he might as well know the truth. "It's so big, so open. It just goes on and on and on and—"

"Yeah," Luke agreed, love, not loathing, resonating in his voice. "A man could ride for days, weeks, and not come across another human being."

Sarah shivered. "Like a lost soul wandering in the desert."

"On a clear day you can see to God and back," he said reverently.

"You're not hearing what I'm saying. It scares the *bejeezus* out of me—"

"Nothing I love more than open country—" He turned to stare at her. "It *scares* you?"

She wrapped her arms around herself, even though it must have been at least a hundred degrees in the truck. "I have these panic attacks," she said miserably. "My heart starts pounding and I get that feeling in my stomach like when an elevator goes up too fast."

"Strewth!" Luke exclaimed, rubbing the side of his jaw. "I've never heard of anything like it. Have you always had this problem?"

"Never until I came here. From researching the Internet, I gather I've got a mild case of agoraphobia, but I don't know what's causing it." She tried to change the subject. "Did Warren ever mention me to you?"

He cast her a sympathetic glance. "We only discussed station business."

She shrugged. "Doesn't matter."

"So these panic attacks are the reason you won't come out on the cattle run?"

"Yes, but it doesn't matter," she repeated. "In less than a week I'll be gone and I won't have to deal with it." She realized somewhat perversely she didn't want her visit to be over so soon.

"Is this how you handle a problem in the city— ignore it until it goes away?"

Sarah shifted on the seat. "It's hardly a *problem*. It's not as though I live here."

"But you'll want to visit your mother when she shifts back to Oz."

That scenario seemed impossibly remote at the moment, but she couldn't pass up the opening. "Does that mean you've decided to sell me your half?"

"I didn't say that."

Sarah sighed. "I have been trying to deal with this…phobia…whatever it is. I've been practicing breathing techniques and meditation and controlled bursts of looking at the Downs, and I'm getting better at it." She paused. "I feel a bit better just talking about it."

Luke slowed as they came upon a mob of several hundred bright reddish-brown cattle grazing by the side of the road, strung out for miles along the verge between the bitumen and the barbed wire fence.

"These are Santa Gertrudis," he said. "Same as our cattle. Pity you never got out to see them."

"Oh, but they're pretty! Why are they loose?" Sarah asked. "Should we do something? Tell the station owner?"

"No, they're grazing what we call the 'long paddock.' During a drought stockmen have to take advantage of whatever feed is available." Luke geared down to avoid a cow and her calf ambling across the road and turned down a rutted track.

"Why are we going down here?" Sarah said. "This isn't even a road."

"We're taking a short cut across Johnston Downs. We'll pick up the road to Rowan a little ways along. It's a bit of a bumpy ride, but we cut an hour off the trip."

"That's the best news I've had all day. How much farther is this restaurant you were talking about? I'm starving."

"Another forty minutes. Can you last?"

"Do I have a choice?" Sarah leaned back and shut her eyes. She'd had enough therapy for one day. "Wake me when we're there."

The rumble of her stomach woke her first. She opened her eyes and saw they were back on a bitumen road and approaching a town. "Is this it?" she asked, stretching and yawning.

"Nearly."

Sarah glanced longingly at the hotel advertising roast lamb for the evening "counter tea" as Luke passed it by.

"Not long now," he promised.

A few miles out of town he pulled off the road and parked in front of an old homestead. Overhung with gum trees and flowering vines, the shaded veranda provided welcome relief from the heat. Luke hung his hat on the pegs outside the front door and they went inside.

The homestead had been converted into a small restaurant, with tables in several rooms, creating a comfortable yet casually sophisticated atmosphere.

Luke greeted many of the other diners by name and introduced Sarah as they slowly made their way through the large main room.

When they were finally seated at a table set with crisp linen napkins and fresh flowers, Sarah said, "We're over a hundred miles from Burrinbilli, yet you know practically everyone here."

"Just about. When your nearest neighbor is an hour's drive away, you get to know everyone within a wide radius."

A pretty blond woman of about forty appeared, wearing a black T-shirt, black pants and a long white apron tied around her waist. "G'day, Luke, how's it going?"

"Not bad. Sarah, this is Inga, the finest chef west of Longreach."

Considering the paucity of restaurants in the area, Sarah thought this was faint praise, but Inga beamed with pleasure. "What'll you folks have? Today's specials are fresh barramundi sautéed in walnut oil, with a semidried tomato coulis, and fillet of emu, with a cream tarragon sauce."

Luke scratched his jaw and appeared to consider. "What I'd really love is a plate of bugs. Have you got any fresh?"

"They were alive and kicking this morning. Good choice."

"Fine then. We'll have two orders."

"Are you okay, Sarah?" Inga asked. "You look a little pale."

"*Bugs?*" Sarah said, glaring at Luke. She felt as though she were already choking on the little jointed legs.

"You said you'd eat them if you were starving,"

Luke reminded her with a grin. "Inga's are the best in Queensland. You wouldn't want to hurt her feelings."

Sarah could have strangled him. "All right, I'll try the bugs," she said through gritted teeth, while he sat there with a smirk on his face. To Inga she added, "Could I have some bread with that?"

"Sure. Focaccia, bruschetta or garlic pita?"

She hesitated, not having expected so many delicious choices. "What the heck, I'll have all three." She could fill up on bread, and if she was lucky the herbs and garlic would disguise the taste of the bugs.

"Okay." Inga exchanged a surprised smile with Luke.

"I like a healthy appetite in a woman," he said, winking at Inga. "Better bring the bread with the main course."

While she sipped an excellent chardonnay, Sarah plotted murder. She would overpower Luke and leave him by the side of the road while she took off back to town for the roast lamb. She might pick him up later. Or she might not. Bugs, indeed. She wasn't some tourist who needed to taste every weird thing just to prove she'd been someplace.

Eventually a waiter bearing a heavily loaded tray approached their table. Sarah spied her three plates of bread as well as two plates of something delectable in a creamy yellow sauce. She eyed those enviously, certain they were destined for another table. To her surprise the waiter placed one in front of Luke and squeezed the other between the plates of bread at her place. "Moreton Bay bugs in saffron sauce. Enjoy."

Sarah gaped at the plump white crustaceans

broiled in their shells and smothered in delicate sauce.

"Hope you're not disappointed this isn't real bush tucker," Luke said, picking up his fork.

Her jaw fell open, but no words came out.

"You going to eat that or outstare it?" Luke's fork strayed toward her plate. "If you really don't like bugs I could help you out—"

The threat brought her out of her trance. Sarah brandished her fork so fast it clashed with his in a tiny *en garde* above her plate. "Touch those bugs and you're dead."

Luke just grinned.

THE BACHELOR and spinster ball was held in a hall constructed of concrete blocks and a corrugated iron roof on the town's rodeo grounds—a seemingly unlikely venue for the several hundred formally dressed men and women. Kegs of beer, flagons of wine and huge bowls of punch sat on tables along one wall. People helped themselves liberally.

They all welcomed Sarah warmly. This she felt was partly because her mother was Australian-born, partly because she was with Luke but mostly simply because these were friendly congenial people who worked hard and played hard.

Luke knew *everyone* including someone's second cousin visiting from Brisbane. The second cousin, an attractive brunette, wasn't the only young woman who had her eye on Luke. But if Sarah suffered pangs of jealousy when other women claimed him for a dance, the pride she felt at spinning around the room in his arms during her turn more than made up for it.

"Having fun?" he murmured in her ear during a slow number. One hand rested at the small of her back, strong and sure, while the other enfolded one of hers close to their chests. Around them couples swayed to the music. Or just swayed.

Sarah stepped over a drunken jackaroo stretched out on the floor. "Fantastic."

She was glad Luke wasn't like some of the other guys, who'd had too much to drink and were now very much the worse for wear. Some of the girls, too. The second cousin from Brisbane was last seen bent over at the waist out in the cattle yards. Sarah was tipsy enough to have that floaty feeling and sober enough to know it was time to stop. Luke's embrace was too precious to waste being unconscious.

Around midnight, plates of sandwiches and cakes plus urns of coffee and tea appeared on trestle tables set up down one side of the hall. The ravenous hordes descended on the food, and when all the refreshments were gone they went back to dancing and drinking.

Finally, at 3:00 a.m., Sarah sagged against Luke. "I can't move another step."

"What's the matter, city girl?" he teased. "I thought you'd be outdancing us all."

"I must be out of shape. I've missed almost two weeks of aerobics classes."

"You actually pay to exercise? Some of the blokes here tonight have put in a ten- or twelve-hour day on the cattle run. Lots of the sheilas, too."

"Are you trying to make me feel inadequate?" She put a light note in her voice, but his words contributed to the growing feeling inside her that she just didn't measure up to the outback life-style.

"You're more than adequate, Sarah." He stroked her hair back from her temple, his lips hovering deliciously near. "I've been thinking, the best way for you to overcome your fear of the open is to spend time out there."

"Oh, sure. Easy as pie."

"I didn't say it would be easy. But I'll help you."

"What did you have in mind?"

"Come on the muster with us."

She couldn't think of anything more exciting—or more frightening. "I can't ride, remember?"

"Yeah, right."

She drew back, to see skepticism written large upon his face. "Okay, so I was lying. I can ride."

"How well?"

"I've had years of lessons. Mom, having grown up on the station, thought her daughter should know how to ride. But I honestly don't see the point in pushing this."

She was bluffing. Deep inside she really wanted to conquer her fear, whether she needed to or not.

"I'm not letting you off the hook," he said, tightening his grip. "I know you can do this if you just give it a go."

She was silent a long time. "Okay, Luke," she said at last. "I'll try."

For you, she added silently, and smiled up at him.

THE BLARE of the music receded as they walked away from the brightly lit hall toward the paddock where utility vehicles and four-wheel-drives were parked in unorganized abandon on the dry grass. Luke's Land Cruiser was at the farthest edge of the field; here the light from the hall barely dented the blackness of the star-strewn sky. A half moon was just peeking above the horizon.

She had wondered where they would sleep. Now she knew. Luke let down the tailgate of the truck and unrolled a couple of thick-padded sleeping bags.

"What is this thing?" she asked, climbing up to kneel beside hers. Short fiberglass poles propped up the head end like a miniature tent and the zipper came right to the top of a square of netting, enclosing the occupant like a cocoon.

"It's called a swag." He pulled off his dangling bow tie and lay on top of his bedding, boots and all.

Sarah kicked off her shoes and lay down next to him, conscious of his warmth and closeness. She gazed up at a sky so thickly studded with pinpricks of light the Milky Way seemed to be a solid band of light. "Where's the Southern Cross?"

Luke propped himself up on one elbow and stretched an arm across her line of vision to point. "There, at about ten o'clock. See it?"

"I think so. It's smaller than I expected."

"Disappointed?" There was a smile in his voice.

"How could I be? It's beautiful." Sarah turned her head, to find his face close to hers. *He* was beautiful—in the most rugged virile masculine sense of the word. She reached up and touched his cheek, feeling the rasp of his beard beneath her fingertips. She'd wanted a real man. But what was she going to do with him now that she'd found him? She smiled to herself as one or two things sprang to mind.

"What's the joke?" Luke moved his head and caught her fingertip between his teeth. The tip of his tongue washed over her sensitive skin and the temperature between them rose by several degrees.

She tugged gently on her finger, drawing him nearer. "Just wondering what it would be to *really* kiss you."

"Only one way to find out."

His lips touched hers and a delicious, enticing warmth suffused her body. He tasted like beer and sunshine, blue sky and red earth. Her lips parted, inviting him in. With a growl, he took her offer. Long callused fingers spanned her cheek and neck, then tangled in her hair as he pulled her closer. Sarah melted into his kiss, wishing it would never end, knowing it must.

He drew back, his breathing shallow, his eyes searching hers. "Well?"

All she could manage was one word. "Good."

His hand moved lower, his wrist brushing her breast as he undid her top two buttons and gently inched back the fabric of her dress. Cleavage, lacy bra, rapidly hardening nipple. Her breathing became shallow and her heart rate sped up, but this was no panic attack. Lowering his head, he kissed a warm path across the swell of her breast while he stroked the softness of her inner thigh where her skirt was pushed up. She pictured in her mind the roughness of his tanned hand against her pale skin. She wanted him. Wanted his heat and his hardness.

His hand stilled on her thigh and he drew back to gaze down at her with a frown. "I don't have any condoms."

Part of her was glad he hadn't taken her acquiescence for granted and come prepared. Most of her ached for him. "In that case, we could..." She trailed off, embarrassed at making intimate suggestions. Which made her realize maybe she didn't know him well enough to make love.

He kissed her again, with bone-melting thoroughness. On the other hand, what better way to get to know someone? Desire clouded her mind. Temptation pushed her toward the easy option.

"I could get off at Redfern," he murmured, his breath shallow against her neck.

She laughed softly. "Huh?"

"It's an expression. Redfern's the last train stop before Central Station in Sydney."

"Oh, you mean..." She sighed, understanding his meaning. Easy options often had unfortunate consequences. "Not exactly foolproof."

"True." He removed his hand from between her legs, leaving a chill behind. As if to compensate, he carefully rebuttoned her top.

He kissed her lightly on the mouth and rolled onto his back, his fingers laced through hers. She heard his long deep sigh, which echoed her own frustration, and almost wished *she'd* come prepared. She imagined the ensuing gossip if she bought a box of condoms in Murrum, and chuckled softly.

"Whatever it is you're wondering now, I don't want to know," Luke rumbled. "There are limits to my self-control."

She'd love to test those limits, she thought as her eyes drooped shut. *Someday. Someday real soon...*

Luke heard the gentle rhythm of her breathing, felt her fingers relax and slacken. Gradually the tension went out of his body, though it didn't leave his mind. He wanted Sarah more than was good for him, but he knew they'd done the right thing by stopping. One thing he sure didn't need was another unexpected pregnancy with a woman who wasn't prepared to share his life.

He couldn't go through again what he'd experienced over Becka. He'd made a mistake leaving her with Abby for so long, not because of Abby's shortcomings but because he'd missed out on so much of his daughter's life. The next time he was responsible for bringing a baby into the world he would be a full-time father right from the word *go*.

Sure there were other ways of making love, but he'd come to appreciate that there were levels and degrees of intimacy. He and Sarah had barely scratched the surface.

They probably never would.

If he'd been smart he would have discouraged her from trying to overcome her fear of open spaces. The less comfortable she felt at Burrinbilli, the less likely she was to hang on to the place. And the longer she stayed, the harder it would be to see her go.

CHAPTER NINE

"IT'S FOR YOU," Sarah said, handing the phone to Luke as he walked into the kitchen Monday morning. "Some Ph.D. student from the university in Sydney wants to know if the tilo-something-or-other is blooming."

"*Ptilotus macrocephalus.*" Luke took the phone. "Is that you, Peter? The *Ptilotus* is flowering on the red soil, but not yet on the clay."

Sarah joined Becka at the table. She herself had eaten earlier before logging on to the computer to surf the cattlemen's Web sites. By now she was used to the steady stream of phone calls from scientists and museum curators, but it still amazed her how blasé Luke was about his expertise.

"What's that all about?" Sarah asked Becka in a low voice as Luke went into detail about the plant species in question. "I thought he was an expert on insects."

Becka swallowed her mouthful of egg and took a drink of milk, leaving twin wings of white at the corners of her lips. She was in her school uniform, a blue-and-white gingham dress buttoned down the front. "Dad's an authority on outback plants, too," she explained matter-of-factly. "Also reptiles and paleo...paleo— You know, fossil stuff. He even has a lizard named after him. A university in California asked him to come and give a talk, but he couldn't go because of the muster coming up.''

Sarah swiveled her head around to stare at Luke. Why hadn't he mentioned the invitation? Quentin would have crowed from dawn until dusk if asked to deliver a lecture at a foreign university. She took in Luke's dusty moleskin pants and chambray shirt and tried to picture him standing in front of an audience of learned scientists. She could see him imparting knowledge, but she couldn't see him liking the attention on himself. Or leaving the station to travel to the "big smoke," as he called it.

"Dad said I could take tomorrow off school for the muster," Becka said, going on to more important matters.

"Won't your teacher mind?"

"Lots of kids do it. I'll make up the work after."

"I'm going on the muster, too, though I don't know how much help I'll be," Sarah replied. She'd called her boss, Ron, and asked for an extended leave, using the flextime due to her. Ron wasn't happy, but he agreed.

That morning Bazza, his brother and the other ringer had gone out to the Lost Thumb Paddock to finish setting up the temporary cattle yards. Just thinking about joining them on the Downs gave her more butterflies than Luke had in his collection. But she had to try.

"You'll need boots," Becka told her, glancing at Sarah's once-white cross-trainers, now dust-red and worn. Becka thrust into view a foot shod in miniature version of Luke's brown leather boots, which had elastic sides and leather tabs front and back to pull them on, tapered toes and Cuban heels.

Sarah adored them. "I want a pair."

"Dad has to go to the feed store so he's taking me right into Murrum this morning. Why don't you come. There's a place that sells boots."

Luke hung up the phone and poured himself a cup of coffee from the pot. As he tasted it, his face registered disappointment. "Are we out of Hawaiian hazelnut?"

Sarah suppressed a grin. He was coming around. "I'll ask Len to order more when we're in town."

"Sarah's driving in with us," Becka piped up. "She's going to get boots."

Luke's glance flicked to Sarah's feet. "About time. Ready, Becka?"

"Just have to brush my teeth."

"Don't forget your lunch." Sarah handed her the bag lunch Abby had insisted on personally preparing for her great-niece. Abby insisted on doing almost everything in the house, a fact that rankled Sarah more each day, though on the upside, it allowed her to avoid Abby and make herself useful outside, feeding the animals and weeding the kitchen garden.

An hour later they'd dropped Becka off at school and were traveling the short distance back to the center of town.

"I think I'll get a hat while I'm at it," Sarah said. This was the first time she and Luke had been alone since the bachelor and spinster ball. Sarah had slept almost the entire trip back, as the "recovery day" had turned out to be just as taxing as the ball, full of athletics and horse races and, for the truly dedicated, yet more drinking.

"Good idea." Luke parked perpendicular to the sidewalk on the wide main street but made no movement to get out of the four-wheel-drive. "Sarah, about the other night..."

She met his gaze and felt the flutter of attraction deep inside. She wished they could simply take their pleasure where they found it. But not only did the unresolved issue of ownership of the station divide them, sooner rather than later, so would the Pacific Ocean. Emotional involvement was a luxury they couldn't afford. "Yes?"

"If I make a trip to the chemist and the wrong busybody happens to see me, the whole town will know. I'm not sure you'd want that."

The knowledge that he was protecting her reputation gave her a warm glow, but he was also asking her indirectly how much she wanted to get closer. "I think we did the right thing. Or rather, we didn't do the wrong thing."

He contemplated that for a moment. "Does that mean you've changed your mind about wanting to make love?"

"I'm afraid it'll complicate things. I can't stay here."

"I know." Almost against his will, it seemed, his fingers slowly brushed her bare arm.

"On the other hand..." her skin tingled at his feather-light touch "—it never hurts to be prepared."

He grinned suddenly. "You're ba-a-ad." He glanced down the deserted street, then leaned over to kiss her on the neck.

She knew he didn't really think her "bad," but talking about sex with him put her on the boil. Laughing, she pushed him away.

Luke tipped his hat back and relaxed against the seat. "We've missed a window of opportunity, anyway, what with the muster coming up. We'll be up before 4:00 a.m., branding and drafting till long after sundown. I'm not Superman.''

Could have fooled her. "Luke?"

"Yeah?" His blue eyes held hers.

"Whatever happens, we'll keep it light, okay?"

Something—disappointment?—flickered in his eyes, then he glanced away. "Sure. Wouldn't want anyone to get hurt."

He jumped out of the truck before she could say another word. Sarah joined him in the shade of the wide covered footpath. "You can get your boots two doors down," he said briskly, as though directing a tourist. "They carry hats, too. I'll meet you back here in about half an hour."

Sarah watched him walk away, lean hipped, broad shouldered, with the rolling gait of one who spent long hours in the saddle. A real man.

But it wasn't his solid build of muscle and bone that made him "real." Not his down-to-earth way of talking or his firm grounding in the land. It wasn't even his astonishing connection to the academic world. It was the fact that he knew exactly who he was and what he wanted from life, and he faced whatever challenge came his way without flinching.

Quietly, persistently, patiently, he'd worked on his relationship with Becka. It still wasn't perfect, but Becka was starting to respond. She wasn't the sullen child she had been a couple weeks ago.

Sarah didn't think she'd ever admired anyone as much as she did Luke. Who could blame her for wanting to share the pleasures and intimacies of love-making with him?

She sighed and entered the clothing store. They'd

assured each other no one would get hurt. She prayed that when her visit was over that would still be true. Because with the boots she was about to buy, she'd one day be walking out of here.

BACK AT THE HOMESTEAD, Bazza was waiting for them on the front veranda. His rifle lay propped against the rail and his face was as long as a funeral procession. "Bad news, mate."

Luke's back went ramrod stiff. "What is it?"

"Old Ripper put a leg down a rabbit hole." Bazza glanced at Sarah and away. "Broken, looks like."

Sarah felt immediately guilty, as though Dorothy had burrowed that particular hole and she, Sarah, had shoved the bull's leg down it.

Luke cursed once and slapped his hat against the post. Then, hands on hips, he glared at the ground, his jaw clenched. "Have you put him out of his misery?"

"Not yet. I rode up just a couple minutes before you got here. Thought you'd want to do the honors."

"Thanks, mate." Luke jammed his hat back on his head, picked up the rifle and headed for the paddock and his horse.

"Wait!" Sarah called, and started after him. "Don't you need another bull right away?" She knew that once they'd mustered the mob and drafted the scrub bulls and weaners, the cows were to have been bred. Old Ripper was overdue for replacement, but the timing of his death couldn't have been worse.

Luke turned, his face as dark as a thundercloud. Sarah knew his frustration and anger weren't just at the inconvenience; she'd seen his deep affection for all his animals. She also knew he wouldn't welcome sympathy. But she could offer practical help.

"If you tell me what you're looking for I can find it on the Internet."

Luke snorted and started walking again.

"You can buy a bull through CALM—Computer-Aided Livestock Market," she said, lengthening her stride to keep up. "I found the Web site the other day."

"I like to see what I'm buying in the flesh," Luke said.

"There are photos and statistics about breeding, growth rates—all the information you need. Purchasing and shipping can be arranged on the computer."

Luke's grip on the rifle barrel tightened. *"I don't have time."*

"I do. What kind of a bull do you want? I'll have a look and show you later what's available."

"Oh, all right." He rattled off some specifications and a price range. Then warned, "This doesn't mean I'm buying."

"Just wait and see." She paused. "And Luke? I'm really sorry about Old Ripper."

He nodded once and pivoted on his heel, bound for his unhappy task.

Pleased to have something truly useful to do, Sarah took her packages into the house and went straight to the homestead office. She never thought she'd go Internet shopping for a two-thousand-pound bull. It was almost as much fun as cruising the online book and music stores.

That night after dinner, she dragged Luke to the

computer and called up her saved files on Santa Gertrudis bulls. ''I like this fellow myself.''

''Let me have a look.'' Luke nudged her out of the way and sat in front of the computer. ''How do you move back and forth through the pages?''

Sarah showed him and left to make them some coffee. She scooped the freshly ground beans into the coffee plunger and inhaled deeply of the delicious aroma. Oddly enough, she didn't drink nearly as much coffee now as she had in Seattle, although she enjoyed it just as much. Not only that, she was sleeping better these days. Must be all the activity and fresh air.

''Well, what do you think?'' she said, setting Luke's cup of coffee on the table well away from the computer.

Luke nodded at the screen. ''This fella is exactly what I'm after.'' He took a swig of coffee. ''Why didn't you tell me about this before?''

THE NEXT MORNING Sarah gazed at her reflection in the full-length mirror on the back of the bathroom door. Rust-brown check shirt, tan moleskins, Akubra hat and R. M. Williams boots. Pretty damn spiffy, if she did say so herself.

It was only 4:00 a.m., but she was pumped. She marched out to the kitchen, expecting to impress.

Luke took one glance at her and grinned widely, which for him was the equivalent of a belly laugh. ''You look like a tourist.''

Abby's tuneless humming preceded her into the kitchen from the backyard. She saw Sarah and put her hands on her hips. ''Well!''

Becka came out of the pantry with the box of Coco Pops. "Wow. You're like, totally brand-new."

"Thank you," Sarah replied, ignoring Abby and tossing her nose in the air at Luke.

Shaking his head, he plucked his well-worn hat off the peg. "When you're ready, come down to the shed. We'll take the shine off those boots."

An hour later, Sarah was riding into the sunrise, her hat pulled firm and low over her brow, her legs slanted forward in the long stirrups and her back slouched, as she mimicked Luke's and Bazza's easy-chair style of riding.

"You'll appreciate it after long hours in the saddle," Luke had assured her when she'd commented how different it was from either English or Western style.

Sarah fixed her gaze on the point between her horse's ears and listened to Luke's low voice telling her about the plants and animals that inhabited the land they were passing through. She knew he was trying to take her mind off her fears and it worked.

They rode across the Downs country to the low breakaway hills where the cattle were foraging for feed among the mulga scrub. Here the fun began as Luke and Sarah and the ringers spread out through the sparse bush to search for the cattle and herd them toward the "coacher" mob of compliant animals that would settle the wilder beasts.

Luckily Sarah's horse, a fiery bay named Kismet, needed little guidance from her; although Sarah knew the finer points of dressage, she didn't know diddly about working cattle. She spotted a scrub bull disappearing behind an outcrop, and with only the mildest encouragement Kismet raced after it, pivoting on his hind legs as the bull darted this way and that through the scrub. After a short chase she and Kismet herded the bull back to the mob. Proud and elated, she rode out after another stray. This was fun!

Hours passed and the mob of cattle grew. Choking dust filled Sarah's nose and throat as several hundred Santa Gertrudis moved over hard-packed dirt. At last Luke gave the signal to drive them toward the temporary yards near a water hole where they would be held until they could be drafted and branded.

Bazza and Kev moved back and forth around the circumference of the mob, keeping the unruly bunch in a tight circle and earning their title of ''ringer.'' Gus, the jackaroo, brought up the rear with Sarah and Becka. This was Becka's first muster, but by the delighted look on her grimy face as she chased after an escapee weaner calf, Sarah predicted it wouldn't be her last. Wal took over the calf and nudged it toward the anxious mother, who was lowing for her baby at the edge of the mob. Bazza's dog, a kelpie named Sue, nipped at the cows' heels to help keep them in line.

At the head of the mob, through the heavy pall of dust that hung over the sea of rounded red-brown backs, Sarah could make out Luke, his stock whip cracking the air as he urged the cattle with shouts and curses to funnel through the gate into the portable cattle yards. He rode standing in his long stirrups, his muscular body moving in concert with the chestnut gelding. At last the steel gate was secured on the bellowing, snorting mass of prime beef and the bore drain opened to give them water.

Luke removed his hat to wipe an arm across his dusty sweaty forehead. ''Time for lunch.''

The horses were watered, then hobbled and left to graze while the muster crew prepared lunch under the shade of a giant coolibah tree. Sarah was contemplating dangling her feet in the water hole, when she saw Bazza filling the billy can from its murky brown depths.

"Ready for a cuppa?" he asked cheerfully around the rollie dangling from his mouth.

"Sure, I guess so."

"The brown color comes from silt that's too fine to settle," Luke informed her. "It's good to drink."

Sarah helped Becka gather twigs and dead branches while Bazza built a small fire in a sandy pit he'd dug out with the heel of his boot. Over it he laid an iron grate and on that he set the billy can to boil.

The tea was hot, strong, sweet and black, and wonderfully thirst-quenching. Sarah perched on a fallen log and proceeded to devour the roast lamb and beetroot sandwiches Abby had packed. Once again she wondered, what was it with Australians and beetroot? Oh, well. She was so hungry she could eat a horse and go after the jockey, as Bazza said. After she polished off two sandwiches she made another billy of tea to have with thick slabs of chocolate cake. She swung the tin pail in a wide circle as she'd seen Bazza do to settle the tea leaves.

"More tea, Gus?" she asked, making her way around the circle.

Gus, who hadn't said a word to her all day, nodded and held out his tin cup. He was eighteen, as skinny as a piece of string and as quiet as Bazza was talkative.

"Do you want to be in the movies, too?" Sarah asked.

He grinned and shook his head.

"What do you want to do, then?"

Gus blew on his tea and shrugged.

"Manage a cattle station? Travel? Go to university?"

This last suggestion brought on vigorous head shaking.

"He oughta start a camel trekking outfit for tourists," Kev said, his grin very white against his dark skin.

"I reckon if Gus wore a sheikh's outfit he'd drive the sheilas mad, but he won't hear a bar of it," Bazza teased.

Gus turned as red as the beetroot. "I just want to live and work in the bush."

Sarah went back to her log to sip her steaming tea. She caught Luke's amused glance and gave him back his smile. But for the first time, the difference between her and them really sank in. Gus's few words had summed up the aspirations of everyone around the fire except her.

"How are your feet holding up in those new boots?" Luke asked a short time later as they saddled fresh horses for the afternoon. Bazza had brought them along in his stock truck, the one he would use later to transport the rogue bulls to the holding yards.

"Feet are fine. Legs might not last." Although she was used to riding, she wasn't used to spending all day on a horse and already her thigh muscles were sore. Tomorrow, she knew, would be a hundred times worse.

He lowered his voice. "And the distances?"

"I'm coping." They were back on the fringe of Downs country, and involuntarily her gaze drifted from the mulga scrub to where the grassy plain stretched endlessly into the distance. She shivered in spite of the heat.

Luke gave her shoulder a quick squeeze. "I shouldn't have mentioned it. You'll be right. You sure know how to sit a horse."

She pulled her hat down low, embarrassed to feel so proud at a few words of praise. But the warmth of his hand and his encouraging words bolstered her flagging spirit and with renewed energy she swung onto her horse.

For the rest of the day they worked with the cattle at the yards. Luke stood at the entrance to a narrow raceway, sending the animals one by one down to a three-way gate where Bazza stood waiting. Luke would shout out "clean skin," "meat works" or "breeder" and Bazza would open the gate that would let the animal into the appropriate yard.

Becka sat on the fence at her father's feet and Sarah helped the ringers move the cattle toward the raceway with a lot of arm waving and shouting, assisted by Wal and Sue in a frenzy of yelping and heel nipping. Occasionally a steer would turn and charge, sending the closest human leaping for the fence.

The dust, red-gold in the morning light, was now bleached to white-hot in the height of the afternoon heat. The din reverberated inside Sarah's head and echoed down her bones. The heat and smell of a thousand cattle filled her senses and the dust clogged her nostrils and seeped into every pore.

She loved it. She hated it. She'd never been so hot

or so exhausted. She'd never felt so full of purpose, so *alive*.

Her romanticized vision of the cattleman's life faltered a little when the bawling "clean-skin" calves were placed in a steel cradle. Gus and Kev held their legs while Bazza singed their flanks with the hot branding iron and Luke snipped out small pieces of the ear in Burrinbilli's distinctive pattern.

Romance disappeared entirely with the dehorning of cattle destined for market and the castrating of young bulls, or "mickies" as Luke called them. But Sarah gritted her teeth and did what she could to help. Whatever the future of Burrinbilli, right now she was part owner and she had a responsibility to the station.

At the end of the day they rode back along the dusty track as the setting sun painted the wide western sky a deep fiery crimson. Ahead the homestead glowed with light in the gathering dusk. Corellas flew high above, screeching as they flocked home to roost in the ghost gums. Between Sarah and Luke, Becka bobbed on Smokey, half-asleep in the saddle.

Luke's profile in the fading light was strong and familiar. He glanced over and gave her a slow smile whose warmth spread over her like the Queensland sun. It was a smile that wrapped up the whole wonderful day of working and laughing together and represented to her a gift and a thank-you at the same time. Sarah was dusty and her entire body ached from the longest day of the hardest physical work she'd ever done in her life. But Luke had looked at her and smiled, and her heart was singing.

SARAH HAD JUST pushed away her plate at the end of dinner when the phone rang.

Abby jumped up to answer it. "Sarah, it's for you."

"Me?" Surprised, she rose from the table and took the receiver Abby held out. Only her mother called her here and then it was on the cell phone. "Hello?"

"Hi, this is Karen. We met at the bachelor and spinster ball. I hope you don't mind, but when I heard you were a computer whiz I thought maybe you could help. I'm having problems with my Internet browser."

"I don't mind a bit," Sarah said, pleased to be of assistance. "One sec, I'll go to the office so I can sit at the computer and talk you through it."

She asked Abby to hang up after she got to the other phone, excused herself from the table with a hurried explanation and walked as quickly as her stiff legs would allow to the office.

"Hi, Karen," she said, as she booted up the computer. "What seems to be the problem?"

A short time later Sarah had instructed Karen on how to reconfigure her Internet setup. They then launched into an amiable post mortem of the bachelor and spinster ball. "Give me your e-mail address," Sarah suggested. "We can keep in touch. Let me know if you have any more problems."

"Thanks, Sarah. Come along for a cuppa next time Luke visits Col."

"I'll do that." But as she said goodbye and hung up she remembered that once they were through with the muster she would be going home.

As if to reinforce the message, when she checked her e-mail there was a note from Ron, asking her to return earlier than they had agreed on, as they were bidding on a big project and he wanted her expertise. She started to reply, then hit Exit, instead, putting off a decision.

She shut the computer down and left the office. As she passed the warmly lit loungeroom she paused in the shadow of the hallway. Luke and Becka were engaged in a humorous argument about the relative merits of satellite TV versus books and conversation. Sarah was torn between wanting to join them and needing time on her own to reflect. Quietly she crept down the hall to her room.

She turned on the lamp and lay across the bed, one arm shielding her eyes from the light. What was she going to do about Luke? It wasn't just physical closeness she wanted. Now she longed for emotional intimacy.

He'd finally revealed his attraction to her, but that didn't necessarily mean he wanted a relationship. He was so reserved it was impossible to tell how he really felt about her. Probably he didn't like to let himself feel anything. One thing was clear, Luke *needed* someone who would be a real partner to him.

Fed up with the futility of her thoughts, Sarah reached for her cell phone and called her mother.

"Hi, Mom, you'll never guess what I did today!" Sprawled across the white cotton bedspread in her mother's old room, Sarah related every detail of the muster.

"I'm glad you're having a good time, darl'. I used to ride out on the muster with my father and Robby. Goodness, that seems a million years ago now. How's the weather? Not too hot?"

"I think I'm acclimatizing. What's it like there?"

"Wet and cool, what you'd expect for this time of year. How are you getting on with Luke? Has he caved in to your demands yet?"

"We haven't had much time to talk about that lately." The longer she knew Luke the less right she felt about buying him out. He belonged here in a way she never could. Not only was he crucial to the running of the cattle, he was involved in long-term studies of the local flora and fauna. What would he do, what would the museums do, if he had to leave the area?

"He's an amazing man, Mom, a self-taught naturalist. People call him up from all over Australia to ask about different species and to get him to collect specimens. He's a world expert on reptiles and he even has a lizard named after him. You should see him handle the animals. Sort of tender but tough. They seem to trust him. And he's tireless. He's physically and mentally the strongest person I've ever met."

"Sarah, darl', the man sounds like a paragon. Are you getting...involved?"

Sarah rolled onto her back and once again covered her face with her arm. Her mother knew her too well. "God, Mom, I think I'm falling in love."

"Oh, Sarah, is that a good idea?"

"*Idea?* Mom, it's not something you think about, then go and do. The question is, how can I stop myself?"

"Just don't do anything rash. Why not have a fling and get him out of your system."

"*Mother!* You're not supposed to say things like that to your daughter. I thought you wanted me to find someone nice and settle down."

"When you're ready. More important, I want you to be happy. Don't rush into anything you might regret."

"Luke isn't someone I could regret. And Becka is a great kid. She just needs a little attention to feel secure. It would be good for her if Luke married again."

"*Sarah.* You're not thinking of marrying him!"

Sarah laughed. "Do a tarot reading and you tell me. Hey, when are you coming down here?"

"I've got to go, darl'. Talk to you soon."

Abby tiptoed away from Sarah's closed door, chilled to the bone by what she'd overheard. In the kitchen she crashed around in the cupboard, looking for the mixing bowl to get a head start on tomorrow's breakfast scones. Fury waged a war with fear; tears threatened, only to be blinked angrily away. Sarah wanted to marry Luke and become Becka's mother. This was terrible. Just terrible. If Luke and Sarah married, Abby wouldn't be needed at all. And she wanted so badly to be needed. She was trying hard to make herself indispensable, doing all the cooking and housework while Sarah gallivanted around on the cattle run.

Abby rose on creaking knees, empty-handed, only to find the mixing bowl right there in front of her on the counter. She stared at it, wondering how it got there. Sarah was no better than her mother had been. She would break Luke's heart when she left. And she *would* leave, Abby had no doubt. But before Sarah left she'd steal Becka's heart, too. Becka already liked Sarah, Abby could tell. But Sarah didn't belong here. She wasn't from the bush. She wasn't even Australian.

Abby refused to let all their lives be ruined by the daughter of Anne Hafford.

CHAPTER TEN

"But Dad, how am I going to get a new dress for the Winton races if you won't let Aunt Abby take me to Mount Isa?" Becka wailed.

"You're staying on the station," he told her for perhaps the tenth time. "We're in the middle of the muster, for crying out loud. Abby's got work to do." He glanced at his watch. He didn't have time for this; the bull they'd purchased over the Internet was being delivered that morning.

"If you'd let her keep the party dress I bought her earlier this wouldn't be a problem," Abby pointed out as she curled strands of Becka's hair around her finger, then let them fall in long ringlets.

Luke pushed away from the breakfast table, chair legs scraping on the slate floor. Bloody oath! The woman would drive him round the twist. From what he'd seen Becka already had a closetful of dresses. All Abby's fussing over Becka's appearance only succeeded in making his daughter more discontented with what she had. Lately he'd thought she was becoming interested in station life—and now this.

"What about that one you were wearing the other day, that blue one?" he said.

"Da-a-a-d. That's *old*. And I want to get a tattoo—"

"Tattoo!" he shouted. "Not in a month of Sundays!"

"Tattoo *choker*," Becka explained with a weary groan. "All the girls wear them."

"You're not a sheep. You don't need to follow the mob." Luke refilled his coffee cup. "The truth is, young miss, we're behind in the bills and until we get the cattle to market there just isn't any money for extras."

Abby pinned Becka's hair at the front with tiny sparkly butterflies. "I said I'd pay for it out of my pension money."

"Where's Sarah?" Luke asked suddenly. He'd hate for her to hear the bickering that was going on.

"Working on the computer," Becka said sullenly.

"Right, I'd forgotten." When he'd expressed interest in a software package for station accounts Sarah had offered to investigate, then join them at the cattle yards after lunch. Thankfully the office was at the other end of the house, out of earshot.

Becka frowned down at her plate. "I still don't see why you won't let Abby take me to Mount Isa."

"Mount Isa is too far, for one thing. It would mean an overnight stay."

"Not a problem," Abby replied. "My friend Jenny always welcomes me whenever I come."

"What about meals for the muster crew?" he growled. "You were hired on as cook." Abby was making him feel like an ogre and he didn't like it.

"I'll make a big pot of stew that will do for tonight and tomorrow. And I can make up extra sandwiches today for tomorrow's lunch. I'm sure Sarah can handle whatever little extras are needed. The boys always help with the dishes."

"*Abby, we had an agreement.* Apart from everything else, there's a bushfire alert for all of western Queensland." He slapped on his hat. "The answer is *no*. And that's final."

"Well, I'm not helping muster today," Becka yelled after him. "And *that's* final."

He ought to wash her mouth out for being cheeky. "Then you can spend the day catching up on your schoolwork."

With that, he turned on his boot heel and strode out the back door. Let Becka stay home this morning if that was what she wanted. Maybe they'd both cool off and she would come out with Sarah when Sarah was finished on the computer.

Luke whistled for Wal and the speckled dog jumped to his feet and trotted over. "Kids, eh, Wal," he said, giving his best mate a quick pat. "They're a constant worry."

Right on schedule, a cattle transport truck pulled around the side of the house. Luke helped the driver unload the new bull into a small paddock. He'd never have believed the purchase could be accomplished so quickly and conveniently. The cattle sales in Longreach were social occasions and he couldn't see himself giving them up entirely, but under the circumstances Internet buying had worked out well. Thanks to Sarah.

As he rode out to meet Bazza and the others at the cattle yards Luke twisted in his saddle to glance at the homestead. Just then Abby appeared out the rear door with a bucket of vegetable scraps to throw onto the compost. They stared at each other, but neither waved. Was he too hard on her? Was he misreading her annoying habits for sinister intent?

Luke turned his gaze ahead and forced his thoughts on the coming day. But at the back of his mind rode the uneasy feeling he shouldn't have left Becka at home.

By lunchtime, though, he had more on his mind than Abby and Becka and new party dresses. They were working Burrinbilli's farthest paddock, full of scrub and rocky terrain. A hot dry wind was blowing down from the northwest and dust devils danced across the dry soil. The cattle were wild-eyed and toey, bellowing their resistance at being mustered, and scattering easily.

At last they got the mob herded into the temporary yards and set up for lunch beneath the meager shade of some mulga trees. Luke took out one of the roast beef sandwiches Abby had packed and hunkered down by the fire to eat it. Steam rose from the blackened billy can and was whisked away in the stiff breeze. Every now and then he peered down the track toward the homestead and wondered when Sarah would show up. He'd thought it would be good for her to ride out on her own, but now he wasn't so sure. What if she had a panic attack?

"Here comes Sarah," Gus called suddenly.

Luke rose, relief quietly filling his chest. While Sarah jumped off her horse and hobbled him, Luke filled a tea mug, the one without the chip, and spooned in plenty of sugar, the way she liked it.

"Nothing wrong with your sense of timing," he said, and handed her the cup.

She grinned immodestly. "What can I say? I'm good."

"I have no doubt about that," he murmured before he could stop himself. Her cheeks bloomed red, but she ignored his comment except for a sidelong look from under her lashes that sent his pulse racing.

She sipped her tea and when she spoke again there was no hint of innuendo. "How much longer will we be mustering?"

Luke gazed squint eyed at the restless mob in the paddock. "We've got less than a hundred head left out here. We should get them into the holding yards today. Cutting, branding, dehorning will take another three days. Then we'll need to separate the weaner calves and handle them...I'd say another week to ten days." He turned to her. "Why do you ask?"

"My boss has e-mailed me twice now. Seems there's a new project on the go and he's anxious for me to return."

"How anxious?" And why did she sound almost relieved?

"My job is on the line." She looked away, avoiding Luke's eyes. "I called a travel agent in Longreach this morning. I can get a flight out of Brisbane on Saturday."

Although he'd known it was coming sooner or later, her announcement was a blow. "That's only four days away."

"I'm sorry, Luke. I feel bad about leaving before the muster's over."

"Don't worry about that." He searched her eyes. *Would she miss him?* "Pity you can't stay past the muster," he said, making his voice deliberately casual. "I could show you the desert country when I go on a collecting expedition for the museum."

"Desert?" She shivered. "No, thanks. I can barely face the Downs."

"But you rode out here on your own today."

She gave him a crooked smile over the rim of her mug. "I'm getting better at hiding my feelings. Must be catching."

His mouth thinned. "Let's climb back in the saddle. We need to get the rest of the beasts yarded before this wind has them completely unworkable.

"Douse the fire," he called to Bazza. "Make sure it's good and out. This is bushfire weather."

"You're not wrong." Bazza poured the last of the billy can on the smoldering embers and kicked dust over the pit.

They unhobbled their horses and cinched the girths tight again. Luke mounted and gathered his reins, glancing in the direction of the homestead. He couldn't shake the uneasy feeling that had troubled him all morning. "Becka didn't want to come?"

"No," Sarah said. "She wants that party dress."

This was not a topic he wished to pursue. He pushed his worries away, dismissing his concerns as nonsense. They were all on edge in weather like this.

A sudden gust of wind sent a flock of budgerigars rising from the ground in a flurry of green wings. Inside the yards, the huddled mob of cattle scattered with outraged bellows and wild eyes. A micky, pushed by the mob, crowded the gate and horned his way through. The rest of the cattle spilled out behind him.

"Hiyah!" Luke cracked his stock whip as he urged his horse forward, cutting off the animal's escape.

Sarah was right with him, and within moments Bazza, Gus and Kev were ringing the mob, pushing them back inside the paddock. Normally Luke accepted a delay as an inevitable part of the job, but today it frustrated him almost beyond endurance. Time was running out on all fronts, it seemed. He was as toey as the cattle and he didn't know if this was due to Sarah's imminent departure or his anxiety over Becka.

Whatever the reason, the rest of the day was fraught with one difficulty after another. Gus's horse lost a shoe in the stony ground and he had to go back to the main yards for another mount. A rogue micky bailed himself up in a blind ravine and charged anyone who came near. Luke damn near got himself gored before he and his horse finally maneuvered behind the animal and sent him roaring out. To top it all off, the bore pump in the paddock into which they herded the animals broke down. The sun was already low in the sky, but no matter how late it was they couldn't leave until they'd fixed it. Without water, cattle—or any creature—would perish quickly in this harsh environment.

It was dark when they finally rode in sight of the homestead. Although the sun was gone the hot wind kept temperatures elevated and the blowing dust entered eyes and noses and caked on sweat-soaked skin.

Luke glanced across at Sarah. She was drooping in her saddle, but for someone not born to the life she'd done all right. He'd heard not a peep of complaint out of her all day, even though he could tell from the way she put her hand to the small of her back that she was bone weary.

"Home soon," he said encouragingly.

He glanced toward the house, searching out the kitchen lights that would guide them in. Strange, the veranda light was on, but the kitchen was dark. Abby should be in there preparing dinner as she did every evening at this time—

The uneasy feeling that had been festering in Luke all day rose to the surface. Despite his horse's fatigue, he spurred the gelding to a canter.

"Luke?" Sarah's wondering call blew away on the wind.

He heeded nothing but his growing sense of urgency. At the edge of the veranda he reined his horse to an abrupt halt and leaped off.

"Becka! Abby!" Even before he pushed through the unlocked door and his cry echoed through the darkened kitchen he knew the house was empty.

Abby had left and taken Becka with her.

IN A NIGHTMARISH DAZE Luke ran down the hall, his boots echoing on the wooden floor as he flung open doors, calling for Becka. Every room was empty and dark. Explosive anger made him slam the door on Abby's room.

Sarah stood at the lit end of the hall. "What's the matter? They've just gone to Mount Isa."

A curse tore from his throat. "You knew about this? Why didn't you say something earlier?"

"I assumed you knew! And I did mention Becka wanted that party dress. But then the cattle escaped and after that we just carried on. Didn't Abby arrange it with you?"

"I told her *not* to go." He whipped his hat off and slapped it against his thigh. "Strewth! I *knew* something was wrong. All day I've had this feeling Becka was in trouble."

Sarah put her hand on his arm, clearly puzzled. "I

don't blame you for being angry, but I'm sure they'll be okay.''

"You don't understand." Luke dragged a hand over his face. "Did she leave a number where they could be reached?"

"I don't know. Let's check by the phone."

Abby *had* left a note, but the information it offered was not what he was after. In her neat up-and-down hand she'd written "Dinner in the fridge," followed by detailed instructions on how to heat it up and what to serve with it.

"Bloody hell," Luke muttered, and went back down the hall to Becka's room. No mention of their destination. No contact phone number. Clearly she didn't want to be located. What was her friend's name again?

Becka's room struck him as unusually neat and tidy. There were no toys littering the floor or books piled haphazardly on the bedside table. Her favorite doll, which normally sat propped atop her pillow, was missing. Luke did a double take. The pillow itself was gone.

He yanked open the door of the wardrobe. The normally crowded rod was half-empty and he reckoned at least three pairs of shoes were missing. This was no overnight trip.

He went back to the kitchen. Sarah was on the veranda, briefing Bazza and the others before they went to clean up for dinner. Luke waited until Sarah returned and told her what he'd discovered.

"Girls always overpack," she said dubiously as she pulled the big pot of stew out of the fridge and placed it on the stove. "Don't worry, Luke. They'll be okay."

"You don't understand," he said, pacing the room.

"That's the second time you've said that." She stopped him in midstride with an outstretched arm. "Maybe you'd better explain."

He heaved a deep sigh. "I believe Abby is...unbalanced."

Sarah gazed at him a long moment then got out a wooden spoon and began to stir the pot. "You've said that before. She's certainly got her quirks—"

Luke stilled Sarah's hand with his own, gripping her fingers as if by doing so he could hang on to his sanity. "Abby tampered with a photo of Becka as a baby in her mother's arms. She cut out Caroline's face and replaced it with her own. Then she denied there was anything strange about her actions."

Sarah's eyes widened. "That is a little creepy."

"It's more than a little creepy. It's bloody scary." Luke removed his hand from hers. "When I agreed to hire her as cook it was on the condition that she never take Becka off the station."

"She told me the day I got bitten that when you meet a snake the thing to do is run," Sarah said slowly.

His gaze veered back to her. "Everyone who lives in the bush knows better than that. Why didn't you tell me?"

"I thought she just disliked me because of my mother. Why didn't *you* tell *me* about the photo? And your rule about Becka not leaving the station? If I'd known I would have stopped them."

The accusation in her eyes was nothing compared with the flogging his own conscience was giving him. "If anything happens to Becka I'll never forgive myself."

"Oh, Luke." Sarah put her arms around him, drawing him to her. Her warmth and sweet softness were comforting and enticing at the same time. For a moment he succumbed to her embrace, before worry and anger made him pull away and pace across the room.

He reached for his hat. "I'm going after them."

"But it's dark," Sarah protested. "Abby said something about a shortcut—"

Luke froze. "Shortcut? There's some rough country between here and Mount Isa. If they break down..."

"Did you ever tell Abby the battery was low?"

"I've never got around to mentioning it. Did you?"

"No. She usually drives her own car."

They stared at each other.

Sarah broke first. "Don't even *think* like that. Try contacting her on the radio phone."

He lunged at the radio phone transceiver in the corner and flipped switches and dials. "Burrinbilli to Redback. Come in Redback. Over."

He heard nothing but the crackle of static on the line.

"Burrinbilli to Redback. *Come in Redback.* Over." His boot tapped out a beat on the slate as he waited. And waited. "Come in, Redback. Damn it, Abby, just answer so I know you're all right. Over."

Silence. He swore and ripped off the headphones. "What time did they leave?"

"Probably just after one o'clock. That's when I left the house to come out to the run. Abby spent the morning cooking this huge pot of stew. She kept saying she didn't want us to go hungry.''

Luke groaned. Abby's motherly concern was frightening. Beneath it lay off-her-rocker madness. ''If they'd left earlier they might have made it to Mount Isa before dark. As it is…''

''Maybe they made it, anyway. Abby mentioned she was going to a friend's house.''

''An old schoolfriend. I've been trying to think of her name,'' Luke said. ''Ginny or Janey or—''

''Jenny,'' Sarah said. ''I overheard her telling Becka.''

''Jenny Ralston.'' Luke grabbed the phone and got the number from directory assistance. He dialed, heart thumping, hope rising. Surely Becka would be there, safe and sound. After he had her back and hugged her within an inch of her life he'd send Abby packing.

The phone picked up. ''Hello?''

''Jenny? This is Luke Sampson.'' He struggled to hold his voice steady. ''I believe you're expecting Abby and my daughter, Becka. Are they there yet?''

His hope faded as he listened to Jenny's reply. Slowly he put down the phone and turned to Sarah. ''Jenny's been expecting them for the past three hours. They haven't arrived.''

''Oh, God,'' Sarah said in a horrified whisper. ''Where could they be?''

Luke paced the kitchen. ''She must have taken a wrong turn on her shortcut. It's easy to do. They could be halfway to Alice Springs by now and not even realize. Abby's got no sense of direction and no bush survival skills.''

''Becka does,'' Sarah said hopefully, though the

knuckles on her clasped hands were white. "She told me you're always instructing her in bush lore."

"She's only a child. A child who deliberately disobeyed me," he added grimly as he dialed Bill Watts, Murrum's lone police officer.

"Don't blame her. She's no match for Abby." Sarah started to set the table.

Bill wasn't in. His answering machine said he was away fighting grass fires raging to the northwest of Burrinbilli.

Luke hung up and relayed the information to Sarah. "That's the direction Abby and Becka would have taken to Mount Isa." His fingertips felt numb and he was sure the blood had drained from his face. "I'll go after them at first light."

This time she didn't argue. Without a word she went to the stove and began scooping stew onto plates. His movements mechanical, Luke sliced bread for their meal, his mind churning with worst-case scenarios—Abby and Becka lost in isolated country, out of water, trapped by fire....

Boots sounded on the veranda and Bazza and the others came into the kitchen. In a few words Luke told them he wouldn't be branding tomorrow and why.

"We'll carry on without you, unless you want us to help search," Bazza offered.

Luke shook his head. "Not yet."

"Then you'd better take my bullcatcher if Abby's gone off with your four-wheel-drive."

Luke started to protest that he could manage with his old ute, then stopped. The ute would never make it over the rough terrain he might encounter. He needed help and he had to accept the fact. "Thanks, mate."

IN THE DARKNESS before dawn Sarah awoke, her heart flooding with a sense of dread. Becka was gone, lost in the outback.

She reached for her cell phone on the bedside table and punched in the sequence of numbers that would connect her with her boss's office. "Hello, Ron?"

"Sarah! Are you back?" Ron barked against the background click of computer keys.

She heard the tension in his voice and winced. "I'm still in Australia. Look, something's come up. I can't come back right away. I need another extension—"

"No way. You're out of time—holiday time, flex-time, by-my-good-graces time. Get yourself back here pronto or your job is toast."

"You don't mean that!" But she'd never heard Ron so stressed.

"Damn right, I do. Stop playing cowgirl," he continued, his voice rising. "This project—"

"A child's gone missing," Sarah interrupted. "She's lost in the outback and I've got to help find her."

"Oh. Sorry to hear that." His voice was less strident, but he still sounded harassed. "This contract is a big deal. Leave it to the search-and-rescue team, Sarah. If you don't come back I'll have to hire someone in your place."

"Then I guess I have no choice but to resign." She waited for him to assure her it wouldn't come to that.

She heard other voices in the background. Ron

said, "I gotta go, Sarah. Sorry about the way things turned out." A loud clunk sounded in her ear as Ron dropped the receiver back in its cradle.

She stared at the phone. Just like that she'd lost her job. Well, tough. There was no question where her priorities lay—Becka was infinitely more important than any job.

She dressed, packed her toothbrush, cell phone and a change of clothing in a small backpack and hurried to the kitchen. Luke stood at the counter, pouring coffee and eating toast. His eyes were sunken and the lines around his mouth deeply etched, testament to a sleepless night. He caught sight of her backpack. "Where do you think you're going?"

She lifted her chin. She hadn't sacrificed her job to sit at the homestead and fret. "With you."

"No, you're not. I need someone to stay here and answer the phone if word comes in about Becka and Abby."

"Can't you ask a neighbor?" Sarah pleaded. "I feel so terrible she's missing. If it hadn't been for me—"

He put down his cup to grip her arms with both hands. "It's *my* fault you didn't know you should have stopped them. And Abby's fault for abducting Becka in the first place. I listened to the radio news this morning. With this wind the fires are spreading rapidly. I'm not going to take you along and possibly put you in danger, as well."

"I'm willing to risk it."

He shook her lightly, his voice intense. "We have to go over the Downs. It's two hundred or more kilometers. Sarah, there's nothing out there. It's flat and featureless as far as the eye can see and then a great deal farther. I can't have you going into a panic attack.''

Sarah felt the blood leave her cheeks. Her whole being quailed at the thought of venturing across the open country. She'd made progress in overcoming her phobia, but she was nowhere near sanguine about the prospect of driving for hour after hour across the plain. Her stomach rolled and tumbled with apprehension.

She plastered on a weak smile that didn't fool either of them. ''If it doesn't kill me, it just might cure me.''

''Sarah, for the last time, you don't have to do this.''

Maybe in his mind, she didn't. But she hadn't realized until this very moment just how much Becka had come to mean to her. Or how important it was to her that Luke be given another chance with his daughter.

''Yes,'' she replied, her voice low but firm. ''I do.''

CHAPTER ELEVEN

AN HOUR LATER she almost wished she'd stayed home. The Downs was so flat she swore she could see the curvature of the earth. Why, she wondered, had Warren hung on to property in this isolated part of the world? After divorcing her mother, what possible sentimental attachment could it possess?

She clutched the dashboard, squinted her eyes against the glare of the blazing sun and prepared to endure the trip.

Then, without warning, her heart began to beat rapidly and erratically. Her palms grew damp as first chills, then hot flushes swept over her body. Her mouth opened and her chest heaved in the effort to bring in oxygen. *No, not now!* Gripped by escalating panic over her loss of control, she curled forward, instinctively taking the fetal position.

"Sarah." Luke's voice came dimly through the thudding of her pulse. "Are you all right?"

How humiliating that he should see her like this. She wanted to die. She curled into a tighter ball and began to recite her mother's mantra. It wasn't working. *Oh, God. Please, no.* She was shaking all over.

She became aware that Luke had stopped the vehicle and was pulling her into his arms. His mouth close to her ear, he spoke to her in low soothing tones. "It's okay, Sarah. You're going to be okay. Relax. Breathe deeply."

How long she stayed in Luke's fortresslike embrace she didn't know, but gradually her heart slowed and breath entered her lungs freely once more.

"I'm sorry," she mumbled, drained of energy. She burrowed her face into his chest so she wouldn't have to look him in the eye.

"Are you all right now?" he said, stroking her hair.

She nodded, even though a minute ago she'd been convinced her life was about to come to an abrupt end. He frowned, seemingly reluctant to let her go, and before he loosened his grip he brushed her lips with his. It was the kiss more than anything that sparked her back to life and sent warmth and tingling awareness to her nerve endings.

"I thought I was getting over it," she said. "It's been almost a week since I had a full-blown attack."

"Something must be triggering these attacks."

Her gaze flickered to the distant horizon and the boundless open country in between. *Empty spaces in the heart.* Was it about her father after all? With a shrug, she slid back onto her side of the seat. "We're losing time."

With a last dubious look at her, Luke restarted the engine. Sarah straightened her hair, adjusted her clothes and tried to get her bearings. They were traveling an even shorter route than Luke surmised Abby had taken, across the neighboring station, heading north and west, ignoring even the rudimentary vehicle and stock tracks to bump across open land. Sarah didn't ask how he knew where he was going;

she just trusted he did. Every now and then he'd glance at the sun and make a slight alteration to their course. Away in the distance a thin line of gray smoke hung over the horizon. Grass fires. Luke changed direction, heading more north than west, and muttered something about hoping the wind wouldn't change.

Around noon they stopped to eat while sitting on the ground in the scant shade cast by the bullcatcher. Sarah's hands and clothes were smeared with dust and the flies buzzed her sweat-dampened face mercilessly. *How much longer?* The words danced on the tip of her tongue, but she kept her mouth clamped. Luke would *not* regret bringing her along. Any more than he already did, that is.

"You right?" he asked, passing her the water bottle.

"Fine." She tipped her head back and drank a little of the precious water, her eyes shutting in the simple pleasure of cool liquid on a parched throat. Drops escaped her lips in her eagerness to drink and slid down her neck. She lowered the bottle and caught Luke's gaze tracing the paths of the drops.

"Are new dresses really so important to women?"

She put the cap back on the bottle. "Depends on the woman. Depends on the dress."

His lips twisted in a smile. "Okay, dumb question." Then he sobered and his eyes, for the instant he turned them on her, looked naked and vulnerable. "I should have found a way to take her to Mount Isa myself."

Aware of what it cost him to reveal his uncertainty, Sarah thought carefully before answering. "It's important to validate her feelings by letting her know she's not bad just for wanting something. But you can't buy her love and she needs to respect you. You had your own sound reasons for saying no. I think you did the right thing.''

"What makes you so sure?"

With a twig she scratched lines in the dirt. "On the few occasions I saw my father he made up for long absences with too many presents. Anything I asked for, he bought me. I loved it at the time, but afterward I always felt like I'd eaten too much Halloween candy—sick and hollow at the same time. Daily contact, affection tempered by discipline—they are what nourish love. When my dad went back to his side of the country there was very little to sustain me until his next visit.''

She stretched her legs out, marveling in one part of her brain that she could sit in the dust, filthy and sweaty, and not care. Some things just weren't important in the larger scheme. "I try not to blame him. I guess he did the best he could. That's all anyone can do.''

But for no earthly reason she could see, tears welled in her eyes and an almost physical pain gripped her chest. Blinking hard, she put down her half-eaten sandwich.

Luke leaned over and carefully blotted the moisture away with a callused thumb. "What's wrong?" he asked in a gently teasing tone. "Don't you like roast beef?''

She smiled, touched by his concern and grateful he wasn't making a big deal of her emotional reactions. "Every day for weeks on end is a bit much. What I wouldn't give for avocado and sprouts and paper-thin slices of smoked turkey.''

"If you want avocado you only have to say so."

"You mean Len can order them in?"

"No, we'll plant a tree in the garden. And sprouts are easy enough to grow on a windowsill."

"And the turkey?"

He pushed back his hat to scratch his forehead. "I reckon we could throw a few gobblers in with the chooks, build a smokehouse in the old meat shed, and Bob's your uncle."

She laughed again. "Nothing's too hard for you, is it?"

"Plenty of things are difficult, but with a little ingenuity and enough determination you can make anything happen." He held her gaze just a fraction long.

Sarah's smile faded. She squinted out at the empty horizon, shimmering with heat haze and bleached by the sun. Was *anything* really possible simply by wanting it badly enough? Maybe. Trouble was, she hardly knew anymore *what* she wanted.

"Come on," Luke said, rising. "Time's passing."

Sarah packed away the remains of their lunch and Luke carried it to the back of the ute. Wedged in beside their swags were two large containers of water, something Sarah now knew was standard equipment on a trip through the outback.

"The only problem with this bullcatcher is that the radio telephone's broken," Luke said, loading the cooler back into the vehicle. "I forgot about that when Bazza offered it to me. We can't call him at the station or check in with Bill in Murrum."

"I've got my cell phone with me."

Luke stared, then a slow smile spread over his tired face. He put his hands on either side of Sarah's face and gave her a big smack on the lips. "You beauty!"

"What'll you give me for the use of it?" she teased, darting away from his grasp.

"A damn good spanking." He lunged for her and missed.

"In that case…" She sashayed back to him.

"Just give me the phone, woman."

Their fun was short-lived. Neither Bazza nor Bill had had any word from or about the missing woman and child. Grim-faced, Luke handed the phone to Sarah. With a deep sigh, she packed it away again.

Light was already fading by the time they were on the road once more. Sarah breathed a sigh of relief as the bullcatcher bumped up the verge and onto the single-lane bitumen. Suddenly the ride felt unbelievably smooth.

"Let's see now…" she muttered, looking at the map and trying to pinpoint their location by figuring out how far and in what direction they'd come. "I think we're about here."

Luke glanced to where she was pointing and shook his head. "Here," he said, indicating a spot on the map several inches west of her guess.

"So if we follow this road we'll get to Mount Isa."

"Yes, but it'll take hours—" He broke off as they came to a junction with a rough dirt road leading north. Quickly he stopped, then got out to take a closer look. "These tire imprints are from the Land Cruiser. See there? The left rear tire has a chunk of tread missing." He lifted his gaze to the track. "If she went up there she's mad."

Sarah thought they'd already established that Abby

was crazy, yet the road looked no worse than the one they'd been following and she said so.

"It's not bad here," Luke told her, "but once you're up into the ridges and gullies it becomes much worse. She wouldn't be able to tell that from the map." He got back in the ute and swung off onto the track.

The only consolation—if you could call it that, Sarah thought—was that they were no longer on the Downs; the land here was broken up with sandstone ridges and sparsely populated with ghost gums and scrubby mulga trees. Her own fear of another panic attack was nothing, however, compared with her worry over Abby and Becka. As the evening light faded and they still hadn't caught up to the Land Cruiser, her concern grew.

"Surely they would have turned back to the road before now," Sarah said, hanging on tightly as the ute bounced over rocks and dry ruts. "This is practically impassable."

"The Land Cruiser would be more comfortable than this old bush basher—" His words were cut off by a sideways jolt so bad that Sarah flew up in her seat and would have been tossed out if she hadn't been strapped in. Gripping the wheel with white knuckles, Luke said, "You right?"

"Fine," she replied, voice wobbling from her being bounced up and down. "Just peachy."

A kangaroo leaped suddenly from the bush directly in the path of the bullcatcher. Luke slewed the wheel sideways, and the vehicle spun through the loose dirt until he slowed to a halt inches from a sharp drop-off.

"We'd better stop for the night," he said reluctantly. "Once dusk falls the 'roos come out. Can't afford to disable the ute by crashing into one."

"No, indeedy," Sarah agreed, shaken.

The ordeal wasn't over. They half slid, half drove down the steep incline, Luke's arms rigid with tension as he maneuvered the vehicle to keep it from overturning. Kangaroos bounded away in the glow of the headlights. Sarah was so intent on watching out for the creatures she almost missed the gleam of chrome hidden behind a stand of coolibah trees.

"Luke!" she shouted. "The Land Cruiser!"

LUKE SKIDDED to a halt and leaped out of the ute. His heart raced as he ran across the short stretch of dirt and grass to where the Land Cruiser was parked at the edge of a dry watercourse. The doors were wide-open and the hood was up.

There was no one in sight.

"Becka! Abby!" he shouted. His voice was lost in the impenetrable quiet of the bush.

He thumped the hood of the Land Cruiser in frustration and slid in behind the wheel. The key was in the ignition, but turning it brought only a faint whirring of the starter motor. Abby had nearly run that down, too. He got out and went around to check under the hood. She'd evidently known enough to scrape the corrosion off the battery terminals, but it hadn't done her any good.

Sarah appeared beside him. "There are no bags or clothing in the back. It looks like they've taken their stuff and tried to walk for help."

Luke stared, amazed she could say that with such bland unconcern. It was a forcible reminder that

Sarah, even more than Abby, was ignorant of survival in the outback.

"Don't you remember what I told you? *Never leave the vehicle.* Wandering away drastically reduces the chances of being found."

She went quiet as the implications sank in. Shivering, she rubbed her arms. "It gets cold once that sun goes down. I'm going to get a sweater."

Sarah went back to the bullcatcher, leaving Luke with gloomy thoughts. Abby had bought Becka's sleeping bag for her seventh birthday. Was it warm enough? Would they remember to check it for snakes before crawling in at night and their shoes for spiders and scorpions in the morning? Did they know enough not to go traipsing through the bush in the dark?

He gazed around the clearing searching for clues, even though it was too dark to see properly. "If they were going to walk, why didn't they head back to the road?"

"I think I know," Sarah said. She'd put on her cardigan and was looking at the map again. "There's a homestead not far from here. It's only a mile or two down the track."

Luke peered over her shoulder. "That's an old map. The Lawrence place has been abandoned since the seventies and was burned to the ground during the last lot of bushfires."

Sarah's shoulders slumped. "Wouldn't Abby be aware of that?"

"Not necessarily. Abby doesn't go out of her way to get acquainted with the station people," Luke said. "But if she and Becka are there, we'll find them tomorrow. How about gathering some wood for a fire while I set up the swags.''

SARAH PERCHED on a fallen limb of the coolibah, sipping hot tea while Luke called Bazza back at Burrinbilli. She listened hopefully at first but could soon tell from his tone of voice that there was still no word from Becka and Abby.

''Fred Walker's station isn't far from where we're camped,'' he said to Bazza before signing off. ''Ask him to drive out here first thing tomorrow with some horses. This country's too rough even for the bull-catcher.''

''We're continuing on horseback?'' she asked when he rejoined her by the fire.

The flickering light threw shadows on his face. ''*You're* going back with Fred. Bazza tells me the bushfires have spread. They're only fifty kilometers west of here and if the wind picks up they'll soon be on top of us. If we don't find Becka and Abby tomorrow...''

He rose abruptly to get the swags from the bull-catcher, then laid them side by side, with hers closest to the fire.

Sarah took her boots off and crawled into her swag fully dressed. Luke did the same. The silence stretched. She rolled on her side to face Luke. Touching his cheek, she said, ''We'll find them tomorrow.''

Luke nodded wordlessly. She wished she could reach deep inside him and touch that part of him that he kept locked away from true intimacy, the place where love dwelled but couldn't seem to get free.

"Were you very much in love with her?" she asked softly.

She sensed him stiffen. "Who?"

"Becka's mother—Caroline."

"Why do you want to know?"

Why *did* she? Was she jealous of a dead woman just because that woman had made love with Luke a long time ago? Or did she hope that by seeing into his heart she might find a place there for herself? "I just wondered."

He was quiet a long while. The embers died to a red glow and stars peeked through the branches of the coolibah. A hush came over the night, as if it, too, were waiting to hear his story. At last, in a low voice, he said, "Yes, I loved her. She was the first woman I loved. The only woman until—" He paused to clear his throat and fell silent.

Sarah found his hand in the dark. "Becka said she drowned."

He sighed and laced his fingers through hers. "We'd left Becka with Abby and traveled to Thailand. Becka was only six months old. I thought she was too young to leave, but... Well, never mind. We got on an evening ferry bound for a resort island off the coast. A storm blew up and the ferry went down. There were no lifeboats and not enough life preservers. Caroline hit her head and was knocked unconscious."

He drew a deep breath. "I kept her afloat as long as I could. The waves were huge. There was so much confusion. It was a nightmare. Pitch-black, people yelling, crying... Someone drowning grabbed on to Caroline, pulled her out of my grasp, dragged her under." Luke's voice shook. His grip on Sarah's fingers tightened painfully. "I dove, but I couldn't find her. All those hands, clutching. I—I *lost* her."

"Oh, Luke," Sarah said softly. Her other hand reached to stroke the hair back from his temple. His eyes were wide and staring, his mouth drawn tight.

"In the morning fishing boats picked up the survivors. Caroline's body washed ashore a few days later. There was an inquest and authorities to deal with. The red tape was all the worse because we weren't married. Abby was her closest relative, but she refused to come out to Thailand, so everything had to be done by correspondence. I was in Bangkok for months, tying up loose ends, when all I wanted was to get back to Becka."

He paused and somewhere in the distance a dingo howled. "By then, Abby had convinced the Queensland courts that Caroline had wanted her to be Becka's guardian in case anything ever happened to her."

"Did she have any documents to prove Caroline's wishes?"

"No. I appealed and won, which didn't endear me to her. In the end we compromised. Abby flatly refused to live at Burrinbilli, but she would stay in Murrum instead of going back to Brisbane and keep Becka while she was small. I didn't like it much, but it made some sense. I couldn't afford a nanny, nor could I look after a baby and work the station, too. When Becka turned nine she was to come to me. Neither Abby nor I realized how hard that would turn out to be for all of us."

Sarah brought the back of his hand to her lips and pressed a kiss on his callused palm. "I'm so sorry," she said gently. "And I'm sorry you lost Caroline."

The sound of his deep sigh came to her through the dark. "We were so young and I had such big dreams to make the station self-sufficient. I wanted to get married. All Caroline wanted was out of Murrum. She didn't want to 'rot on the station,' was how she put it."

Sarah thought about her mother, who'd also wanted to see the world. Station life wasn't for everyone. But the women she'd met here so far all loved the bush. In spite of the isolation they insisted they were never lonely or bored.

"And your dreams?" she asked. "Do you still have them?"

"Yes, but they're a long way off being fulfilled." He paused. "What about you? Got a boyfriend?"

"I did, but in hindsight...I don't know, it was a pretty shallow relationship." She paused to reflect. "A lot like my life. I'm in a responsible job, yet it's not like I'm responsible for anything...I don't know, *big*." She extended one arm, encompassing the whole of the universe. "Life-and-death issues, passionate love—these things simply haven't come my way."

He spoke quietly. "You're lucky."

She started to deny it and then remembered that his daughter was lost in the bush, maybe alive, maybe not. "In some ways I guess I am."

A twig snapped close by and she jumped. "What was that?"

Luke didn't even lift his head. "It's nothing."

"It had to be *something*." She strained to listen.

"Your problem," he said, "is that you look on the bush as a hostile environment."

"Well, isn't it? Snakes, spiders, bushfires—"

"Are all just part of nature. The bush is neutral. It's your attitude that's hostile."

She thought about that for a while. Maybe he was right.... Then some creature crashed through the bushes nearby and she buried her head under the blankets.

Luke rose onto one elbow and tugged the swag away from her face. "Open your eyes, Sarah. Look at the beauty of the night."

"Do I have to?" Slowly she sat up and peered around.

Moonlight silvered the coolibah tree and cast an ethereal glow over the dry watercourse and the bushes along its banks. Cool air swirled around her face, bringing with it the scents of the bush, eucalyptus and earth and mysterious smells she could only guess at. She heard a scrambling in the branches above and glanced up to see a small bushy creature leap from tree to tree.

"Possum," Luke said. "The night comes alive in the Australian bush. With daytime temperatures so hot many creatures are nocturnal."

"Possums are cute," Sarah conceded.

"Unless they're dining on your fruit trees."

Sarah put an arm behind her neck and gazed up at the moon and the ancient stars above an ancient land. She began to relax and the night filled with a mystical beauty. She recalled her mother telling her creation stories from the aboriginal dreamtime and she thought of her own childhood dreams about a place where love was a law of the universe and commitment was forever.

Slowly, she drifted asleep.

Hours later she awoke in the night to the distant

howl of a dingo. Her frisson of alarm gave way to a feeling of warmth and security when she realized she was wrapped snugly in Luke's arms. A smile curved her lips as the sound of his deep even breathing lulled her back to sleep.

LUKE AWAKENED LAZILY, tucked deep within the covers of the swag, melded with Sarah. He ascended toward consciousness with his nose buried in her hair and his arms holding her close. Breathing deeply, he inhaled her sweet musky scent. His body responded...tightening and hardening as his blood stirred.

Then he remembered Becka and fear for his daughter's safety brought his head up sharply. He sucked in a breath of morning air. Every hair on his body stood on end. Throwing back the covers, he turned his face into the wind.

"What is it?" Sarah asked sleepily.

"Smoke!"

He leaped to his feet and banged his boots together upside down. "The wind's shifted. The fire's heading this way." Somewhere out there were Becka and Abby. If he didn't get to them before the fire did... His foot jammed as he dragged on his boot and he cursed, hopping and tugging.

Sarah extricated herself from the tangled blankets of the swag. Luke had just gotten his foot into his boot, when she leaned up and without a word placed her mouth on his in a brief firm kiss. "We're going to find them."

"Sure." She had no idea of the extent of the danger. The blazing heat, the flying embers and the suffocating smoke that stung the eyes and burned the throat. The way an uncontrolled fire could outrun a vehicle in a strong wind or leapfrog over firebreaks, trapping anyone unlucky enough to be caught in between.

Nor was he about to tell her. "When Fred gets here with the horses, you're going back with him."

"No, I'm not." She bustled around their campsite, rolling blankets and picking up the dishes from last night's Spartan dinner.

"It's not open for debate, Sarah."

"I'm not debating," she said calmly. "I'm simply going. What if one of them is injured? You'll need help."

"I can handle it."

She dropped the bundle she was carrying and took a step toward him, her eyes blazing. "*You* can handle it. Who are you God? If you are, then just blow this bushfire out, snap your fingers for Becka and Abby to appear and we can all go home. But you can't, can you? You're a man. A hell of a man, but still not in possession of superpowers."

She advanced farther toward him, her voice rising. "Admit it, Luke, you need me."

"I don't want to lose you, too."

His words shocked her into silence. For the first time she seemed to realize the seriousness of the situation. *Good,* he thought grimly. Now she'd have to accept his decision.

"Let's not waste time arguing," she said at last.

"Amen to that."

They ate a quick breakfast of bread and cheese, then loaded the gear into the Land Cruiser. Sarah got behind the wheel while Luke attached jumper cables from the Land Cruiser to the bullcatcher. Relief flooded through him as the Land Cruiser's motor caught and roared. They might need to beat a quick retreat and the bigger vehicle could carry all of them more comfortably than the bullcatcher.

Luke got out to undo the jumper cables. Birds flitted through the treetops away from the direction of the fire. He sniffed the air. The smoke, still faint, smelled like burning rubber. Spinifex grass. Hard to say exactly how far away the bushfire was, but there was no time to lose.

"Turn it off and come on," he said to Sarah. "We'll leave the Land Cruiser here and go to the road to meet Fred."

He gunned the bullcatcher's engine, put the vehicle in gear and plowed up the rise to the track. Their jolting ride back over the rutted track was rewarded by the sight of a truck hitched to a four-horse trailer waiting at the junction with the road.

Fred Walker climbed down from the cab of the truck as they pulled up. He was a thickset man in his early forties, with a permanent squint from gazing into the sun and a jaw that would have done a bulldog proud. "G'day, mate," he said to Luke. "Got a message you needed some horses."

Luke schooled his anxiety into a stoic expression. "Becka and Abby are up there in the hills. Track's pretty rugged. I reckon I'll find 'em easier on horseback."

Fred glanced up at the ridge. "Fire's headed this direction."

Luke nodded. "How far?"

"Forty or fifty kilometers. That'll change quick the way this wind's picking up."

"Not much fuel out there after this long drought," Luke said, wanting to believe it.

"There's enough. Local landholders are being called out. Soon as the fires are under control we'll come back and help you search."

"I expect I'll have found them by then." Or it would be too late. Luke nodded toward Sarah. "This is Sarah. She's going back with you."

Sarah smiled politely. "No, I'm not."

Fred gave her an appraising glance, then turned to Luke. "Didn't know how many horses would be needed so I brought four, all saddled and ready to go."

"Great," Sarah said.

Luke shook his head. "I'll take two of the horses—I'll ride one and lead one."

Fred sided with his friend and neighbor, as Luke had known he would. He went around to the back of the horse float and dropped the ramp to unload a tall roan and a smaller black. "There're food and a first aid kit in the saddlebags, and I've strapped on a couple of water bottles."

"Appreciate it, Fred." Luke checked the girths and cinched the straps tighter.

"No worries. Coming, Sarah? I'll run you back to my place. You can wait there for Luke or take a vehicle and go back to Burrinbilli." He climbed in the open door of his four-wheel-drive and started the engine.

Luke forestalled Sarah's outburst with an upraised hand. "I know you want to help, but I can go faster alone." He cupped her face in his palm, felt the angle of cheek and jaw. "I appreciate all you've done—"

She pushed his hand away. Then clung to it. "You know you need me."

More than she guessed. "I'll see you soon."

He swung onto his horse and the tall roan danced away in a skittish sidestep. "If you want to help, you and Frank's wife can make sandwiches for the fire-fighting crew."

"Ohh!" Sarah's rigid arms formed fists as she realized he wasn't going to relent.

Luke grasped the reins of the black and wheeled his horse to plunge back up the track. The smell of smoke was getting stronger and the brisk wind carried wisps of black against the blue sky.

CHAPTER TWELVE

HE RODE BACK to their campsite and dismounted, scouring the ground for clues to the direction Abby and Becka had taken. It made logical sense they'd keep to the track, but so far Abby hadn't shown either logic or sense. Moving in ever-widening circles from the Land Cruiser, he searched for footprints in the dust.

Eventually two pairs of prints, one large and one small, separated themselves from the muddle. They branched off down the dry watercourse instead of continuing up the track. Maybe instead of heading for the burned-out homestead they'd gone down the watercourse, hoping to find water. From years of exploring the countryside for specimens of native flora and fauna Luke knew there were no permanent water holes along here. There *was* water to be found in the bush—if you knew where to look—but he'd bet his last dollar Abby didn't.

He suspected they would quickly run out of whatever water they'd brought with them. They'd only been gone a day, but the heat was fierce. If the bushfires didn't kill them they could die of thirst. The thought of Becka dehydrated made his throat close up. From sheer force of will he pushed his worries aside. Nothing was going to help his daughter except a clear head unobstructed by anxiety and fear. Thank goodness Sarah had stayed behind.

No sooner had the thought entered his brain than he heard the thud of horse hooves cantering through the dust.

Sarah! Bloody hell!

She reined in her dapple gray horse and skidded to a halt in front of him. Her face wore an anxious smile as she searched his face for the slightest sign of welcome.

His scowl deepened in direct proportion to the height to which his heart lifted. "How the hell did you get Fred to unload that horse for you?"

Her expression turned smug as she patted the backpack strapped behind the saddle. "I told him I had the phone."

Luke pinched his nose between two fingers and muttered a curse. Not at Sarah but at himself, for forgetting to ask for what had become a survival tool.

"Fred's already turned back so you can't send me away again," she said, her chin lifted defiantly.

"All right," he sighed, "you can come. But don't get hurt, don't get lost and don't get in the way."

He nudged his horse into motion and side by side they rode down the empty watercourse. After a few minutes of silence, Sarah turned to him. "Admit it, Luke. You need me."

"Strewth, woman! What do you want from me?" he growled. He was having the devil of a time stifling a smile.

"An apology and an acknowledgment that I have something to contribute to the search," she replied maddeningly.

He allowed one corner of his mouth to rise. "I'm

sorry I forgot to take the phone. It'll be handy to have along." He glared at her from beneath his hat brim. "And that's all you're getting, so don't ask for more."

"It'll do," she said, tilting her nose in the air. "For now."

Although it was tempting to hurry, Luke restricted the horses to a fast walk, not wanting to miss any signs of the lost pair veering off the track. The dust underfoot turned to rocks as the watercourse narrowed through a gorge and the footprints disappeared. As the riverbank rose Luke tried to calculate how long Abby and Becka had been walking and how far they'd get. If they'd arrived at the watercourse the previous afternoon and set out immediately they might have covered five or six kilometers before stopping for the night. Had they found shelter? Had they had anything to eat? If Abby had planned on reaching Mount Isa yesterday she might not have packed much.

"Did Abby take lunch with them?" he asked Sarah, breaking the heavy silence.

"I think she made extra sandwiches when she prepared lunch for the mustering crew. Yes, I'm certain she had a lunch. I remember Becka filling a container with water."

"One of the big ones?"

Sarah looked as though she'd rather not answer that question. "No, one of the small ones. Speaking of water, I could use a drink." She started to reach for the water bottle strapped to her saddle.

Luke stopped her with an outstretched hand. "Let's try to conserve that in case..." In case Becka and Abby needed it more. In case they were out in the bush for days. "Don't worry, I'll find us some water."

"Okay," she agreed dubiously.

As the morning wore on the heat built and bounced off the rock walls of the gorge. Sweat dripped down Luke's temples and snaked down the hollow of his back. His mouth grew parched.

Gradually the watercourse widened again and farther upstream it split into two. This was the western fringe of channel country, where during the Wet, floodwaters flowed in a spiderweb network of temporary rivers toward Lake Eyre in the dry heart of the continent. Now everywhere was dry, the channel bed hard-caked mud. On either side gidyea scrub and mulga formed sparse vegetation, which would nevertheless burn fast and hot.

Luke gazed around. The right bank of the main watercourse was formed of a tumble of large rocks grading to gravel farther upstream. On top of a large boulder he glimpsed a pile of small stones. His pulse quickened. If that was what he thought it was…

Dismounting, he dropped his horse's reins on the ground and climbed the bank. A closer look confirmed that the waist-high pile of rocks was no natural formation.

"What's that?" Sarah asked, coming up behind him. She wiped the perspiration off her forehead with the back of her wrist. Her cheeks were flushed with the heat.

"Aboriginals mark their water holes this way." He scrambled up the rocks and, with a bit of searching, located a large flat stone. When he lifted it he uncovered a two-foot-deep hole. It was dry.

"Oh," said Sarah, her disappointment tangible.

Luke crouched and began to dig, scooping out handfuls of dry gravel. He was up to his elbow and seconds away from giving up, when his fingertips encountered moisture. Digging harder, he scrabbled away a few more centimeters of gravel and was rewarded by water seeping into the hole.

He cupped his hand and scooped out a handful. The water, although lukewarm and murky, was wet and refreshing. Life giving. He backed away and motioned for Sarah to have a drink.

"It will never replace Perrier," she said, wiping her wet hand over her face when she was done. "But it tastes damn good when you're dying of thirst."

His face froze. "Don't even joke about that."

"I'm sorry," she said, her smile fading.

They went back to the watercourse and started up the main channel, riding ten feet apart, searching the substrate for any sign of people having passed this way. They hadn't gone far, when Sarah shouted, "Luke, look at this!" She held up an apple core. "There are footprints here, too," Sarah added, peering at the ground.

Luke inspected the smudged prints. "Those are wallaby tracks." Sarah appeared disappointed. "The apple core suggests *someone* came this way," he said. But for some reason he couldn't explain, he had a feeling it wasn't Abby and Becka. "Let's check the other channel before we go too far in this direction. Just to be sure."

As they backtracked the short distance to the secondary channel, he prayed Becka and Abby hadn't taken it, for it branched off in the direction of the bushfires. His gaze roved across the channel and along both banks, searching for broken vegetation or minute disturbances in the rocks or dirt. He was about to give up and go back to the main channel, when something about the pattern of the stones ahead made him pause.

"Look at this," Luke said, gesturing Sarah over.

"What?" she said. "I don't see anything."

With the toe of his boot he indicated a straggly row of stones capped by two diagonal rows. The arrow pointed down the secondary channel.

"Do you think it's them?" Sarah said doubtfully. "The water doesn't seem to have flowed here for months. This arrow could be old."

"Could be, except for *this*." He indicated a smooth hollow in the dirt where a stone had been recently overturned and the sharp edges not yet worn by wind or trampled by animals.

The pall of smoke hanging over the western horizon was bigger. And closer. It might have been his imagination, but the heat of the day felt more intense, as though stoked by flames. "Let's get moving."

He swung onto his horse, Sarah close behind. Her gray mare danced and snorted, jumpy with the smell of smoke and the hot gusty wind. Side by side they trotted up the channel, their horses' shoes ringing on the small stones in the rocky dirt. The spare horse followed reluctantly behind Luke, dragging on the reins.

"Becka! Abby!" Luke called repeatedly, slowing every few minutes to listen—in vain—for a reply.

"How close are we to the fire?" Sarah asked.

"Maybe only a kilometer or two. Maybe less."

"But there's no sign of the firefighters."

His mouth set in a grim line. "There's more than one bushfire burning."

"Becka! Abby!" Sarah joined him in calling.

They'd ridden like that for fifteen or twenty minutes, when from somewhere close by he heard the crackle of flames. "Let's go," he yelled, spurring his horse on.

They rounded a bend in the watercourse and the horses shied as a lick of intense heat blasted them. The fire was burning not fifty yards from the bank. Over the rustle of flames and the frightened twitter of birds they heard a cry.

"Help!"

"Becka!" Luke shouted. Heart pounding, he turned his horse and scrambled up the dirt bank of the channel toward the fire.

They rode along the bank parallel to the fire, eyes squinted against the smoke as they searched for a glimpse of the lost pair. The dry grass rippled with half-invisible orange flame, the blackening of the bleached brown stalks sometimes the only sign of the fire's advance. Marsupials no bigger than rats hopped past, and a lizard, his gray-green frill raised in alarm, skittered away and down the bank.

Luke undid the handkerchief knotted around his neck and retied it around his mouth, motioning to Sarah to do the same. The heat was palpable. Smoke seared the throat and drew streaming tears. Embers flew through the air as the sap exploded in the branches of the gum trees. The fire licked the exteriors of the trees, singed off their leaves and moved on, whipped along by the wind.

"Becka! Abby!" Luke yelled, his voice hoarse from smoke and from calling.

"Help! Help!"

The cries sounded louder, but it was difficult to

tell exactly where they were coming from. Then, a few hundred yards away, through the smoke and flames, he glimpsed a scrap of purple-and-gold. Becka's Winnie-the-Pooh T-shirt. Next to her was Abby in her lilac print dress. They were alive!

Then he took in the scene and his elation disappeared, overtaken by new heights of terror. Becka and Abby were trapped by the fire in a breakaway gully, huddled against the face of a crumbling dirt cliff. The fire was burning around both sides of the gully, curving to meet in the middle. There the band of fire was still narrow, but it was spreading fast. Soon it would be impassable.

"Daddy!" Becka screamed.

The horses trumpeted their terror, rearing and prancing. Sarah struggled to control her gray mare. Luke leaped from his horse and threw Sarah both sets of reins.

"Run, Becka. Run toward us." He fumbled for the water bottle and soaked his handkerchief.

Becka started to run, but Abby curled an arm protectively around her shoulders. "No!" she shrieked. "You'll be burned."

Luke cursed and yelled again, "Run, Becka. If you go fast enough you'll make it." He tied the handkerchief over his mouth.

Becka broke free and started toward her father. Then she realized Abby wasn't following. Hesitating, she glanced over her shoulder at Luke. Then turned to run back to Abby.

"*Becka!*" Luke bellowed his fear and frustration and plunged into the burning scrub. Abby was scared witless and unless he physically forced her and

Becka out they could die there in the fire—if not from flames, then from smoke.

Luke leaped and dodged through the burning bush, never leaving his feet in one spot long enough to catch fire. There was enough space between the bushes to avoid most of the flames, but red-hot embers were flying everywhere. Mixed with the smoke was the hot resiny scent of eucalyptus.

He made it to the rapidly diminishing area of unburned scrub and dropped to one knee to catch Becka as she catapulted herself into his arms. Tears of joy washed away the sting of the smoke. "Come on, possum, let's go home."

"Abby won't come," Becka wailed. "I can't leave her."

"Come on, Abby," he shouted, his voice rough with smoke and impatience. "If you stay here you'll be trapped."

Abby shook her head, stark terror sharpening her cheekbones and pinching her mouth into a thin line. "You can't tell me what to do. We're not on the station now."

She'd completely lost her senses. Desperate, Luke took her roughly by the arm and dragged her toward the burning no-man's-land. Whimpering, Becka followed.

He glanced across and saw Sarah. She'd put the horses on the other side of the watercourse and was about to enter the burning scrub. He shook his head sharply. She hesitated, then to his relief, stayed where she was, clutching the saddle blanket she'd unstrapped from her horse.

At the edge of the flames Abby balked again, so firmly Luke couldn't budge her. "Goddamn it, Abby, you've got to come *now*. Don't make me go through the fire twice, once to take Becka out and once to save you."

She put her hands over her face. "I can't. I won't."

A burning spark flew against her bare leg. She shrieked and leaped back. More embers fell around them, igniting the grass. They were out of time. And out of choices.

Luke picked up Becka and ran with her across the burning scrub, while she screamed over her shoulder for her aunt. He heaved her onto the spare horse, then went back for Abby. As he ran toward her a gust of wind flung a burning branch against her head and arm. Flames licked up hot and fresh, burning cotton and singeing flesh. Abby's hair was on fire. Behind him, Becka screamed.

Then suddenly Sarah was beside Abby, wrapping the horse blanket around her head and shoulders, dragging her by the arm. He hurried to help Sarah pull the sobbing woman to safety.

Sarah quickly mounted her horse and reached down to help Luke as he lifted up Abby. Sarah's face turned pale at the sight of Abby's blistered flesh, but he saw her jaw set and knew she wouldn't let him down.

"Can you hold on to Sarah, Abby?" Luke asked.

Abby nodded weakly and clung to Sarah's waist.

Luke swung onto his horse, then gathered up the reins of the black, where Becka clung to saddle and mane. His horse reared and leaped forward. "Hang on tight, Becka. Let's fly."

The horses, free of restraint at last, galloped down the dry watercourse. On the opposite bank, trees burst into flame. Triumph surged through Luke as he urged his horse on faster. Against the odds, they'd found Becka and Abby and would bring them home safely. Abby was burned, but she would survive. They came to the junction of the two channels and turned right to head downstream along the main channel. All they had to do was ride through the gorge to the vehicle and get out to the road—

"Luke!"

He glanced back at Sarah's desperate cry. Bloody hell! Abby's hold was slipping and she'd slid halfway off the horse. Sarah was hauling on the reins with one hand and hanging on to Abby with the other, but she couldn't halt the woman's downward slide. Luke wheeled in the middle of the main channel and charged over, but before he could grab her, Abby slid semiconscious from the back of the horse and fell to the ground.

Luke leaped from his horse and crouched beside Abby, checking her pulse and lifting her eyelids in a quick assessment of her condition. She was badly burned on her arm, scalp and back and just barely alive.

"Aunt Abby!" Becka cried, and jumped off her horse.

Luke shot a glance at Sarah, who dismounted to hold the weeping Becka in her arms while he tipped the water bottle to Abby's cracked and unresponsive lips. *Damn it, Abby, don't die now.*

"Sarah, call 000 for Emergency Services." He turned to his daughter. "Becka, get me the first aid kit from the back of my horse."

Becka ran to do as he asked. Thank God she was safe. He'd so nearly lost her. And he didn't have a moment to scold her or to tell her he loved her. After fishing in his pocket for his penknife, he began carefully cutting away Abby's dress around the burned area.

Sarah jabbed the buttons on her phone and then spoke in urgent tones to the dispatcher, explaining in terse sentences the predicament they were in. And what a predicament, Luke thought. The fire was raging all along the right bank of the main channel. How long before it leaped to the opposite bank? How long before it cut off the narrow gorge farther downstream, trapping them?

Abby's pulse was weak and she drifted in and out of consciousness. Probably just as well, considering how much pain she must be in. Luke ripped open the paper protecting the sterile gauze pads in the first aid kit Becka handed him and gently laid them on Abby's burns.

"Where exactly are we?" Sarah called to him.

On the road to hell. "When we get to the road we'll be at the junction of the Lawrence Track and Rodney's Road, roughly one hundred kilometers north of the developmental road. Tell them to send the Flying Doctor."

Abby's eyes fluttered open. Tears welled, then flowed down her cheeks, leaving streaks in the sooty grime.

"Becka? Where's Becka?" she rasped.

"Becka's okay. Quiet now. Everything's going to be fine." He'd finished covering her burns with sterile dressings and begun to lightly secure them with gauze tape.

"I'm right here, Aunt Abby," Becka said, putting

a small hand on her aunt's unburned arm. "Don't worry. Sarah's calling the Flying Doctor."

Abby's eyes closed and she muttered something unintelligible. Luke tied off the gauze tape and instructed Becka to offer Abby more water. This time she was able to drink.

Becka tugged at his sleeve. "Daddy?"

Luke glanced at his daughter and his heart turned over. Her blond hair was a sooty tangled mess and she had ash smeared from forehead to chin. "What is it, possum?"

"I'm sorry I went with Abby." Her voice wobbled, but she held his gaze. "I knew it was wrong."

He gripped her hand hard. "When I found out you'd left the Land Cruiser and gone off into the bush—"

Tears spilled down her cheeks. "Please don't hate me."

"*Hate* you?" Lord, what had he done to make her think that? Rather, what had he *not* done? He pulled her into his arms and held her close. "Becka, I love you. I was so afraid I'd lose you."

Her arms tightened around his neck, bringing tears into his eyes. Healing tears that washed away the grief and dissolved the barriers between them. They clung together for a long precious moment. Finally Becka pulled away and a fragile smile lit her grimy face. "I love you, Daddy."

A warm glow curled around Luke's heart as he returned her smile. He had his little girl back.

A gum tree cracking brought him back to the urgency of their situation. He rose to his feet and joined Sarah, who was shoving her cell phone in her backpack. She touched his cheek and her finger came away streaked with red. She started to reach for the first aid kit.

"Daddy! Sarah!" Becka's urgent cry stilled her hand and they both turned. Becka was pointing to the middle of the main channel, where flames engulfed a clump of gidyea.

Luke glanced at the burning bush, then over his shoulder at the far side of the channel. As quick as that the bank was alight. Intense heat seared his face as the hot wind whirled ash and embers through a merciless white sky.

"Sarah, help me lay Abby over the front of my horse," he called. "Becka, do you think you can ride by yourself?" She nodded vigorously. "Then let's go!"

When they were mounted Luke wheeled his horse and dug in his spurs. The horses needed no urging to escape the fiery bush. Necks stretched and nostrils flaring, they took off at full gallop down the dusty watercourse in a race against time.

At the gorge, Luke, Sarah and Becka were forced to rein in to prevent the horses from breaking legs in the rocks and debris from previous floods. Panting and snorting, their coats shiny with sweat and flecked with lather, the horses picked their way through, emerging just as the fire lit the trees on the high banks overhead.

Back on the flat again they broke into a gallop. Luke glanced over at his daughter, a tiny thing clinging to her horse like a limpet. Beyond her, Sarah leaned forward in the saddle, her hair streaming from beneath her broad-brimmed hat. City girl or not, she had guts. She was a battler, all right; a survivor. And he was damned glad she was with him.

Luke didn't waste time transferring Abby to the Land Cruiser but galloped past the campsite, up the bank to the rutted track and out to the road. There he slid Abby off his horse and laid her gently in the grass beside Bazza's bullcatcher. "I'll go back for the Land Cruiser," he said to Sarah. "You wait with Abby and Becka for the Flying Doctor."

Twenty minutes passed in tense silence and Luke had returned with the Land Cruiser, his horse trotting behind, before they heard the sound of a small plane engine. He stood in the middle of the road and waved his arms to signal their location. Out of the vast blue sky the white plane descended, raising swirling clouds of red dust as it landed with a series of light bumps on the road and taxied toward them.

The plane came to a halt and the door opened. Out stepped a pretty young nurse in a whiter-than-white uniform, followed by the doctor with her black bag. From the other side stepped the pilot in his navy pants, peaked cap and white shirt with epaulettes. Luke felt like cheering and Becka actually did yell "Hooray!"

"Will she be okay, Doc?" Luke asked the serious-faced woman with short-cropped brown hair, as she crouched beside Abby with a stethoscope. Close by, the nurse prepared an IV.

The doctor rose. "She'll live. There'll be some scarring, undoubtedly. Let's get her on board."

Luke helped her and the pilot load Abby onto a stretcher and into the plane. He felt a small hand on his sleeve and turned to see Becka looking worriedly after her aunt. To let his child out of his sight so soon after near tragedy would be a wrench, but...

"Would you like to go with her and make sure she's okay?" he said to Becka.

Becka nodded, a smile beaming through her tears. "Thank you, Daddy." She turned to climb aboard, then paused and said anxiously, "Will you come and get me later?"

"No worries." Luke blinked away the moisture in his eyes.

CHAPTER THIRTEEN

SARAH HESITATED outside the door to Luke's bedroom. It was past midnight, two days after they'd safely emerged from the burning bushland. Abby was in the hospital, her condition stable. Becka had had her cuts and bruises tended to and was tucked up in bed after a story from her father. All was once again right with the world at Burrinbilli.

But Sarah couldn't sleep. The bushfires might be under control, but she had a fire burning inside her that was as big as western Queensland.

And Luke was the only man who could quench the flames.

Two days ago, after making sure Becka and Abby were okay, Luke had downed a quick meal and gone back to help fight the bushfires. As a landholder he was a member of the rural fire brigade and called upon in emergencies. Once the fires were under control he'd staggered home, fallen into bed and slept for fourteen hours solid.

Sarah thought that for a man of Luke's strength and stamina that should be plenty of time to recover. Now she wanted to know if the promise of intimacy she and Luke had begun to explore under a moonlit sky was real. And she didn't want to wait another moment to find out.

She'd been lying sleeplessly in bed when she'd

heard the shower running in the bathroom. She'd waited, hoping he'd see the light under her door and come to her. He hadn't, so she had come to him.

Just as she lifted her hand to knock, the door opened. Luke's hair was damp and brushed straight back, one lock escaping to fall over his brow. He wore cotton drawstring trousers of deep indigo that looked as though they came from Thailand and a white cotton singlet that gleamed against his bronzed skin. The glow of the bedside lamp highlighted the curve of his muscular shoulders and sculpted his biceps with shadows.

His blue eyes were intensely focused on her and his slightly curving mouth was dead serious. He was inside-out gorgeous, and Lord, she wanted him. More than that, she wanted him to lose himself in her and emerge changed, the way she'd been changed by him. "Luke…?"

His gaze swept down her, taking in the thin cotton knit nightgown that clung to breasts and hips. "Come in."

Sarah stepped into the room, her gaze locked with his as he reached around her to shut the door. She was totally joyous things had finally come to this. And she couldn't stand another second without touching him. They had to get physical before they singed each other's skin off with their eyes.

Luke grasped her around her waist and his fingers seemed to burn her skin right through her nightgown. She slid her hands beneath the front of his singlet and shut her eyes at the deep rippling shudder that went across his stomach muscles. He smelled of sandalwood and smoke and she reveled in the glory of hard muscles and hot skin. His hands stroked down her hips to slide up under her nightie.

"Sarah," he said, his voice low and hoarse, and kissed her.

His lips were warm and tender and deliciously firm, his mouth and hands light upon her. Beneath the haze of desire she began to realize he was keeping himself under rigid control. Surely the time for control had passed.

"Touch me," she whispered.

Luke groaned and moved his hands lovingly over her back and down her legs, making her feel all hot and soft inside. Through the thin cotton of their clothing she could feel that he himself was hot, but oh, so hard. Mercy on her, he wanted her, too. This moment wasn't going to end with a simple kiss. Oh, no.

Luke murmured something sexy and sweet in her ear, and her breasts ached under his caress as he teased her with devouring kisses that stoked the need growing inside her.

Sarah pushed his singlet up and over his shoulders and began planting kisses across his abdomen. The drawstring of his pants yielded to her tug and they slid down to reveal the top of a curling mass of dark blond hair. Her hands splayed against his hips; her tongue took a leisurely trip south. With a gasp he gently drew her back into his arms.

"I won't even make it to Redfern if you carry on like this," he said.

"We're no longer on the Redfern line," she said, and pulled a small package from the waistband of her panties. "*I* made the trip to the chemist."

"Well, now aren't you an enterprising young

woman,'' he said with a delighted smile. "Did you meet up with any of the town's good-hearted gossip-mongers?"

She chuckled. "Not a one. I timed my visit to coincide with a meeting of the Country Women's Association."

"Pretty clever for a city girl. How did I get so lucky?" Without waiting for an answer, he grasped the hem of her nightgown and pulled it slowly over her head. Her lightly freckled breasts glowed against his darker skin and their rosy tips brushed his chest.

Sarah met his mouth in a long deep kiss that left her knees as weak as a newborn lamb's. As she sagged against him Luke swung her into his arms and carried her to his bed. "Give me a second," he said, taking the packet from her. "Okay."

He moved over her and Sarah moaned as his naked body brushed hers. She ran her hands over him and he felt to her as though he were burning up, hotter than a bushfire, harder than the horns of his new bull.

"I want you." His voice was husky as he teased and caressed her with his lips, his hands, his body.

"Luke," she breathed, "I'm way past want and into need."

He parted her legs with his knee and slowly filled her, stretching her, making her long for everything only he could give her. Perspiration beaded at his hairline with the effort he was making to control his movements. She moaned and pushed upward with her hips, pulling him down, urging him closer. Holding her gaze, he set his hips in motion, slow at first, rocking, rocking, moving in time with the beat of their hearts.

She gazed into his blue eyes and her heart seemed

to pause to look at him. This was what she'd yearned for, this oneness with Luke—mind, body and soul.

Then he dipped his head and sucked an erect nipple into his mouth. It electrified her, and her movements became jerky and uncoordinated, her need more urgent. Luke put his hands on her hips and brought her back into rhythm, rocking faster. He himself was on the very edge, his body rigid with tension, yet controlled in order to give her pleasure. She gazed down at their joined bodies, glistening in the lamplight under a sheen of perspiration. A moan escaped her throat as pleasure built into pressure that couldn't be contained but clamored for release.

"Come with me, Sarah," he said hoarsely, as if the words had been torn from him.

"Yes...oh, Luke. Luke."

He moved inside her with long strong strokes. Her body slick with sweat, matched his rhythm, pushing against him, straining, holding back, then reaching for the peak moment, for the blissful leap into the unknown.

His cry mingled with hers as the moment came when light expanded and time stood still with hallucinogenic clarity. Sarah tumbled into chaos, ears ringing, eyes dazzled, body melting, heart saturated with love. *Luke. Luke. Luke.*

When Luke awoke, hours later, the bedside lamp still burned and his head was cradled on her breast. Opening his eyes wider, he gazed with pure pleasure at the expanse of lightly freckled skin curving away from his line of sight. Arousal stirred his body and he shifted higher to drop kisses randomly over her shoulders and down her breast.

"What are you doing?" she murmured, her voice soft with sleep.

"I'm on a mission to kiss every one of your freckles. I reckon if I start now I'll be done by the end of the Wet."

She smiled. "Then what?"

"Then—" he kissed his way to the tip of her breast "—I'll start all over again."

Twisting in his arms, she turned to face him. "I won't be here at the end of the Wet. I won't even be here at the beginning." Her voice was light, but her eyes were sober. And questioning.

He met her gaze with one equally serious. Now was the moment to say what was in his heart. That he loved the way she was so natural and direct, so generous with love and laughter, so courageous and determined. How he sensed her longing for a meaningful life and shared that desire, and ached to share the journey with her, as well. He ached to tell her she was strong and beautiful and very, very special.

In the few short weeks she'd been at Burrinbilli he'd leaped the chasm between not feeling and feeling and now his heart was so full of love he thought it would burst like a seed pod in spring. He'd be more than proud and beyond happy to be her man.

Yes, now was the time to say all this and more, he thought, gazing into her honest, loving eyes. Now was the time to ask her to stay. To marry him. He swallowed, opened his mouth. Something seemed to block his throat.

This was Sarah, he reminded himself. For her he longed to move mountains, to overcome his deep reserve. But how to express the unfamiliar and intense emotions swirling through him? He was desperately afraid he'd say the wrong thing. There were too many unresolved issues between them that couldn't be disposed of with "I love you." If he spoke now, without thinking through what he wanted to say, his clumsy words might ruin everything.

Better not to speak at all.

"Then I reckon I should cut to the chase." He pulled her to him, relieved to hear her soft laughter and feel her arms close around his neck. With all the tenderness and passion he possessed he made love to her again. And again.

Later, as Sarah slept, her auburn hair spread across his pillow, Luke lay awake and contemplated the future. Burrinbilli belonged to her by right. Sure, he had a claim, too, but by all that he believed in, all the moral and ethical values he held close to his heart, he had to acknowledge that she had the stronger claim. Even if she didn't realize now how important Burrinbilli was to her—not her mother but *her*—she would one day, and then how could *he* be the one who had taken it away from her? She was looking for her destiny and more than anything he wanted her to find it and be fulfilled.

Because he loved her, he would give up Burrinbilli.

The miserable catch was, it meant he would have to give up her, as well. For, once he'd sold his half, he would have nothing to offer her. A man who couldn't give his woman a home and a life didn't deserve to ask her to marry him. And if he couldn't support Sarah, how could he ask her to give up all she had in Seattle to throw her lot in with him?

Restless, now that he knew what he had to do, Luke threw back the covers and pulled on his pants.

He moved through the dark house, running his fingertips across the timber door frames, gazing around at the familiar and much loved, already grieving for its loss. In the kitchen Wal lifted his head in his corner by the stove and whimpered a puzzled greeting. "Too early, Boss, even for you," he seemed to say.

Luke poured himself cold water from the fridge. "Am I hopelessly old-fashioned to want to provide for and support my family, Wal?"

Wal licked his bare foot. Luke took that as a qualified yes; he might be old-fashioned, but there was nothing wrong with that.

He hunkered down to scratch the dog behind his ears. "You know, Wal, there's an old saying that the quickest way to own a station is to marry the owner's daughter. Or in this case, the owner herself. That's not my way." He lifted Wal's muzzle and spoke directly to him. "*You* understand, don't you, mate?"

Would Sarah understand? She was a woman of the new millennium and probably felt it didn't matter which partner brought wealth to the family. But pride and self-sufficiency were part of who he was, and if Sarah loved him at all, she had to love that aspect of him, too. He could only hope that their relationship would endure with time, renewed during her visits to her mother. Eventually he would find another station he could afford and he would ask her to marry him.

If she hadn't married someone else by then.

SARAH AWOKE in the pale dawn light, blinked at the unfamiliar bedroom, then smiled as memories flooded back of the previous night. Outside, magpies warbled in concert with her singing heart. She rolled over, reaching for Luke.

The space beside her in bed was empty.

Disappointment stabbed through her, but she quickly set it aside. He'd probably gone to the bathroom and would be back any minute. She dozed a little, concocting dreamy delicious fantasies of what they'd do when he did return.

When she opened her eyes again, light flooded the room and she was still alone. Damn. She'd missed him again. She grabbed her watch on the bedside table and groaned. Ten o'clock. He'd be out on the cattle run and she wouldn't see him till lunchtime.

Ten o'clock! Becka would be up. Sarah knew they would want to tell the girl about their relationship soon, but she was pretty sure Luke wouldn't want his daughter accidentally coming across her in his bed.

She got up, threw on her nightgown and quickly made the bed. Then she peeped around the door to see if the coast was clear and ran lightly down the hall, back to her own room.

A few minutes later she was singing in the shower, her spirits bubbling along with the foaming bath gel. When she'd told her mother she wanted a "real" man she hadn't really believed the creature of her fantasy existed. Now she knew different. Luke was everything she'd ever wanted and much more. He was strong yet vulnerable, passionate yet tender, full of moral and physical courage. He was bigger than her fantasy; he was his own man.

She turned off the water and stepped out of the shower. With the heel of her hand she cleared the fogged mirror to peer at her reflection. Luke's evasion of her oblique query about the future was somewhat less than reassuring, but she pushed her nervousness aside. This was Luke. If it took him a little time to get used to being in love, well, she could be patient.

Smiling again, she emerged from the bathroom wrapped in a big fluffy towel, with another around her wet hair turban style. Down the hall she ran into Becka coming out of her room. "G'day, Beck, how ya goin'?" she said gaily, practicing an Aussie accent.

"Uh, okay." Becka stared at her. "Are you all right?"

"Couldn't be better. An' never a word of a lie." Pivoting, she grinned at the wide-eyed girl over her shoulder and sauntered back to her room to dress.

She met up with Becka again in the kitchen. "Where's your dad?" she asked, spreading jam over a slice of apricot-and-macadamia nut bread.

Becka got the cold water from the fridge and made herself a glass of cordial. "He's gone to Longreach."

"Longreach! What for?"

Becka shrugged and sipped her drink. "I don't know."

Sarah took a bite of toast and chewed thoughtfully. She was surprised Luke had undertaken the long trip without mentioning it to her. Surprised and a little hurt. On the other hand, Luke wouldn't have given up a working day except for some very important reason. No doubt he'd tell her about it when he got home.

"In that case, maybe you and I should go visit Abby this morning."

"Oh, can we?" Becka's eyes lit. "Poor Aunt Abby, she didn't mean to cause trouble."

Sarah bit her tongue. Becka and her aunt loved each other and she didn't want to damage that. But Abby had real problems that needed to be addressed.

After breakfast they gathered a big bouquet of flowers from the garden and headed for the Murrum Bush Nursing Hospital in the utility truck.

"Doesn't driving on the Downs bother you anymore?" Becka asked after they'd gone some distance in silence.

Sarah was startled out of a daydream about Luke. The road was so straight and empty she'd gotten used to focusing only a hundred yards ahead. As long as her peripheral vision was on the alert for road trains it seemed to work. She hadn't had a panic attack since they'd gone after Becka and Abby, but she never knew when one would strike next.

"I'm learning to cope. When I'll really be over it, I can't say. How did you know about that?"

"Dad explained it to me when I asked why you couldn't take me shopping." Her blond brows knitted anxiously. "He didn't want to tell your secret, but he didn't want me to think badly of you, either."

"It's okay, honey," Sarah assured her, reaching out to stroke her head. "It's a little embarrassing, but I don't mind *you* knowing."

Becka smiled shyly. "Thanks."

"Your dad is a pretty special man, you realize. He really loves you a lot. I've never seen anyone so worried as when you went missing."

Becka sighed. "I was never so glad to see anyone as him when we were trapped by that fire."

"You were very brave. And smart."

"What do you mean?"

"That arrow of stones you made led us right to you. Your dad taught you that, didn't he?"

She nodded. "He's taught me a lot of useful things about the bush."

"Because he wants you to feel at home there. He'd be very sad if you didn't want to live at the station with him."

Becka stared at her hands, linked in her lap. "I want to live with him. But I want Aunt Abby, too."

"Maybe Abby will come and live there with you." Sarah flinched at the thought of Abby in permanent residence.

Becka shook her head. "Abby won't live at the station."

"Doesn't she like the station life? Too isolated?" Once upon a time Sarah would have understood that very well. Now the station seemed not only a haven from the toils of the city but a rich and varied existence.

"It's not that. She wants to be boss of her own house. And she doesn't want to be a burden on anyone else."

Self-sufficiency seemed to be a common virtue out here, Sarah thought. And just as commonly carried to a fault. But Becka's revelation gave her an idea.

Abby was covered in bandages on her upper right side and propped up in the big hospital bed. Tears filled her eyes when she saw Becka and she gushed with gratitude over the flowers. Sarah stood back, fighting lingering feelings of anger for the danger in which she'd placed Becka.

"Becka, will you go ask the nurse for a vase?"

Abby said after a long hug and mutual exchanges of affection with her great-niece. Becka skipped off.

"I'm sorry about your burns," Sarah said, taking a step closer to the bed. "How are you feeling?"

Abby eyed her warily. "I'll be okay."

"Becka would have been very upset if anything had happened to you."

Tears filled Abby's mismatched eyes. "Are you going to take my darling girl away from me?"

"What on earth are you talking about?"

"You'll marry Luke and then you'll be Becka's mother," Abby blurted, dabbing at her watery eyes with a crumpled tissue. "And I'll be nobody with no one to love me."

"That's not true," Sarah protested, though she wasn't sure which part she was denying. Did she want to marry Luke? Yes! Would he ask her? She had no idea. "Becka loves you."

"You won't be good for Luke, you know," Abby continued spitefully. "He needs a wife who can be a help to him, not a hindrance. Your mother was Australian, but you're not. You're not from the bush and you never will be."

Sarah was silent, thinking of Luke's dreams of self-sufficiency. As much as she hated to admit it, Abby was right. For all that the outback was part of the modern world, computer skills weren't very useful when it came to milking cows or canning fruits and vegetables.

"You'll ruin his life and you'll take her away from me," Abby stated accusingly.

"No, I won't," Sarah said firmly. She would never do anything that would be harmful to Luke. "But you'll have to learn to share Becka, and respect Luke's authority.''

Abby sniffed and glanced away, clearly not wanting to take advice from Sarah. A moment later, her mouth twisted and her face crumpled. "I won't run off with her again—I promise. I wouldn't ever hurt my baby.''

"I'm sure you wouldn't do it deliberately," Sarah said in a rush of compassion. She put a hand on Abby's where it rested on the coverlet. "You'll find the help you need and everything will be okay.''

Abby took a deep breath to get herself under control. "I—I'm sorry about the snake. I didn't think you'd actually encounter one. Fewer people are bitten by snakes in Australia than foreigners tend to think, you know.''

"Tell it to the tourist bureau," Sarah said dryly. "But you're probably right. Just don't be surprised if I double-check any bush survival tips from you.''

Abby gave her a wan smile. "I don't know many, anyway.''

As Sarah drove back through Murrum she realized she was looking at its wide streets and colorful buildings with new affection. She waved to Len, who was sweeping the footpath outside his store; slowed to let the sheep amble off the road and stopped to say hello to someone she'd met at the ball. Although she hadn't been here long she felt she belonged. Her ancestors' history in the area helped and people seemed to accept her for herself.

But Abby had cultivated the seed of doubt lying in a dark corner of Sarah's mind.

With the best will in the world could she be what Luke needed in a wife? Even if she mastered the diverse tasks—cook, nurse, teacher, accountant, stockman—the list was endless. Would she be able to handle the way of life in the long term? Or would she quit the first time they were cut off by floods for months at a time during the Wet? Could she handle the heat and the dust and the isolation? Or would she miss her old life in Seattle too much? She'd worked hard to build a career. Could she really just give it all away?

How could she be sure she was up to the challenge of station life? And if she wasn't sure, was it fair to Luke to attempt it? *Luke, I'll give it a shot, but I can't guarantee I'll still be here this time next year.* What kind of a vow was that? And what about Becka's feelings? Sarah wiped sweaty palms on her short skirt and regripped the slippery steering wheel. She didn't even want to think about what such an upheaval would do to Becka.

Back at the station she left Becka working on the computer and went to her room. There was only a page or two left of the diary. Propped on one elbow she leafed through it till she found the place she'd left off:

December 5, 1971. We did it. Warren and I. We actually did *It.* Down by the water hole, among the river red gums. It was wonderful. I'm so in love with him I'm over the moon. The only bad part was seeing Abby sneaking off through the trees afterward. Hateful girl, she was spying on us! She thought that when I broke up with Len she would get him, but Len's gone off to Sydney and no one knows when he's coming back now that his mum had to sell the station and go to work in the store.

April 8, 1972. I'm pregnant. Warren and I are getting married and we're going to live in Seattle. I've never been so happy. I've longed to leave for so long and now it's really happening. I'll miss Mum and Dad something fierce. And Burrinbilli, too. But this is my chance. I love Warren and I'm going to love having his baby. I feel bad about Len. He's a good man and I'd hate to think I ruined his life as Abby says— but I feel like my life has finally begun.

Sarah closed the diary and rolled onto her back to stare at the ceiling. Suddenly she missed her own life with a sharp stabbing sense of loss. She missed her work and her friends and her mother. She missed Seattle: the stores and the traffic and everyone speaking with the same accent as her. She missed the soft cool rain, the dark green trees and the deep-blue waters of Puget Sound on a sunny day.

She wanted to go home.

She picked up the phone to call her mother. She'd spoken to Anne briefly a few days earlier to let her know the runaways had been found safely. Now Sarah needed a heart-to-heart.

Anne answered on the second ring. Her warm, welcoming voice only reinforced Sarah's homesickness. "Hello, darl'. Have things settled down a bit?"

Sarah relaxed on the bed. "The bushfires are under control. Becka's fine. Abby's recovering in the hospital."

"Good. Is Abby going to see a doctor?"

"Yes, Luke and I both talked to Dr. Murchison. He contacted a psychiatrist in Longreach and they'll work together. Her biggest problem is she can't ask for help." God, didn't she know someone else like that!

"Are you coming home soon?" Anne asked. "Don't you need to get back to your job?"

"I no longer have a job. Ron gave me an ultimatum when I asked for extra time to join the search for Becka."

"Never mind, darl'. You did the right thing. You'll find something else just as good."

"I'm not worried about that. I could probably sweet-talk him into giving me my old position back if I wanted it."

Sarah rolled over so she could gaze out the window at the gum trees. This was actually a much nicer view than city streets, when you thought about it. "I finished your diary. Mom. What happened to you and Warren? You seemed so in love."

Anne sighed heavily. "I don't know, darl'. I *thought* I loved him. But I think I was really in love with what he represented—a new and exciting world that I wanted to explore. He was my ticket to that world."

"How did he feel when he realized that?" Sarah asked slowly.

"He asked for a divorce."

There was a very long silence while Sarah readjusted her whole perspective on her parents' brief marriage.

"Oh, Sarah, I'm sorry. I realize he wasn't much of a father to you, but that was partly my fault. To his credit he bought Burrinbilli and hung on to it all those years for you.''

''For me? I thought he bought it as an investment.''

''A run-down cattle station was not a good investment in the seventies, not with beef prices rock bottom the way they were. No, he bought it because he knew that if he didn't I would sell it to someone else and you would never know your Australian heritage. He couldn't give you much, but he could give you that.''

Tears welled in Sarah's eyes. ''I wish I'd realized that. I always thought he didn't love me. If only I could have thanked him before he died.''

''Oh, Sarah, can you ever forgive me?'' Anne was crying, too. ''He never mentioned the station again all those years. I thought he must have sold it and I didn't want to raise your hopes only to have them dashed.''

''It's okay, Mom. *He* should have told me.'' She wiped her eyes with the back of her wrist. ''I still haven't figured out what to do with the station, and now that it's time for me to come home I think—''

''What, darl'?''

''I...nothing.''

''Is it, Luke?'' Anne guessed correctly. ''Outback life is a good life, Sarah. You're your own boss, the air is clean, the rat race a million miles away. It's a wonderful place to raise children.''

''A few weeks ago you were telling me it was the dusty back of beyond.'' It was also the center of the universe.

''But if you love him...'' Anne suggested gently.

Sarah got up to pace her room. ''He hasn't said

anything to me about staying. He needs and wants someone who'll be a real partner. I had fun doing the muster, but when the novelty wears off, then what?''

"Then you'd better hope that what you feel for him is real."

"Do you want the station, Mom?'' Sarah asked point-blank.

"I know you wanted to do something special for me,'' Anne said slowly, "and I love you for it...but it's not the life for me. I hope you understand.''

Sarah was oddly relieved. "I do, Mom. Now that I've spent some time here I can see why you might not want to take on the responsibility. I'm asking, because if you don't want it, I'm going to sell it to Luke.''

"Oh, Sarah, are you sure?'' Anne said, dismayed. "Once you let it go you'll never get it back.''

Sarah felt tears seep into her eyes again, for Luke and for the station and for all she would lose when she left.

"'Who seeks, and will not take, when once 'tis offered, shall never find it more,''' Anne quoted.

Sarah wiped the back of her wrist across her eyes. "Who said that?''

"Shakespeare, of course. Honestly, darl', you ought to read more instead of always sitting in front of a computer. It seems to me you've traveled a very long way in search of something and now that you've got it almost in your grasp you're backing away from it. That's not like you.''

"I want to be fair to Luke. He deserves his dreams, too.''

"Well, if he asks you to stay, then you'll know you're part of those dreams."

That was a mighty big *if*. And one Sarah was afraid to put to the test. Yet deep in her heart she cherished the hope that he *would* ask her to remain.

CHAPTER FOURTEEN

SARAH SAID GOODBYE to her mother and went to the kitchen to make a jug of iced tea. The Land Cruiser pulled up beside the house, sending her heart into double time. Becka was still at the computer. Now was her chance to talk to Luke.

But when he came through the door and cast her a brooding glance instead of taking her in his arms Sarah felt he was already someone she'd lost and would never find again. Silently she poured two glasses of iced tea and brought them to the table.

"We need to talk," they both said at the same time.

"Go ahead," Sarah said with a nervous laugh.

Luke shook his head, obdurately polite. "Ladies first."

"Okay. Well, I—I've made a decision. I'm going to sell you my half of the station." She sipped her iced tea and hurried on, ignoring the incredulous look on his face. "I've talked to my mother. She's not coming back here to live. It's not her 'thing.' And please don't say 'I told you so.'"

He smiled. "Did I say that?"

"No, but you were thinking it."

"So…" he said slowly, "is it *your* thing?" His eyes were opaquely blue, his thoughts hidden.

There was only one way to answer him. Honestly.

"I don't know. That's why I'm going back to Seattle."

He was silent a long time. "You've already decided."

"I still have that plane reservation. I forgot to cancel it when we went after Becka and haven't given it a thought since. Until this morning when I realized I would have to leave today in order to make my flight in Brisbane."

"And last night? Doesn't that mean anything?"

"It was wonderful. I'll never forget it—or you." She dropped her gaze, afraid to look at him in case she broke down. "If you wouldn't mind getting an evaluation of the property so we can negotiate terms by e-mail…"

Luke took a folded paper from his top pocket and spread it on the table. "I've just come from a rural property agent in Longreach. He knows Burrinbilli and this is his official estimate of its worth, including livestock."

Sarah stared at the paper. "But…?"

"I'm selling you *my* half," he explained, his voice neutral. "It's yours by birthright. Land isn't something you let go lightly. You keep it—for your children, if not for yourself."

Her children, not *their* children.

"I daresay some around here will be disappointed there won't be a local computer expert to call on," he added. "Jacqui over at the School of the Air— sorry, Distance Education—was asking if you'd consider teaching computer skills to the kids from home. I told her you had a job in Seattle and I wasn't sure you'd be here."

Sarah shrugged, not bothering to inform him she

no longer had a job. She would have loved to teach kids over the air, but if Luke didn't care if she stayed or not, doing so would be too painful to bear.

"I'll see if I can find you another manager—"

"I don't want to buy," Sarah interrupted. "I want to sell."

"Well, you can't if I refuse to buy."

"If *you* won't buy, then someone else will." Argh, shades of her mother. But this was different. Wasn't it? "Forget I said that. I don't know what I'm saying anymore." And she didn't. Her emotions were up, down, all over the place. She had no idea what she felt or what she thought. One minute she wanted to marry Luke, the next minute she couldn't climb on that plane fast enough. She pushed away her iced tea and got up from the table. "My offer stands. I won't change my mind on *that*."

Luke rose, too. "Are you really going back to Seattle?"

"Is there any reason I shouldn't?" She looked him in the eye, silently challenging him to say what was on his mind, in his heart. And wished she had the courage she was demanding of him.

After a long moment, he dropped his gaze and shook his head, unable or unwilling to answer. Then he crossed to take his hat off the peg. "As I was telling you—I'll stay on until you find another manager, or until I find another station, whichever comes first."

Sarah bit her lip to keep it from trembling. What had happened between last night and this morning to change him so utterly? Where was their hard-won intimacy? Had he awoken this morning feeling too close for comfort? Or was it simply *her* he was afraid of? A woman who could share a laugh, even his bed, but who would never share his dreams.

To see her fears substantiated in Luke's estimation hurt more than she could have guessed.

"*You* buy it, Luke." Her voice sounded colder than she'd ever heard it, but who cared? If he wanted to deny all that had passed between them she could be as tough as he. "Keep it for Becka. You told me yourself properties small enough to be affordable don't often come on the market."

He paused at the door. "There's an obvious solution to our dilemma."

"Yes?" She waited, *knowing* what he was about to suggest. Praying it was so, yet not really believing it.

"We get married, equal partners in the station."

Yes! She waited again, for some mention of love. Nothing.

She turned her head, lest he see the depth of her disappointment. "I can't marry unless it's for love."

He was quiet a moment, then he nodded, deferring to her feelings. The window of opportunity closed.

Inside, she wanted to scream; outwardly, she remained cool. "It won't take me long to pack. Can you drive me into town?"

"I'll drive you to the train station in Longreach."

"It's not necessary. The bus comes right into Murrum."

"You don't have to take the bus. I'll give you a lift."

"I *want* to take the bus." Did she have to spell it out? Even the bus was preferable to spending any longer than she had to in the company of a man who could make love to her and then treat her like a stranger.

"Luke?" she added when he started to leave.

He turned. "Yes?"

Was it her imagination or did his face lighten? No, maybe not. "I think I know a solution to the Abby problem."

"Oh, that." He frowned and shifted his weight. "Well, let's hear it."

"Becka told me it's not the town Abby doesn't want to leave but her house."

Luke shrugged. "So?"

"So why not move her house onto your property? Somewhere between the homestead and the road."

Head down, hands on hips, he considered her suggestion. "It would solve a lot of problems," he conceded. "I'll have a think about it and talk to Becka and Abby."

Clapping his hat on his head, Luke stepped onto the veranda and whistled for Wal.

Sarah sat on at the table in the quiet of the big kitchen. She gazed around the homey room at Becka's drawings on the fridge, the feed store calendar tacked to the cork board, a notice of the Winton race meeting. The vase of pink-and-yellow carnations Becka had picked yesterday. The radio phone with the portable radio stacked on top. The big brown Betty teapot and the quilted framed photo of Luke and Becka on their horses. All of it dear, and none of it hers.

The grandfather clock in the loungeroom chimed the hour. Time was running out on her outback adventure.

Wearily, Sarah rose, took her hat from its peg and

walked across the baking yard to the shed. It was time for Dorothy to go home.

"Come here, you wascally wabbit," she muttered. "You don't belong in captivity any more than I belong in Oz."

The skittish bunny thumped its hind feet twice and sped around the cage. Sarah reached in with both hands, snatched it up and cuddled it firmly in the crook of one arm, soothing its trembling body with her other hand. "There now, everything's going to be okay."

Becka appeared around the side of the shed. "Where are you taking Dorothy?" she said, running a gentle finger along the rabbit's flattened ears.

"Back to where I got her. She's completely healed. It's time she went home."

"I hope Bazza doesn't shoot her again."

"I think she'll know to be extra careful." Sarah hesitated. "Do you want to come with me?"

"Thanks, but Dad said I could go around the bores with him this morning."

Sarah smiled. Becka was hard to pry away from Luke's side these days. "That's okay. I'll see you before I go." At Becka's puzzled frown she added, "Didn't your dad tell you? I—I'm going back to Seattle."

Becka's eyes widened and she tucked her bottom lip under her teeth. "When?"

"Today. After lunch." Suddenly the immediacy of her departure hit her. With her free arm she crushed the girl to her side, bowing her head to kiss Becka's temple. "I'm going to miss you."

Becka's arms went around her waist. "Do you have to go?" she said, her voice muffled against

Sarah's shirt, her hat tilting so far it fell off into the dust.

"I'm afraid so." Sarah glanced up and saw Luke pause a hundred yards away. He looked over at them, then very deliberately turned his back and walked on.

How could he be so stoic? Didn't her departure mean anything to him? She stroked Becka's hair and sniffed back her tears. "You'd better go. Your dad's waiting."

Becka ran off, blond braids flying. Sarah felt her heart crack. "Let's go, Dorothy," she murmured to the rabbit, rubbing her cheek against its soft fur.

She walked along the creek bed until she came to the spot where Dorothy got caught in Bazza's trap. There she sat in the shade of the river gums and set Dorothy on the ground. "Off you go."

Dorothy stood on her hind legs and snuffed the air. Then without so much as a backward glance she hopped away into the long grass.

Sarah watched until the rabbit disappeared, brown coat blending into the endless dry plains of the Downs. She would never see the land in the Wet, when it was green and bursting with life. Stillness settled over her, and with it, a great sadness.

She lay in the grass and gazed up at the broad smooth limbs of the gum tree. Its slender sickle-shaped leaves fluttered silver and sage-green against the vaulted blue sky. She breathed in their mentho-lated scent and listened to the breeze wring their se-crets from them.

Something about this wide brown land had seeped into her soul. Maybe it had always been there. She felt an attachment so deep it was as though she'd been born here, right out of the ancient rust-red earth.

Now that she was leaving, she didn't want to go. But go she must. With an immense effort she shook off her lethargy and turned her face toward the homestead.

The house was cool and welcoming after the noonday sun. The overhead fans whirred quietly, moving the warm air in a semblance of a breeze. Sarah sliced cold meat and prepared a salad for lunch. Then she packed, showered and dressed for travel in the cotton skirt and top she'd arrived in. She put her bags in the entrance hall and waited for Luke and Becka.

When the others returned Sarah quickly saw that unless she set the tone, their last meal together would be a sober affair indeed. Rather than give in to tears and regrets, she forced herself to chatter gaily in the face of terse comments from Luke and gloomy sighs from Becka. By the time they were loaded in the Land Cruiser for the trip to Murrum she was emotionally exhausted.

In town they had a few minutes before the bus arrived so she went into Len's store. Bazza was there, too. Saying goodbye to them was harder than she'd thought, like leaving old friends.

Len came around the counter to grip her hand. "What am I going to do with fifty kilos of flavored coffee beans?"

"Open the first drive-through coffee stall in western Queensland?" She smiled through watery eyes and hugged him hard. "Thanks for everything, Len."

She turned to Bazza. "Don't take any potshots at Dorothy, you hear?"

"I reckon I'll give up rabbit hunting for a while. Come back and see us." When she went to hug him he reddened and thrust out a callused hand. "Cheers."

Sarah laughed and pumped his hand. "Send me your press kit. I know someone who knows someone who knows an agent. Just don't forget me when you're a big Hollywood star."

Outside, she heard the rumble of the bus down the main street and then the soft sigh of its brakes as it pulled up at the bus stop. Sarah glanced from Len's sloping shoulders to Bazza's youthful cocky stance and felt the tears start. "I'd better go."

She pushed through the plastic strips that lined the open doorway and hurried across the street to where Luke and Becka waited in the dappled shade of a gum tree. While Luke helped the driver load her suitcases onto the bus, Sarah hugged Becka.

"Promise to e-mail me?" she said to Becka.

"I promise."

"Good girl. Tell your dad if he wants to survive in cyberspace he'd better let you teach him a few things."

Becka giggled. Then pleaded, "Will you come back to visit?"

Sarah straightened, her smile fading. "I don't know about that, honey. But one thing is certain, I won't forget you. Ever."

Becka sat on the bus stop bench, put her arms around Wal's neck and buried her face in his rough black-and-white fur. Sarah blinked back the moisture in her eyes and glanced up as a tall figure stepped between her and the sun. Luke. How do you say goodbye to the man you love?

His arms went around her and she leaned into his embrace, pressing her cheek against his scratchy jaw and breathing in his scent of leather and dust and warm skin.

"Goodbye, Sarah." His voice broke on her name.

"Oh, Luke." She held him tightly and her lips found his in a too brief kiss. Then she pushed him away, even as he was about to kiss her again. She dug into her purse, pulled out a card wallet and began handing him cards. "Here's my home address and phone number and my cell phone number. This card's from the café where I hang out when I'm not working. This is my mother's home number and the number at her import store. Shall I write Mom's cell phone number on the back?"

He shook his head. "This is more than enough. I reckon I could find you if—"

What? she wondered frantically. *If you need me? Want me?*

"I'd have thought you'd have a business card."

Her mouth twisted. "I kinda got the old heave-ho. Asked for one too many leave extensions. You know how it is in the corporate world these days, no employer loyalty."

"You gave up your job for Becka," he said, his voice low and husky. "Thank you for that."

"It's nothing." She forced herself to smile to keep from crying. "Something else will come along. It always does."

The bus driver beeped his horn.

Sarah eased away from Luke and climbed onto the bus.

"Sarah?" Luke called.

"Yes?" *Too eager, girl, get a grip.* But the bus driver had started the bus and she leaned out, anxious not to miss a word beneath the drone of the diesel engine.

Luke shook his head. "Nothing. Enjoy your penthouse."

She nodded, swallowing hard. "Sure."

The doors clanged shut. From the window seat opposite the driver she waved to Luke and Becka, who stood with arms around each other, watching her leave. *Goodbye. Goodbye.* Becka wiped her eyes on her arm and waved wildly. Sarah waved back, although she could barely see for tears.

The big bus slowly moved away from the curb. Len and Bazza stood in the shade of the footpath outside Len's store as they rumbled past. *Goodbye. Goodbye.* She pressed her forehead against the glass and tried to smile. Farther up the street, people came out of the pub to wave farewell. Even the chemist in his white coat stepped onto the footpath and raised a hand as the bus passed.

By the time she was out of town she was blubbering. The driver, the same one who'd brought her out three weeks earlier, glanced sympathetically in the rearview mirror. "Some people don't take to the outback. Others have red dust running in their veins. I came here for a three-month stint. That was twenty-five years ago. I reckon you'll be back."

Sarah heaved a deep sigh. "I don't think so."

"WELCOME HOME, SARAH." Anne threw her arms around her daughter amid the swirling airport crowd. "My word, you're as brown as a berry!"

"Mom! It's so good to see you." Sarah hugged her back.

"You look like a jilleroo in that getup," Anne said, laughing with delight. "Very *outback*."

Sarah wheeled her luggage trolley toward the automatic doors that opened to the outside. "I guess my Akubra will keep off rain as well as sun," she said when she saw the rain sheeting down.

Anne unfurled a big blue umbrella and held it over both of them. "You're back in the Pacific Northwest, darl'."

"Burrinbilli could use a little of this wet stuff." She pulled her hat down low. "Shall we make a run for it?"

Back at her apartment Sarah relayed to Anne the details of her Australian trip. "Mmm, this coffee is wonderful," she said, dunking a hazelnut biscotti and slurping up the crumbling sweet softness.

"I'll bet you can't wait to drive through a coffee stall and have a night out at a jazz bar with your friends," Anne said. "Seattle has *so* much more to offer than Murrum."

"Oh, Mom, that's not fair. Seattle and Murrum are like apples and oranges. No one would ever claim Murrum has all the amenities of Seattle. But the outback has other things of value—a sense of community, fresh air, wide-open spaces...."

Anne laid a finger aside her jaw and gazed into the air with an affectation of puzzlement. "Was that *my* daughter who professed a horror of open spaces a few short weeks ago?"

"Okay, forget the open spaces. They still give me the heebie-jeebies." Sarah set her coffee cup on the table. "But people can be their own boss, make their own decisions. There's so much wildlife and bird life. The sunsets are out of this world, and the *stars!*"

"I grew up there, remember?" Anne said mildly.

"And it's a *wonderful* place to raise children. They learn to be so much more resourceful and mature than city children. Becka is only nine, but Luke is already teaching her how to drive the farm vehicles."

Anne laughed. "Sarah, you obviously think the outback is pretty fantastic. What I wonder is, why on earth did you leave?"

WHY, INDEED? Sarah wondered for the thousandth time later that week as she drove home from a day of job interviews. Several had been promising and one potential employer had offered her a position on the spot. She'd asked for a couple of days to think it over, but she was already framing her refusal. Why didn't she want to take it? Why this reluctance to get on with her life?

The wipers swished rain off the windshield. Her fax machine rang and a second later spewed out a page. Sarah glanced at it and tossed it aside. A message from an old client who obviously hadn't heard she no longer worked for the software company. Hohum. Her cell phone rang, but she couldn't be bothered answering it.

Maybe a coffee would perk her up. She spotted a drive-through stall ahead and signaled her intention to pull into the right lane so she could exit. A cherry-red BMW in that lane beeped its horn and sped up, not only refusing to let her in but clearly intending to get to the coffee stall first.

"Oh, no, you don't." She stepped on the accelerator and zipped in front of the BMW, as sweet as if she were cutting a steer from the mob. She grinned into the rearview mirror.

Her elation quickly turned to self-disgust. Was this all her life was about? Going from one drive-through coffee stall to another? Her biggest challenge beating an obnoxious Beemer to the head of the line?

Unfair, she scolded herself. There were countless rewarding and meaningful things with which she could occupy her time in the city. Less-fortunate people she could help, environmental problems she could tackle…

The real problem, she decided as she drove off with a double mochaccino, was that since coming home she'd felt hemmed in—*claustrophobic*, in fact. She couldn't breathe surrounded by all these tall buildings and low clouds. The very hills Seattle was built on seemed to be crowding her.

How ironic that now that she was back, she longed for the very open spaces she used to fear. She wondered if recognizing the connection in her mind between the Downs and the void Warren's death left would cause the anxiety attacks to abate. She might never know. But knowing her father had cared enough to keep Burrinbilli was a start in filling that void.

Yet it wasn't enough. The night before, she'd gone with friends to a favorite jazz bar and sat isolated in silence while the people whose style and taste she'd once admired squawked endlessly about trivialities. What a bunch of galahs.

Checking her e-mail had become the highlight of her day. Most days there'd be a message from Becka, occasionally one from Luke. His were mostly a dry transfer of information relating to station business.

Thin rations when she longed for so much more from him.

Hunched over the steering wheel, she gazed up as she passed the once-coveted penthouse, now with a ragged Sold sign fluttering from its roof. How could she ever have wanted to live way up there, cut off from the trees and the birds? The most wildlife she'd see from the fiftieth floor would be seagulls wheeling in search of garbage or gimpy-legged pigeons inching along the ledge like would-be suicides.

She'd been correct in thinking that all her emotional ups and downs would disappear when she got back to Seattle. Trouble was, now she felt nothing. No joy, no laughter, no pain. Just emptiness.

Without warning the tears she'd held back burst forth, filling her eyes, obscuring her vision. She pulled to the side of the road, her shoulders shaking. Her cell phone rang again. Blindly she jabbed the button to turn it off. Her coffee sat cooling in its special holder, utterly forgotten, as tears streamed down her face.

She loved Luke. And Becka. And Burrinbilli.

It didn't matter where they were on the face of the earth. *Love* was another country. You could read all the guide books you wanted, but you still have to take a leap of faith to surrender your passport and cross that border.

She was ready to make the trip.

"IT'S NO FUN anymore around here without Sarah," Becka complained, stirring her food around on her plate.

"She's back where she belongs," Abby said tartly.

"Mark my words, she'll forget about you soon enough."

Luke held his tongue. A week had passed since Sarah had left and he was still waiting for the pain of saying goodbye to recede. He guessed he'd be waiting a little longer.

"She thought I had talent," Bazza said. "I wonder if she remembered to send my press kit to that Hollywood agent."

Luke was roused from a slump over his half-eaten dinner. "*Bazza!* You didn't ask her to find you an agent, did you? Seattle is a thousand miles from Los Angeles."

Bazza shrugged. "She offered." He jabbed at his stew. "I miss her. And her little rabbit, too."

Luke had never felt this low, not even when he had to shoot five hundred head of cattle dying of thirst during the four-year drought. But he wasn't going to wallow in the muck of self-pity; he had to set an example for Becka. "Sure it's tough without her, but we can survive on our own."

Becka threw him a skeptical glance. He had to admit, his words sounded hollow. A deep sigh lifted his chest. There was a difference between mere survival and happiness.

"Why should we *have* to survive on our own?" Becka demanded. "Especially since Sarah wanted to stay with us."

"Did she *say* that?" Luke asked.

Becka wriggled in her chair. "No, I suppose not."

"You told her you loved her, didn't you?" Bazza said.

Now Luke shifted uncomfortably. "Are we going

to finish our meal or natter all night?'' he replied gruffly.

"For crying out loud, mate,'' Bazza chided. "I don't know much about sheilas, but I know that's the one thing they all want to hear. Besides 'Will you marry me?' that is.''

"Really, Bazza,'' Abby said. "I'm sure a modern young woman like Sarah has no wish to get married. Or if she does, she would prefer her own kind.''

Tired of the futile discussion and heartsore at constantly being reminded of Sarah, Luke pushed away from the table and went outside. Wal jumped to his feet, his nails clicking against the wood as he followed Luke off the veranda and across the yard.

"I reckon I stuffed up royally, Wal. What has being strong got me this time except an empty future? And if I'm such a tough guy, why couldn't I tell Sarah I loved her?''

Wal whined and gave a low yip.

"You're right, Wal, I'm a coward.''

From the rise beyond the shed he leaned on the fence and watched the sky turn bloodred with sunset. *Burrinbilli.* It was all he'd ever wanted and now it was his for the taking. Trouble was, it would always remind him of Sarah. Painfully. The way his leg ached during the Wet from a bad spill he'd taken off an unbroken horse ten years ago. Some hurts just didn't go away.

Damn it, why hadn't he told her he loved her?

SARAH PULLED HERSELF together and drove to her high-rise apartment building where she lived on the fourteenth floor, neither up nor down. Her heart weighed so heavy she felt as though her spirits would never lift again. She used to love this apartment block—before she'd been to Burrinbilli and discovered out what it was like to live in a real home.

She parked below in the car park, but instead of taking the elevator to her floor, she ran up the stairs to the lobby and from there into the café next door. She wasn't ready to go back to her cold empty apartment yet.

The waiter behind the polished mahogany counter smiled when she pushed through the door. "The usual, Sarah?"

"Yes, please, Sam." She went to her favorite table and sat with her back to the window. The café was rapidly filling with the afterwork suit crowd. How could she be among so many people and feel so lonely? The answer was easy; because Luke wasn't there.

Sam brought her coffee over. "You look tanned. Where've you been?"

"Visiting my cattle station in Australia," she replied, and smiled when his jaw dropped. She started to explain and halfway through realized her compulsion to talk about Burrinbilli was more a longing to talk about Luke. She had an overwhelming craving just to say his name.

"Next time you go bring me a boomerang," Sam suggested.

Sarah smiled noncommittally. "Sure."

If there ever was a next time.

She unfolded her copy of the *Seattle Post Intelligencer* and settled down for a long session. She *never* wanted to go back to her cold empty apartment.

Ignoring the front page, she turned to the world news and scanned the printed columns for mention of Australia. She sighed. Nothing today. The Internet carried the big newspapers from Sydney and Melbourne, but what she really longed for was news of Sandy Ronstad's baby and whether Bazza had heard from that agent yet. Whether Becka ever got that new dress. And how a certain station manager was managing without her.

A gust of cool air blew through the open door as someone entered the café. Whoever it was caused a brief but palpable pause in the buzz of conversation. Sarah idly lifted her gaze. At the counter stood a man in a rain-spotted chambray shirt and hip-snug moleskins, his streaky blond hair bare of the broadbrimmed hat tucked between the fingers of one hand.

His back was to her, but she'd know those shoulders anywhere. "Luke!"

He turned, his gaze sweeping the room. Sarah rose, still hardly daring to believe her eyes. The newspaper drifted to the floor as her chair scraped backward and she edged out from behind the table.

Luke pushed through the crowded café to meet her. "Don't you answer your cell phone? I've been trying to call."

She would have thrown herself into his arms, but some shred of pride made her stop inches away. "What are you doing here?"

"I want you to come back to Burrinbilli."

Sarah's instinct was to leap into his arms and shout "Yes!" But she wasn't settling for anything less than love. "Why should I?"

By now, Luke's deep Aussie twang had drawn the attention of the entire café. He glanced around at the avid faces surrounding them and shifted uncomfortably. "Bloody oath, woman! I left the sale mob in

Bazza's hands and traveled twelve thousand miles just to bring you home. Do I have to shout the reason in front of all these people?''

"Darn tootin'."

"Shout it out, cowboy!" someone called.

Luke pressed his eyes shut in a brief moment of private agony. When he opened them again his eyes seemed a brighter blue than before. Sarah held her breath, gladly yielding her hands as he grasped both of them in his.

"I love you, Sarah," he said. "I want to marry you and have your children."

The café patrons roared with laughter.

"I mean," he amended, his face and neck flushing brick red, "I want you to be the mother of *my* children. *Our* children," he finished on a softer note.

Joy rang through Sarah, taking away her breath and all possibility of speech. Until she remembered what had brought her back to Seattle in the first place.

"Luke, I can't be all you want in a partner," she said, pulling her hands away. "I don't know how to do all the things you need a wife to do to make the station truly self-sufficient. And—and—I'm not sure I *want* to spend all my time just surviving. I'm a computer programmer, not a modern-day pioneer like you."

"I need *you,* Sarah, not a housekeeper or a milking machine. I need your smile and your quirks and your warmth." He took a deep breath. "If you have to compromise your life-style so we can be together, then I reckon it's only fair I do the same."

It sounded as though he'd rehearsed his speech all the way over on the plane, but to Sarah that just made it even more endearing. "Then you don't mind if I can't preserve the vegetable patch and milk a cow?"

"How about, I'll teach you to milk a cow and you can teach me about the Internet. We'll build a life that suits us *both*, doing as much as we can with the talents and skills God's given us." He pulled her into his arms. "What do you say, Freckles? Give it a go?"

She nodded so hard tears spilled down her cheeks.

"Well?" he demanded, still holding her in his iron embrace. "Don't you have something to tell me?"

"I love you...partner."

"And...?" the crowd around them prompted.

"Yes, Luke, I'll marry you."

"Beauty!" Luke grinned, his teeth white against his tanned skin. He bent his head and took her mouth in a kiss that sent Sarah's heart soaring into the stratosphere.

The crowd went wild.

CHAPTER FIFTEEN

"If I'd known that a wedding was all it took to get you back to Burrinbilli I'd have gotten engaged right away," Sarah teased her mother as they bumped down the red dust track toward the homestead in the Land Cruiser.

Sarah had returned to Burrinbilli two weeks earlier to prepare for the wedding. Now she'd picked Anne up from the train station in Longreach and all the way back to the homestead her mother had exclaimed in delight over fondly remembered landmarks and dismay over changes she perceived not to be for the better. Delight or dismay, however, there was no doubt that now that she'd come, Anne was pleased to be here.

"Sh, darl', if I remember right it's just over this next little rise." Anne leaned forward in her seat, craning for the first glimpse of her childhood home in almost thirty years.

And then they topped the rise. Afternoon sun gilded the ridges of the corrugated iron roof and lit the brilliant purple-flowered vines twining around the slender iron poles supporting the veranda. Anne's eyes filled with tears. Sarah felt her own eyes become moist, too; she was overjoyed that her mother had finally come home and bursting with pride that this was now *her* home, too.

"Look at the bougainvillea, how it's grown!" Anne exclaimed. "And there are the palm trees my grandmother planted and granddad said would never survive. Oh, and the house…" Anne smudged at her tears with the back of her hand. "Damn it, I can't see," she said with a choking laugh.

"Your old bedroom is all ready for you," Sarah said, slowing to a halt. "Abby made new curtains and I painted the walls."

Anne turned in the seat and put her arms around Sarah. "Thank you, darl'. I'm so happy. I never thought I'd see this place again."

"Oh, Mom. I'm so glad you're here." Sarah hugged her back. Maybe, just maybe, now that Anne had made the long journey home she'd want to stay.

A WEEK LATER, final preparations for the wedding were complete. Between them, Abby, Sarah and the women on neighboring stations had cooked enough food for the whole of western Queensland. Abby had worked like a Trojan—and made sure everyone knew it.

With Anne's arrival, tension levels rose. Abby greeted her graciously, then spent the next six days bizz-buzzing around the kitchen like a deposed queen bee.

"You go ahead and bake your chocolate brownies first," she said to Anne with exaggerated politeness when they'd both gone to use the oven at the same time the morning of the wedding. "My scones can wait."

"That's all right," Anne said cheerfully, setting her pan back on the counter. "You go first."

"No, *you* go first," Abby insisted in martyred

tones. "You're Anne Hafford and Burrinbilli is your rightful home." She turned to Becka, who was innocently licking the spoon Anne had used to stir the brownie batter. Abby whisked the spoon out of the startled girl's hand and replaced it with a beater thick with cream for the scones. "Here, Becka, I know how you love whipped cream."

Sarah cravenly hid in the walk-in pantry, mixing up salad dressing and listening to every word. She wasn't surprised when Anne marched into the narrow room, scowling.

"That woman is driving me out of my mind," she said in a low voice through gritted teeth. "No matter how hard I try to get along she always finds some way to push my buttons."

"She's like that," Sarah said sympathetically. "I think she's feeling a little insecure. I'll see what I can do." She glanced at her watch. "And then we'd better stop cooking and start getting ready."

Wiping her hands on a towel, she went into the kitchen, where Abby was resetting the temperature on the oven. "Abby?"

"Yes?" Abby said coolly. Since Sarah's return she'd treated the bride-to-be with poisonous courtesy. In her mind, the worst-case scenario had happened and her fears were vindicated.

Sarah had avoided a confrontation with her long enough. "Abby, *I* am the mistress of Burrinbilli."

Abby's jaw dropped.

Sarah almost spoiled it then by laughing, she sounded so much like a character from an old Lucy Walker novel, though possibly not a heroine. Setting her mouth into a stern line, she continued, "*You* are the station cook. *You* are in charge of preparations for the wedding lunch. *You* will decide what goes in the oven first.''

Abby didn't say a word, just stared at her, her one brown eye and one blue eye wide.

Sarah swallowed. Had she gone too far? ''Please?'' she added.

''Oh, well,'' Abby huffed, smoothing down her apron. ''If you put it that way.''

Anne moved back into the room, ready to hear what the chief cook had to say.

''Let's see,'' Abby said briskly, glancing at her watch. ''The scones take less time. But...Anne, I presume you're going to help Sarah get dressed, so why don't you put your brownies in now and set the timer. I'll take them out and then bake the scones. The fresher they are the better, anyway.''

Anne obediently placed the brownies in the oven. Abby bustled around the room, clearing counters and piling dirty mixing bowls in the sink, her entire demeanor changed. ''What are you doing mucking around in the pantry, Sarah?'' she scolded. ''You're getting married this morning. You should be having a shower and readying yourself. Off you go now, the pair of you.'' She shooed Sarah and Anne right out of the kitchen.

''What about me?'' Becka demanded.

''You can help me clear up and then we'll get ready.''

For a moment Sarah and Anne stood transfixed outside in the hall, listening to Abby run water into the sink, humming happily and tunelessly.

Then, giggling like a schoolgirl, Anne hustled Sarah down the hall. ''You were brilliant!'' She glanced back once. "Should I have stayed to help? Will there be enough food?"

"The tables are all set up in the garden. Karen and Jacqui will be here any second to help out with last-minute stuff. And there's enough food to last till next Easter."

It was very nearly true. The fridge was stocked high with salads, the pantry was filled to bursting with baked goods and the meat house was stacked with chops and steaks and sausages. Luke had borrowed three barbecues in addition to his own and set them up in the side yard. He'd put a side of beef on the spit and it had been cooking since dawn, sending the tantalizing aroma of roasting meat wafting through the screened veranda and throughout the house.

The wedding ceremony was to be held in the front garden under an awning of white-and-silver-blue shade cloth. Another larger awning in sage-green provided shelter from the sun for the tables that Becka had covered with white linen cloths and decorated with lush pink peonies. Sarah had been touched to tears at the offers of help that had poured in from the graziers and their wives of the surrounding district, offers that ranged from such basic items of crockery and linen to a professionally iced cake. If this was how they did things in the bush she was pleased and proud to become part of such a community.

Someone had even offered to make her wedding dress, but this Sarah had gratefully declined. She'd found her dream dress in a little wedding boutique in Seattle. Sewn of the finest white polished cotton, it had capped sleeves, a scoop neckline, fitted bodice and a full skirt that swirled around her tanned legs at midcalf. It was perfect for the heat of an outback summer and so feminine and pretty that Sarah felt like a ballerina. Now she pulled it over her head with her mother's help and gazed at her reflection in the cheval mirror.

"You look absolutely beautiful, darl'," Anne said as she did up the row of tiny pearl buttons at the back. For perhaps the twentieth time in the past week her eyes filled with tears. "My goodness," she said, wiping them away with a smile. "I'm not going to have any tears left for the ceremony."

Sarah pressed a hand to her stomach. "It's really happening. I can't quite believe it."

"You're not getting cold feet, are you?"

"Not about marrying Luke. I've never been more sure of anything in my life. I'm just excited."

"Luke's a wonderful man and Becka's a darling. Now, don't move. I'll go get the veil." And she hurried to the wardrobe.

"Veil?" Sarah spun on a nervous swish of polished cotton. "Mom, this is the twenty-first century. I'm not wearing a veil." Honestly, for all her mix of hippie and New Age voodoo weirdo mysticism Anne sometimes made astonishing reversals to traditionalism. Then the opening chords of organ music sounded from the garden. "We don't have time…"

Her voice trailed off as Anne turned, her arms full of a bouffant confection of white netting sprigged with tiny satin rosebuds. "I thought you might object. That's why I saved this till last. It was my mother's. I wore it, too."

"It's beautiful," Sarah breathed, her protests forgotten. She bent her knees and Anne reached high to position it over her upswept hair.

The door pushed open and Becka poked her head in. "They're waiting for you—" the flower girl announced, her voice high with excitement, then stopped with a gasp. "Oh, Sarah, you look like a princess!"

"So do you, sweetheart. Come in and let us see you."

Becka obligingly twirled around to show off the dress Abby had bought for her on a shopping expedition sanctioned by Luke. Pink lace on pink satin, the dress was a surfeit of frills and ribbons that were at last appropriate to the occasion. Becka's hair curled softly around her shoulders, pinned at the front with pink daisies.

"Come on," Becka urged, beckoning them into the hall with her bouquet of more pink daisies and white rosebuds. "Quick, before our flowers wilt."

"We're right behind you," Sarah said, and picked up her own bouquet, a mixture of white roses, gardenias and baby's breath.

Halfway down the hall, Becka suddenly stopped and turned to gaze up at Sarah with a solemn expression. "Should I call you Sarah or Mum?"

"I would like it if you called me Mom, but only if you want to," Sarah said carefully.

"Mum," Becka said decisively, then turned and gave a hop and a skip. "Yippee, I've got a mum!"

Laughing, Sarah followed the small figure with the glowing blond hair. Becka was a jewel, a bonus that was good enough to be the prize, if the prize— Luke—wasn't already the pinnacle, the triple mochaccino with whipped cream and cointreau and lashings of cinnamon and chocolate....

She reached the open front door and stopped dead, suddenly breathless, her stomach churning. The guests were seated in two long banks of folding chairs on the grassy lawn. A woman from a neighboring station was seated at a portable organ, playing softly. Faces turned toward her, some familiar, some belonging to new friends; all were smiling.

Then the music changed. *Here comes the bride....*

This was it. *Keep cool.* Her stomach fluttered. Her palms grew damp. Her mother arranged the veil over her face. Kissed her on the cheek. Firmly tucked her arm in hers. And urged her forward when her feet felt rooted to the spot. "I wish Dennis could be here," she whispered to Anne.

"So do I." Tears sprang into Anne's eyes again.

"And I wish my real father..."

"I know, darl'. I know."

Since neither of her fathers was there to give her away, Sarah was to travel the grassy path between the chairs arm in arm with her mother. But before she began that long walk she silently thanked the man who'd unwittingly set her on this path. *This is the best present ever, Daddy.*

Blinking, she took a deep breath and turned her gaze to the tall, handsome man in the tuxedo who waited for her at the end of the aisle. Luke, who held her heart in the palm of his hand. And who loved her so thoroughly she knew she would never want for anything that was truly important.

Standing to one side of Luke was Bazza, stiff and red faced in a rented tux and almost unrecognizable without a rollie hanging out of his mouth and a rifle or a stock whip in his hand. Wal sat at his master's feet, grinning around a lolling tongue, quietly confident that *he*, not Bazza, was best man.

Although Sara was dimly aware that all eyes were on her as she followed Becka down the aisle she saw nothing and no one but Luke. She might have residual doubts about her ability to traverse the wide-open spaces, but she had no doubt at all about her love for this man or that they would have a long and happy marriage.

And then she was by his side, where she belonged.

"'Dearly beloved....'"

As the minister spoke the marriage service Sarah's butterflies settled their wings. The heady sweet scent of the gardenias, the liquid warble of magpies in the gums by the creek, the heat and the vaulted blue sky—all crystallized into a moment of pure happiness.

She found herself listening to the familiar words and discovering a depth and beauty that gave extra meaning to the new life she was about to begin. She stole a sideways glance at Luke. Solemn and intent, he sensed her gaze and gave her a reassuring smile and made a promise with his eyes. The inner commitment that had begun weeks before culminated in a soul-to-soul glance she would remember forever.

She returned his smile and made her own promise. *I'm yours, now and always.*

"Do you, Sarah Jane Templestowe..." The minister's resonant voice intoned.

"I do," she proclaimed, soft and clear.

"Do you, Luke Nicholas Sampson..."

Husky voiced, Luke pledged his love and commitment to her before God and man. "I do."

An expectant hush fell over the assembled guests as he lifted her veil and dropped his lips to hers. Their first kiss as man and wife went on…and on…. Cheering and good-natured catcalls erupted, and finally Sarah and Luke broke apart, laughing, arms twined around each other as they faced their family and friends. The music swelled. The guests rose as one and showers of rose petals followed them down the aisle to the rising, joyous strains of the organ. Everyone was laughing and hugging and kissing.

Bazza shed his tie and jacket, and several beers later his shirt, as well. By the time everyone was seated at the tables under the awning he'd stripped to singlet and shorts and was delivering a raucous and ribald toast to the newlyweds that had Sarah holding her sides, laughing.

When the laughter died down Len stood and asked to say a few words. He cleared his throat and began by welcoming Sarah to the district in his official capacity as Mayor of Murrumburrumgurrandah. "She hasn't been here long, but already she's offered her friendship and special talents to the community. We're all extremely fond of her and very glad she's chosen to make Murrum her home." He paused. "And we're bloody glad she married Luke so we get to keep our good friend and neighbor."

Blushing at the rousing applause, Sarah rose and took a bow. "Thank you, everyone. You've all been so wonderful and made me feel so welcome. And now that Len stocks gourmet coffee beans I wouldn't want to live anywhere else." She glanced down at Luke. "Of course," she added in a sultry murmur, "Murrum has one or two other special attractions."

The jackaroos let out a volley of whoops and yells.

Spoons tapped on glasses, setting them to ring like bells, urging Luke to stand beside his bride. He kissed her long and sweet and Sarah felt her knees begin to buckle.

Len, still standing, cleared his throat. "Ahem. I wasn't quite finished, young Luke."

Amid more laughter, Sarah and Luke sat down.

"I'd also like to welcome an old friend, Anne Hafford," Len continued, his voice softening as his gaze sought Anne, seated at the head table. "She left us as a bride almost thirty years ago so it's right and fitting that her daughter has returned as a bride to Burrinbilli, where Haffords have lived for four generations."

Sarah's gaze went from Len to her mother as he spoke. There was a generosity of spirit in Len's words that transcended the years and the heartbreak. There was affection and gratitude on Anne's face. And something more? Sarah wondered.

Anne rose and made a little bow. "Thank you, Len. It's wonderful to be back, to catch up with old friends and to meet all your sons and daughters." She glanced at Sarah. "Sarah told me before she left Seattle she wanted a 'real man.' I'm happy to say she's found him. I couldn't wish for a better son-in-law. I'm glad, too, that she's come home to Burrinbilli." Anne's voice caught. "Luke, take care of my baby."

Luke rose. "Anne, I will do my best. And I hope you'll always consider Burrinbilli your home." To the crowd of smiling faces seated around them, he said, "Thank you all for coming and sharing our special day. It's times like these a man knows what's important in life.

He gazed into Sarah's smiling upturned face. "I want to thank Sarah for not selling Burrinbilli to me over the phone when I asked, for not giving up when times got rough and for taking one lonely cattleman and his estranged daughter and turning us into a family."

Sarah felt the tears welling and the lump in her throat forming and reached for his hand. She kissed his palm and then pressed it to her cheek. She wanted to speak but couldn't seem to find the words, even though complete silence had fallen over the wedding party.

"You don't need to say anything," Luke told her softly, as though reading her mind. "Your actions in forsaking your old life for a new one with me and Becka speak louder than any words." He raised his glass. "To Sarah—my love, my life, my bride."

EPILOGUE

"ALMOST HOME, girl," Sarah said to the blue heeler pup beside her on the bench seat of the utility truck. The dog was a wedding present from Luke and went with her everywhere.

Ahead of her the long narrow strip of bitumen stretched to the flat horizon, bordered by wide shoulders of red earth and, beyond that, by endless open land. Sarah gazed freely at the plain and felt nothing but affection for her mother's country and a feeling of soaring freedom at the vast open spaces. A person had room to breathe out here. It was *her* country now.

And it was changing as the year wore to a close. The once blue sky was heavy with towering gray clouds and moisture hung thick in the air. Any day now the Wet would begin. Sarah couldn't wait to see the Downs turn green and come alive with wildflowers and frogs the way Luke had promised.

She hummed along to the country song on the radio and reminded herself to order that new software package for Karen as soon as she got home. Everything that needed to be brought in from the outside had to be arranged before the Wet. If there *was* a decent Wet, Luke would always say, but Sarah just knew that this year the drought would break.

She turned off the road at the fridge-cum-mailbox

onto the Burrinbilli track. A hundred yards farther on she slowed as she came upon Abby toiling in the garden outside her transplanted weatherboard cottage. Luke had planted saplings around the yard and it wouldn't be long before the house would look as though it had always been there.

Becka ran out of the cottage at the sound of Sarah's truck. The school bus dropped her at the mailbox every day and she walked up to Abby's to spend time with her aunt before coming back to the homestead for tea.

"Sarah!" Becka called, and ran over to the car. "Look at the friendship necklace I got from Lucy." She thrust one half of a golden heart dangling from a chain into the window of the utility truck. "She's got the other half. Isn't it cool?"

"Totally." Sarah grinned and pulled on a blond braid. "Are you coming up to the house with me?"

"I'll bring her up in an hour if that's okay," Abby said as she wiped the sweat from her brow with a scarred hand.

"That's fine," Sarah said easily, knowing Abby wouldn't risk losing her privileges with Becka by failing to bring her home at the appointed time. Counseling and medication had resulted in significant improvement, although Abby still had many problems to resolve. "By the way," Sarah added, "I talked to my mother this morning. She's coming for Christmas."

Abby's thin lips pursed. "She's setting her cap at Len again."

Sarah just laughed. Abby was as irritating as ever, but now Sarah refused to let it bother her. "Actually, she's thinking of retiring to the Gold Coast. She's going to check out condos while she's in Australia.''

She didn't mention that Len was taking a holiday on the Gold Coast at the same time. Anne insisted they were just friends—and maybe that was all they would ever be. Still, it was enough for Abby to have to deal with sharing Becka with her new grandmother.

''Even if Anne does move back to Australia she'll be a thousand miles away,'' Sarah added. ''It's nice for Becka that you live so close.''

Abby started to smile, then seemed to think better of it. ''Humph. Well, I'd best get back to the garden.''

Sarah shook her head and put the truck into gear. ''I'll catch you later.''

And then she was barreling down the track, over the rise, eagerly awaiting the first glimpse of Burrinbilli nestled among the ghost gums glowing golden in the setting sun. And Luke, standing tall and lean on the front veranda, welcoming her home with a kiss and whispered words of love.

The first fat drops of rain fell from the lowering sky as she pulled up in front of the house. She jumped down from the truck and ran over to Luke, into his arms. Within minutes the rain was so thick it streamed over the edge of the bullnose roof and they couldn't see as far as the gate.

Luke drew her close for a kiss. ''That little dance you did for me last night in your sweet nothin's must have been a rain dance.''

Sarah blushed and grinned. ''You're just angling for a repeat performance.'' She heaved a happy sigh as they watched the downpour. "At last our problems are over."

Luke gave a bark of laughter. "Over? They've just begun. The floods will cover the land, take out the bridges and cut us off from the town. The animals will founder and some will be lost. But we'll battle on the way we've always done."

He gazed searchingly into her eyes. "Do you ever regret giving up your life in Seattle?"

Sarah shook her head. "Not for a second."

Life in the outback would never be an easy life. But it would be a life worth living because it held challenge and demanded dedication and passion. And because it contained Luke and Becka and all their friends near and far. Even Abby.

"There's no place like home." She reached down to ruffle her dog's fur. "Isn't that right, Toto?"

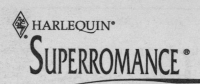

HARLEQUIN
SUPERROMANCE

You are now entering

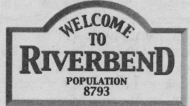

WELCOME TO RIVERBEND
POPULATION 8793

Riverbend...the kind of place where everyone knows your name—and your business. Riverbend...home of the River Rats—a group of small-town sons and daughters who've been friends since high school.

The Rats are all grown up now. Living their lives and learning that some days are good and some days aren't—and that you can get through anything as long as you have your friends.

Starting in July 2000, Harlequin Superromance brings you Riverbend—six books about the River Rats and the Midwest town they live in.

BIRTHRIGHT by Judith Arnold (July 2000)
THAT SUMMER THING by Pamela Bauer (August 2000)
HOMECOMING by Laura Abbot (September 2000)
LAST-MINUTE MARRIAGE by Marisa Carroll (October 2000)
A CHRISTMAS LEGACY by Kathryn Shay (November 2000)

Available wherever Harlequin books are sold.

HARLEQUIN
Makes any time special ™

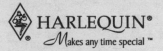

**Don't miss
an exciting opportunity
to save on the purchase of
Harlequin and Silhouette books!**

Buy any two Harlequin or
Silhouette books and save
$10.00 off future Harlequin
and Silhouette purchases

OR

buy any three
Harlequin or Silhouette books
and save **$20.00 off** future
Harlequin and Silhouette purchases.

**Watch for details
coming in October 2000!**

PHQ400

If you enjoyed what you just read,
then we've got an offer you can't resist!

Take 2 bestselling love stories FREE!

Plus get a FREE surprise gift!

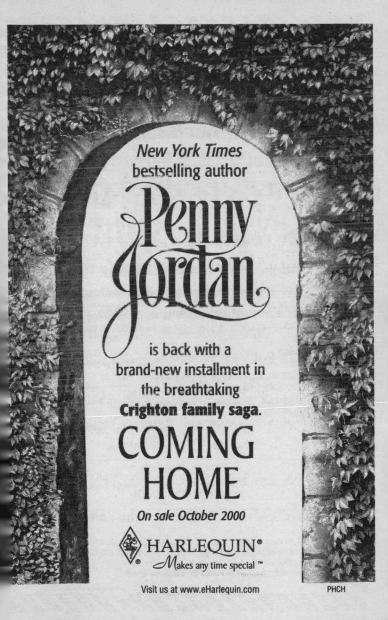